Both thei
shattered
tragic tru

A truth Clay was striving to understand.

All he asked was that Lainey do the same. Compared to what he had suffered, it seemed a small price to pay.

But in Scarlet, the walls really did have ears. If anyone in that tattling town ever learned her secret, Lainey would die of shame. From church pews to street corners, from canasta games to quilting bees, the entire population would be gossiping. Lainey would be reviled, an outcast among the only people she'd ever known.

Clay's insistent questions frightened her. She swallowed a lump of panic. Dear God, what would happen if he somehow managed to find out? Then everyone would know.

And the cruel whispers would begin....

SCARLET WHISPERS

Diana Whitney

SILHOUETTE
JASMINE
Published by Silhouette Books Australia

First Australian Paperback Edition 1995

ISBN 0 373 07603 7

Published by
Silhouette Books
3 Gibbes Street
Chatswood, NSW 2067
Australia

Printed and bound in Australia by
Griffin Paperbacks, South Australia

DIANA WHITNEY

says she loves 'fat babies and warm puppies, mountain streams and California sunshine, camping, hiking and gold prospecting. Not to mention strong, romantic heroes!' She married her own real-life hero twenty years ago. With his encouragement, she left her long-time career as a municipal finance director and pursued the dream that had haunted her since childhood – writing. To Diana, writing is a joy, the ultimate satisfaction. Reading, too, is her passion, from spine-chilling thrillers to sweeping sagas, but nothing can compare to the magic and wonder of romance.

To my handsome son Jeff,
who is—in my unbiased opinion—
true hero material!

Chapter 1

The lonely little girl wandered through the meandering circus crowd. She was crying quietly, searching the ground. No one spoke to her. No one noticed her tears. Then a black kitten appeared, meowing in fear. The child called out, but the tiny cat scampered between wheeled cages. As the frantic girl followed, she suddenly found herself in a frightening forest of legs, some trousered, some bare, all looming like disembodied tree trunks. Her lip quivered. Everything was so huge, and she felt so very, very small. The big-top calliope drowned out her feeble attempt to call her kitten, and she began to cry. No one spoke to her, no one offered comfort.

There were no people anymore. There were only legs.

A black blur caught her eye as the kitten dashed through the opening of a striped canvas tent. With a childish giggle, she ran into the darkened arena, scooping the little animal into her arms just as a ragged, pale-eyed boy stepped from the shadows. He tugged insistently on her elbow, saying nothing, although she knew that he wanted her to leave.

A single spotlight illuminated the center ring.

Still clutching her furry prize, the little girl watched the circle of light with increasing trepidation. There were more legs now—clown legs clad in puffy trousers that were spat-

tered with crimson polka dots. Trembling, the girl turned to the ragged boy for comfort. But he was gone. She was alone again. And the spotted legs were moving closer.

With a terrified gasp, Lainey Sheridan bolted upright in bed and pressed an icy palm against her chest. Her racing heart pounded against her ribs. She tried to catch her breath.

Not again, she screamed silently. Dear God, not again.

Stiff with fear, she stared into the black void, her brain throbbing with remnants of the nightmare. Tears stung her eyes yet she dared not blink, fearing a return of the hideous image, the prelude of madness....

"You Ben Cooper's kid?" Without waiting for an answer, the desk clerk shifted a narrowed gaze from the motel registration card to the pale-eyed man leaning on the counter. "You got some nerve, coming back after what your daddy done to this town."

Although stung by the desk clerk's contemptuous expression, Clayton Cooper managed a cool reply. "I believe you have that backward. The correct statement would be that I have some nerve coming back after what this town did to my father."

The clerk's mouth twisted as if he were preparing to spit on the counter. Instead he settled on a venomous stare. "Dying in prison was too good for Ben Cooper. That murdering bastard shoulda been hung twenty years ago, with his whorin' wife dangling in the next loop."

"You're certainly entitled to your opinion." Clay casually pocketed the motel key, then spun around without warning and hauled the startled clerk across the scarred counter. "As I said, you're entitled to your opinion, but if you ever speak another unkind word about my mother, you'll spend the rest of your life with your nose growing out of your forehead." A quick shove propelled the stunned man against a key-studded pegboard behind the counter. "Have I made myself perfectly clear?"

When the squat-faced fellow issued a jerky nod, Clay smiled pleasantly, wished the dazed clerk a nice day and walked out of the office.

Shaken, Clay crossed the parking lot, angry at himself for having lost control. The desk clerk was an idiot but his attitude was no different than anyone else's in this smug little town. Some things never change, he thought, gazing beyond the cracked asphalt to the rolling meadows and lush woods surrounding the picturesque hamlet of Scarlet, South Carolina.

Through the pink glow of a crimson sunrise, the town exuded an unsettling sense of having been plucked from a bygone era. The first blush of dawn also concealed the blemishes of age, the peeling eaves and stained clapboards that evidenced a lethargic populace.

Once, Scarlet's economy had been dependent on coal—when the mines closed, the town had nearly died. After Lloyd Reeves convinced a chemical conglomerate to build a manufacturing plant on the outskirts of town, Scarlet had boomed again. So with a collective sigh of relief, the self-righteous citizens had handed their town, their economic future and their souls over to ChemCorp management before settling back into comfortable complacency.

Now Clay had the means to test that complacency. Tucked inside his sleek gray minivan were cartons of research material meticulously gathered in anticipation of his crusade. After years of preparation, the moment had finally arrived. Clay's quest had begun.

With a shiver of satisfaction, he began tediously unloading the precious documents. Finally finished, he grabbed his trusty laptop computer, tucked a cellular phone into the pocket of his tweed sport coat and retreated into the austere motel room.

After clearing a place for his computer between stacks of file folders on a wobbly wooden desk, Clay tested the mattress—extra firm, only slightly lumpy—and stared around the room. A couple of dime-store prints adorned the faded plaster walls; a lamp table was flanked by two cheap vinyl chairs; the narrow hallway accessed a cramped bathroom and a closet not quite wide enough to close without tipping the hangers.

All in all, the room was an extension of the town itself—too old, too small, with a clean surface and dirt-caked corners.

As Clay gazed out the smeared window, he was overcome by a flood of memories. He'd expected that, of course, but the accompanying surge of emotion took him by surprise. The past had suddenly become more than vague recollections of poverty and violence. It became real; a living, breathing entity consuming his thoughts, devouring his carefully concealed adult emotions. In that moment Clay relived the childhood shame, recalling the cruel taunts and scornful whispers that had been the penance he'd paid for having been fathered by the town's most infamous resident.

Ben Cooper had been a hard-drinking bully who'd eked out a living hustling pool and, some said, picking the pockets of drunken patrons at the tavern where he'd tended bar. If it hadn't been for his wife's job as a ChemCorp accounting clerk, the family would have starved. Life had been hard, but at least they'd had a life before the rumors had begun—a whispered scandal campaign that had shaken the town to its foundation had ripped the fragile family apart.

As the town's contempt swelled, Lloyd Reeves had used his power as ChemCorp's chief executive officer to rally the townsfolk. Reeves had labeled the entire Cooper family as a canker on the town, human malignancies destined to infect the entire populace.

Clay, who'd been only eleven at the time, had been forced to watch helplessly as Reeves and his ChemCorp lackeys had systemically destroyed his mother's reputation, her self-esteem, and eventually, her life. The memory of how she'd been snubbed and defiled by Scarlet's sanctimonious citizens still brought a bitter lump to Clay's throat. He remembered silent tears staining her porcelain-pale cheeks as she'd stared straight ahead, pretending not to notice the scornful glances and lewd remarks from those gathered at the courthouse steps.

Young Clay would have waded into the crowd with skinny fists flailing, except his mother had made him promise to ignore the taunts. "Be strong," she'd told him. "Be proud. Show them the courage of your heart." So he'd endured without confessing that his heart was filled not with courage but with hatred and a thirst for vengeance.

Over the years he'd kept the promise to his mother. Now it was time to keep the silent promise he'd made to himself. Clay knew that returning to Scarlet would fuel renewed speculation and reopen old wounds. In fact, he was counting on it. He sought justice, not for himself or for the father he'd despised, but for the memory of his sweet and gentle mother.

Inside his briefcase was enough evidence to clear her name and rub the town's nose in its own hypocrisy. Once the truth was exposed, all Scarlet's dirty little secrets would be revealed to the world. If a few upstanding reputations were trampled along the way, that was all part of the game. For Clay, it would be the best part.

Yawning, Lainey Sheridan tiredly shoved a limp strand of brown hair from her eyes, dragging an iron skillet onto the chipped porcelain stove. Right on cue, the kitchen pipes vibrated to announce that Uncle Russ was in the shower. On a routine morning, the antiquated plumbing would whine for exactly three minutes, after which Russ would emerge, spend eleven minutes dressing himself, then stalk into the kitchen and expect a steaming, three-course breakfast.

Today he would be disappointed. Lainey was already six minutes behind schedule and couldn't muster the enthusiasm to move any faster. With an audible sigh, she rubbed her stinging eyes and tried to get back on track.

After arranging two thick ham slices in the pan, she flipped on the burner and glanced out the kitchen window, vaguely aware that the sunrise was particularly striking. Ordinarily she'd have reveled in such beauty—dawn had always been her favorite time of day—but this morning she was exhausted, physically and mentally drained by another bout with the nightmare that had haunted her since childhood.

Each time she had the awful dream, it was more vivid, more terrifying. As a child, she'd tried to escape the hideous images by crawling under her bed and muffling her sobs with a pillow. But she was a big girl now, a grown woman who was much too mature for such childish nonsense.

Besides, she didn't fit under the bed anymore. God knows, she'd tried often enough.

A loud thud emanated from her aunt's bedroom. "Lainey!"

With a pained sigh, Lainey turned off the stove, braced herself with another swallow of strong black coffee, then hurried down the hallway and found her aunt sitting stiffly on the edge of the bed, grimacing in pain. The woman was clutching one of her wooden canes; the other had fallen onto the floor, out of reach.

Lainey's heart sank. "Oh, Aunt Hallie. Another spasm?"

Hallie nodded grimly. "My... pills."

"I'll get them." Lainey retrieved the fallen cane and wrapped one of her aunt's bony hands around the smooth wooden handle. "There. Now lean forward...that's good. Let the canes support your weight." Although the seated woman was now bent like a safety pin, the awkward position apparently alleviated some spinal pressure, and the stress lines bracketing Hallie's thin mouth eased considerably.

After sorting through the array of prescription bottles on the nightstand, Lainey shook two fast-acting muscle relaxants into her palm. Supporting her aunt's gaunt shoulders with one arm, she gently put the tablets in the woman's open mouth, then held up the water glass that was always filled and ready. In spite of the unwieldy position, Hallie managed to swallow the pills before her head lolled forward.

Lainey returned the glass to the nightstand and used a tissue to gently dry her aunt's damp chin. "Perhaps you should lie back in bed for a while and give the medication time to work."

Hallie stubbornly shook her head. "It's Thursday."

Lainey nearly moaned aloud, but managed to keep her voice even. "It might be best if you skipped the ladies' auxiliary this morning."

The woman looked up, horrified. "And let those old biddies talk about me?"

"I'm sure they wouldn't say anything unkind," Lainey murmured, glancing away to cover the lie. If gossip had been an athletic event, Scarlet's citizens would have been destined for Olympic gold. Anyone unfortunate enough to miss a social function automatically became *topic de jour,* which explained why even the dullest occasions were so well attended.

Despite the fact that Aunt Hallie's concern was not misplaced, Lainey begged her to reconsider. "All that sitting will just aggravate your back, and besides, you can't possibly drive until you're feeling better."

"Then you'll have to take me."

Stiffening, Lainey glanced at the wall clock and was acutely aware that the water pipe had stopped whining. "The *Banner* has been understaffed all week. I can't be late again."

Hallie issued a haughty snort. "Poppycock. It's your newspaper."

Lainey flinched at the curt reminder. Under the terms of her father's will, she'd inherited the *Scarlet Banner* on her twenty-fifth birthday. Although that had been more than a year ago, what Lainey knew about running a newspaper could still be etched on the head of a very small pin. Fortunately the *Banner* had been ably managed for the past twenty years by Broddie McFerson, who'd become as dear a friend to Lainey as he'd been to her father.

Broddie was an old-time newsman who'd honed his steely ethics in Capone's Chicago during the height of Prohibition. Lainey adored him, partly because she admired his crusty, renegade style and partly because he'd never faulted her for not having printer's ink in her veins. To her, the newsroom was a hectic, noisy place filled with beeping computers, ringing telephones and the annoying buzz of a dozen voices all talking at once. From noon on, the rhythmic clatter of the press vibrated the entire building, adding to the miserable din.

Lainey loathed it.

But since there wasn't any other burning career in her future, she'd reluctantly immersed herself in the business that had been her father's passion. Despite the impressive title of Publisher flanking her name in the credit box, she'd insisted on learning the trade from the ground up. Like any other *Banner* employee, Lainey considered Broddie to be her boss. The possibility of incurring his disapproval made her shiver.

"Maybe Ethel Johnson can give you a lift. She's only a few blocks away—"

"No!" Hallie's thin lips drew a hard line. "I won't be beholden to her or anyone else."

An angry male voice resonated from the adjoining bedroom. "Where'n hell are my blue socks?"

Lainey replied absently. "If they're not in the drawer, they must be in the laundry. Don't you have any black ones?"

"I don't want black socks." Wearing only gray trousers and a freshly laundered undershirt, Russ Clemmons loomed in the doorway waving a fistful of clean black socks. "I want blue, dammit, blue! For crying out loud, is expecting clean socks too much to ask?"

"Of course not, Uncle Russ." A surge of resentment was quickly swallowed by guilt. After Lainey's father died, she'd have spent her formative years being shuffled between foster homes if the Clemmonses hadn't taken her in. Since they'd never had children of their own, raising a grief-stricken little girl hadn't been easy for them. Still, they'd done the best they could, and Lainey was deeply grateful. She gave her uncle a reassuring smile. "I'll put a load in the washer before I leave for work."

"What good is that going to do?" Russ growled. "I need socks *now.*"

Hallie, unable to contain her irritation, fixed her husband with an unsympathetic stare and spoke through clenched teeth. "There are more important things in this life than the color of your feet."

Russ blinked as though noticing his wife for the first time. "But I have a meeting with Hunicutt—"

"That sniveling pip-squeak." Hallie's derogatory snort turned into a grunt of pain.

"Your back again?" Frowning, Russ entered the room and laid a solicitous hand on his wife's shoulder. "Maybe I should call Dr. Reynolds."

With a stoic shake of her head, the haggard woman shifted her weight to her stiff arms. "I'll be fine."

Obviously concerned, Russ knelt beside the bed and studied his wife's drawn face. Under the best of conditions, Hallie was not an attractive woman. Her pale complexion and sharp features were emphasized by drab, ash-colored hair that was usually skinned back into a severe, schoolmarm bun. Now, however, a few stringy strands had escaped the twisted clump and clung to the damp hollow beneath her cheekbones.

With a rare display of affection, Russ smoothed the displaced strands back into place. The unexpected gesture both startled and touched Lainey. In the twenty years that she'd lived with Russ and Hallie Clemmons, she'd seen little evidence that they even liked each other. Sporadic personal conversations between the couple frequently deteriorated into childish bickering, problems exacerbated by the fact that her aunt and uncle were so different, in personality as well as appearance.

Russell Clemmons was a block of a man, square-jawed and solid, with a thinning thatch of crinkly red-gold hair that glowed like an amber traffic light. His bushy brows and stubby eyelashes exuded a similar incandescence, drawing attention to a pair of bright hazel eyes that wanted to twinkle yet didn't seem to know how.

Between occasional flares of temper, Russ was undeniably demanding. All things considered, he'd treated Lainey well enough over the years, although she'd always sensed an undercurrent of resentment, an emotional distance that had never been alleviated by her extraordinary attempts to please him.

Aunt Hallie, too, was a bit of an enigma, so diametrically opposed to the gregarious nature of her only brother—Lainey's father—that there had once been speculation that one of the siblings might have been adopted. Lainey doubted that. Her father's angular features were much like those of his sister, but whereas Gerald Sheridan's dark eyes had constantly danced with amusement, Hallie's were bleak and angry.

As a child, Lainey had considered her aunt to be a grim disciplinarian with a tight mouth, tight hair and a tight heart. Over the years, however, she'd recognized that much of Hallie's snappishness was caused by the unrelenting pain of scoliosis, a spinal malformation that had tormented the poor woman since early adolescence.

Although doctors hadn't offered much hope, a Greenville neurosurgeon once offered to try a new spinal fusion technique. Since Hallie didn't find the prospect of being a human guinea pig particularly appealing, she'd conveyed that opinion with trademark bluntness and sworn that no bloodthirsty, chicken-carving quack would ever get another dime of her money. So far, none had.

Russ stood suddenly, cleared his throat and clasped his hands behind his back. "I, uh, can't be late for the meeting." He slid Lainey a covert glance, seemingly embarrassed that she'd witnessed the tender moment between him and his wife. "Lainey, help your aunt with her back brace."

As he turned to leave, Lainey touched his arm. He stepped beyond reach and eyed her coolly. "Yes?"

Lainey's hand dropped to her side. "I ironed your embossed white dress shirt yesterday. It would be a handsome complement to that suit." She gestured limply toward the gray wool trousers he wore.

Russ frowned. "I always wear a blue-striped shirt with gray."

"I know, but as a change, a crimson tie and matching pocket handkerchief would be striking accents. You'd look quite impressive."

Russ considered that, then shook his head. "Hunicutt don't want anyone to look more impressive than him."

Lainey was startled by the bitter edge on her uncle's voice. For reasons she'd never understood, there had always been a palpable tension between her uncle and Sandborne Hunicutt, who'd only recently taken over as ChemCorp's CEO. For decades, Lloyd Reeves had ruled the company and the town itself with an iron fist. When Reeves had retired, Russ had expressed both disappointment and disgust at the appointment, remarking with surprising candor that Hunicutt possessed none of his predecessor's strengths and all of the flaws.

Suddenly Russ announced, "I'll stick with the blue stripe." With a resigned shudder, he glanced at the cloth wads in his fist. "And *black* socks." With that, he spun abruptly, strode into the bedroom that as far as Lainey knew had never been shared with his wife.

As Russ closed the door behind him, Hallie tightened her grip on the dual canes and stood painfully. "Get...my brace."

"Of course." Lainey scooped the elasticized spinal truss from a chair beside the bed, then expertly positioned the stiff brace beneath her aunt's flannel pajama top. After tightening the Velcro fasteners, she was rewarded by Hallie's soft sigh of relief. "Shall I help you with your hair?" Lainey asked.

"Later." The canes thumped across the worn carpet. Hallie moved stiffly into the hall, grumbling. "You'd best get cracking, girl. Breakfast should have been on the table ten minutes ago."

Wondering what it would feel like to do something right, Lainey blew out a breath and returned to the kitchen.

Five minutes later, the phone rang. Since Lainey was scrambling eggs with one hand and buttering toast with another, she glanced over her shoulder. At the kitchen table, Hallie was stirring her thickly creamed coffee with maddening precision while Russ meticulously folded an unread copy of the *Wall Street Journal* into the compact package that could be tucked under his arm for display. Neither looked up as the telephone continued to ring.

Lainey dropped the butter knife, grabbed the receiver and dragged the stretchy cord toward the stove. "Hello?"

A pinched male voice responded curtly. "Let me have Clemmons."

"Just a moment, please." Lainey flipped off the burner and held out the receiver, responding to her uncle's annoyed glance with a helpless shrug.

Obviously pained by the interruption, Russ pushed away from the table and snatched the phone. As he impatiently announced himself, Lainey returned her attention to the skillet and the overcooked yellow mass that was congealing before her eyes. She was wondering whether she dare serve the disgusting mess when Russ suddenly exclaimed, *"What?"*

Startled, Lainey turned quickly and saw that her uncle's ruddy complexion had paled three shades. His voice dropped to a whisper. "When?" He slid a worried glance at his wife, who'd finally laid down her stirring spoon and was listening intently. "Is Peterson sure? I mean, it's been a helluva long time...what? Yeah...I know." Russ looked at his watch. "I'll be there. Fine."

He cradled the receiver and stared at the floor for a moment before returning to the table.

Since Lainey had recognized Sandborne Hunicutt's nasally voice on the telephone, she tensely followed the conversation with increasing trepidation. Her uncle had never been comfortable in a management position and frequently issued gloomy predictions about the imminent demise of his career. For reasons Lainey never understood, he constantly fretted that hidden inadequacies would suddenly emerge, forcing him to return to the backbreaking work and abysmal conditions of the manufacturing facility. Lainey held her breath, hoping the news wasn't as bad as her uncle's dismal expression would suggest.

Hallie, too, seemed worried. She anxiously leaned forward. "What is it?"

Russ laid his head in his hands and answered without looking up. "Cooper is back."

The skillet slipped from Lainey's fingers and crashed to the floor.

Russ slid her a disgusted glance. "Dammit, girl! What'n hell's wrong with you? Look at that mess."

Trembling violently, Lainey was vaguely aware of the gloppy egg clumps scattered across the linoleum floor. She steadied herself against the counter. "I—I'm sorry," she murmured, absently grabbing a roll of paper towels.

As she scooped up the remnants of the ruined breakfast, the terrifying name from her childhood echoed through her mind. Town folklore had extolled Ben Cooper as a rabid killer, a murdering mad dog who had stalked the streets of Scarlet in a frenzied thirst for innocent blood. Over the years there'd been various rumors about the nefarious criminal—including a disgusting piece of gossip that Lainey found particularly offensive—but she'd heard that the man was dead. Her hands trembled as she eavesdropped on the hushed conversation around the kitchen table.

"Maybe it's not really him," Hallie said urgently. "It's been so long—"

"It's him, all right." Russ drummed his thick fingers on the tabletop. "Mike Peterson is telling anyone who'll listen that Cooper sauntered in without so much as a howdy-do and signed his name big as life, like he was proud of being the son of thieving trash."

Although Lainey was aware that Mike Peterson worked at the motel and was a major source for the town's incorrigible grapevine, it was the word "son" that stuck in her mind.

"Clayton?" She looked up hopefully. "Is Clay back in town?"

Ignoring the question, Hallie dunked the spoon into her mug and stirred so hard that the milky brown liquid sloshed over the rim. "What can we do?"

"We don't have to do a damn thing." Russ issued a derisive snort and folded his thick arms. "He'll learn quick enough that his kind isn't welcome around here."

"That's an awful thing to say." Lainey stood and tossed the soiled towels into the wastebasket. "Clay Cooper can't be held responsible for what his father did. For heaven's sake, he was just a little boy—"

Lainey gasped as her uncle's fist slammed the table. "He's a Cooper, dammit!" Russ stood so quickly that his chair lurched backward and crashed to the floor. "This town's got no room for the likes of him." Then Russ snatched up the folded newspaper and yanked open the back door.

Still stunned by her uncle's outburst, Lainey stammered, "Wait! You haven't had anything—" she winced as the door crashed shut "—to eat." Lainey glanced toward the table where her aunt was staring into space, still stirring madly and apparently oblivious to the puddled mess spreading around the base of her coffee mug. "Aunt Hallie?"

"Hmm?" The woman blinked.

"You're white as a bed sheet. Are you all right?"

"Truth be told, I am feeling a mite peaked." Hallie absently laid the spoon into the cold coffee pooled on the table and reached for the canes propped against a neighboring chair. "Think I'll take a rest."

Instantly concerned, Lainey rounded the table and helped Hallie to her feet. "If your back is hurting that badly, you really should let me call the doctor."

The canes bumped across the linoleum. "I'm tired, that's all."

"What about the auxiliary meeting?"

"It doesn't matter," she murmured, then disappeared down the hall. In a moment, her bedroom door clicked shut.

Feeling suddenly drained, Lainey sat in the vacated chair and tried to sort out the morning's strange happenings. She'd never seen her uncle so upset and couldn't remember the last time her aunt had missed a meeting of the ladies' auxiliary. They'd both seemed shaken to the core by news of Clay Cooper's return.

Lainey couldn't understand why they should care, but then, the Clemmonses had always been a secretive couple. She'd long since given up hope of ever sharing a meaningful dialogue with either of them, particularly about the senseless tragedy that had taken her father's life. Questions about that fateful night had always been greeted with evasiveness and a brusque change of subject. Eventually she'd stopped asking. Clay Cooper's return offered a tiny, albeit tenuous hope that some of those questions might finally be answered.

Leaning against the counter, Lainey closed her eyes as a vague image floated out of the past. She remembered the staid youngster on the courthouse steps wearing a frayed shirt, freshly starched and ironed, and patched trousers with immaculately pressed creases. The boy had defiantly positioned his skinny frame to shield his delicate mother from the taunting crowd. Lainey recalled being frightened by the raw hatred burning in his pale eyes.

Since she'd only been six at the time, memories of that arduous period were somewhat elusive. She could, however, recall sitting in the front row of the stifling courtroom where

Hallie had occasionally pinched her leg so the jury could see her cry. Young Clay had been there, too, seated stiff and stoic throughout the grueling ordeal. Lainey remembered feeling that he, too, had been swept away by the same powerful, incomprehensible force that had destroyed her own young life.

Then their eyes had met. For one shining moment, little Lainey had connected with someone who understood her pain. She'd never forgotten the warmth and comfort of that fleeting moment or the silent ally with whom she had so briefly bonded. Now that he was back in town, she looked forward to seeing him again. In fact, she could hardly wait.

Chapter 2

By the time Lainey rushed into the *Banner*'s buzzing newsroom, the morning's deadline crunch was in full swing. A dozen desks overflowing with untidy stacks of paper and books had been crammed into a work space only slightly larger than a three-car garage. Harried staff members bustled through the narrow aisles or hunched over telephones as though oblivious to the surrounding din. Dotting the cluttered hodgepodge were computer terminals, most displaying electronic reproductions of news columns and classified advertisements that would soon be printed, pasted and processed into the afternoon edition.

Lainey swiveled through the jumbled maze toward her own heaped desk, tossed her purse into the bottom drawer and glanced anxiously through the glass wall of the editorial office, hoping Broddie hadn't noticed that she'd been late again. The crusty old editor was standing beside his desk, arms folded, seemingly engrossed in conversation with a dark-haired man who was dressed like a banker.

With a sigh of relief, Lainey slid into her squeaky swivel chair while keeping a wary eye on the glass office. There was something unsettling about Broddie's somber expression, a guarded look in his eyes that made her uncomfortable. A casual observer would see a white-haired man in his mid-sixties with a puckered mouth and a weathered face well grooved by the claws of time. But Lainey saw so much more—rheumy blue eyes shining like tiny sapphires at a little girl's birthday party, swollen fingers brushing away childish tears, and wizened lips stretched in a proud grin at her high school graduation.

Long before Broddie McFerson had become Lainey's boss, he'd been a friend, confidant and surrogate father. Because she loved him dearly, she recognized the subtle arc of his wrinkled brow and a nearly imperceptible tautness bracketing his rumpled mouth. Most people would interpret Broddie's solemn expression as one of polite interest. Lainey saw grim worry. She turned her attention to the apparent source of that worry, the man in the banker's suit.

Although facing away from her, she noted that the man's thick ebony hair was neatly cut, barely touching his collar. He wore an expensive charcoal gray suit, perfectly tailored to compliment a well proportioned, six-foot-plus frame. A crisp white shirt with a subtle golden glint on each cuff completed the tasteful ensemble.

Even from the back, this guy just oozed class and distinction. Lainey wondered if he was half as impressive from the front. She was wishing the anonymous man would turn around when Broddie looked past his visitor, spotted Lainey and gestured for her to come in. Startled, she glanced around, then pointed questioningly at herself. Broddie issued a terse nod. She swallowed hard, crossed the busy room and stood in the doorway.

As was his habit when preoccupied, Broddie absently fingered the forest of writing instruments jutting from the pocket of his nerdy, short-sleeved plaid shirt. Although not much taller than Lainey, Broddie's thick black brows gave him a fierce expression and provided a startling contrast to the cottony mass of hair exploding from his scalp.

At the moment those brows were knitted together in an ominous scowl. "In with you, lass."

As she complied, her practiced explanation came out in a hurried rush. "I'm really sorry I was late. It was just another one of those mornings—"

The dark-haired man turned, and Lainey's breath backed up her throat. She couldn't speak, couldn't move, was totally transfixed by his silvery gaze. He was strikingly handsome, with smooth skin and patrician features that seemed too perfect to be real. But it was his eyes that riveted her attention—iridescent, mysterious, like pools of moonlight on an exotic sea.

Feeling oddly benumbed and besotted, Lainey vaguely realized that the pale eyes were returning her candid appraisal, reflecting both surprise and a sudden apprehension that made her blink. After what seemed an eternity of silence, she tested her voice. "Welcome home, Mr. Cooper."

Clayton Cooper hesitated, sliding a guarded glance at Broddie before taking her proffered hand. "Thank you, Miss Sheridan."

As the warmth of his lingering touch radiated throughout her body, Lainey was aware that the polite handshake had evolved into something altogether different. She vaguely wondered if she should withdraw her hand, but instantly dismissed the notion. At that moment breaking this fragile link would be like severing a limb. Over the lonely years she'd thought of the young Cooper as a kind of spiritual guardian; when the circus nightmares came, it was Clay's image that tried to save her, to pull her away from the frightening clowns. It was only a dream, of course. Still . . .

Lainey moistened her lips and managed what she hoped was a friendly smile. "It's nice to see you again."

Clay's eyes warmed a little but lost none of their cautious intensity. "It's nice to see you, too."

As the atmosphere thickened, Lainey suddenly realized that Broddie was stiff as a broomstick. Apparently Clay noticed, too, because he released Lainey's hand—a bit reluctantly, she thought—then took a step back.

Ignoring the telling glance that passed between the two men, Lainey clasped her hands together. "So, is it business or pleasure that brings you back to Scarlet?"

Clay's smile was overly polite. "A bit of both, actually."

"Really? And what business are you in?"

He shifted uncomfortably. "I write."

"You're a journalist? That's wonderful. Are you going to join the *Banner*'s staff?" she asked hopefully.

It was Broddie who answered. "'Tis books the man writes."

"Oh." She concealed her disappointment with forced interest. "So, you're a novelist?"

"Of a sort. I write biographies."

Biographies. The word brought a glimmer of recognition, the discomforting feeling of something lurking just beyond the mind's reach. After a moment's concentration, her head snapped up. "You're not C. C. Cooper."

Looking decidedly pained, he managed a self-conscious shrug.

"Oh, my gosh." Lainey's stunned glance went from Clay to Broddie and back again. C. C. Cooper had the reputation of being forthright and honest, a writer of unquestioned integrity who refused to embellish facts to satisfy the public's thirst for scandal. "Imagine that," she murmured, duly impressed. "One of Scarlet's own, a nationally renowned author."

Clay made a wry face. "That's certainly an overstatement."

"Now don't be modest. *The Glass Dome* was on the *Times*'s list for months and the furor over *Greasepaint and Garlic* is still raging on every talk show in the country. After all, it's not every day one learns that a grande dame of the theater believed in vampires."

"Yes, well . . ." He absently tugged at his collar. "Apparently I underestimated interest in the bizarre. As a matter of fact, one of the reasons I'm here is to—"

A sharp buzz cut off his words.

With a muttered curse, Broddie snatched up the phone. "I'll not be taking calls until— What's that you're saying?" His brows furrowed in annoyance. As he looked through the glass wall, Lainey followed his gaze and saw Marge Slattery, telephone to her ear, glaring into the office. She was obviously the person to whom Broddie was speaking, but Lainey was taken aback by the woman's viperous gaze.

Plump, pleasant and unfailingly loyal, Marge had been with the *Banner* for twenty-five years and still kept Gerald Sheridan's photograph on her desk. Although increasingly challenged by modern computerized procedures, Marge had repeatedly refused retirement offers—much to Broddie's consternation—and vowed that when God was ready to take her, He'd find her waiting in the *Banner* newsroom.

Lainey had seen Marge express frustration, confusion and even annoyance. She had never, however, seen the normally placid woman express overt fury. It was startling, to say the least.

"And how is it, I'm wondering, that Mr. Reeves is knowing about my visitors? Well, of course I'll be talking to him. I've little choice now, have I?" Covering the receiver, Broddie glanced up with a helpless shrug.

Lainey took the hint. "Perhaps you'd enjoy a tour of the newsroom, Mr. Cooper?"

"I'd like that very much." His smile was utterly devastating as he politely opened the office door. "But only if you promise to drop the formality. My name is Clay."

With a nervous smile, Lainey led him into the busy newsroom and conducted the tour with as much dignity as her pounding heart would allow. After pointing out the wire service photo-fax, she showed Clay the darkroom where photographs were screened to add the dot patterns necessary for transferring the image onto burn plates.

Later, while she explained how printed computer text was arranged on page-size, grided poster board, Clay stood so close that his subtle scent made her dizzy. Steadying herself on the counter, she continued the explanation with feigned confidence. "When the pasteup is completed, it's taken into the processing area."

As Clay looked over her shoulder, his cheek brushed her hair. "I see," he murmured huskily. "What happens then?"

Lainey closed her eyes, suppressing a shiver. The man was exuding enough body heat to be protected as a national resource. She swallowed hard, took a deep breath, then stepped away and managed a bright smile. "Follow me and I'll show you."

Somehow she managed to explain the production process without tripping over her tongue more than half a dozen times. She explained that the pasteup was taken to a vertical camera, a massive thing resembling an upside-down Polaroid. The resultant negative was processed chemically, proofed on a light table, then inserted into a plate burner that transferred the image onto full-size aluminum plates.

Although Clay expressed polite interest, he seemed more engrossed with the tour guide than the tour. Several times Lainey caught him watching her with an intensity that took her breath away. His gaze was mesmerizing and so deliciously erotic that she feared her skin might start to glow. Her cheeks were still burning as they entered the production area, which was completely filled by the huge printing press.

Resembling an amusement park roller coaster, the twelve-foot-high press was a mass of ladders, girders and conveyers extending the entire length of the thirty-foot room. One pressman was climbing the giant machine, inspecting gauge settings and preparing for the afternoon run. Another man was hunched underneath, threading newstock from a giant spool into a complex system of rollers.

In one corner was the beating heart of the system, the powerful pump that propelled ink through an arterial maze of tubes from a vat the size of a small bus to the working core of the press itself. Soon that pump would be humming, the press would be spitting pages and the entire room would be swarming with activity. At the moment, however, the place was about as exciting as a tombstone.

Lainey offered an apologetic smile as they returned to the newsroom. "I'm afraid there's not really much to see until the press is running."

"It's still a fascinating process. Thanks for the tour." Clay held her gaze for several moments, then sighed deeply, slid his hands into his pockets and glanced toward Broddie's office. "Looks like Mac is off the telephone."

She was startled by the personal nickname for a man whom Clay had supposedly just met. Before she could question the casual reference, she saw Broddie meet Clay's eyes with a nearly imperceptible nod. Clay tilted his head in acknowledgment, then politely thanked Lainey for the tour and disappeared into the editor's office.

Having been effectively dismissed, she meekly returned to her desk, acutely aware that she was being scrutinized by members of the staff. Some of her co-workers—Marge in particular—were glaring with undisguised hostility.

The angry stares were unsettling. Evidently her colleagues, like the majority of Scarlet's citizens, had chosen to paint Clay Cooper with the same broad brush used on his father. Although that was grossly unfair, Lainey understood the town's hatred for the elder Cooper. In fact, she shared it. Ben Cooper's brutal crime had robbed a heartbroken child of the only person who'd ever loved her. The man had been cruel and vicious. And he'd murdered Lainey's father.

* * *

Clay slid a stealthy glance at the stunning woman beside him. "A penny for your thoughts."

Stepping over a prostrate thistle, Lainey gazed down the tree-lined residential street. "I was just thinking how difficult this must be for you."

"How difficult what must be?"

"Coming back to Scarlet, facing so many sad memories." A dried poplar leaf crunched beneath her sensible loafers.

"Memories are a product of the mind," Clay said. "Not of any particular place."

The comment about memories seemed troubling to her. "It's just that people around here haven't given you an especially warm welcome."

"Some people have." He stopped abruptly. "You have."

A wary cloud veiled her dark eyes. "You sound surprised."

"I am."

"Not everyone in Scarlet feels like Marge Slattery."

"Most do." Clay didn't expect her to dispute that, and she didn't. They both knew that although the Slattery woman had admitted calling several people to announce Clay's arrival, the newsroom phones had been jammed by indignant citizens demanding that Ben Cooper's son be ridden out of town on the proverbial rail. Yet the one person in this godforsaken place who actually had reason to hate a Cooper had seemed completely stunned by the uproar. Lainey Sheridan had, in fact, seemed deeply hurt by the cruel comments—not for herself, but for Clay. That had astounded him.

But on second thought, it probably shouldn't have. Until this morning, Clay and Lainey had never exchanged a single word, yet he *knew* her. Once they'd shared something far deeper, a spiritual communication that had touched his soul and carried him through the darkest days of his life. He'd never forgotten her. Although the child of his mind had evolved into a lithe, beautiful woman, a shadow of the bewildered girl he remembered still lurked in those enormous brown eyes.

Now, however, those eyes scrupulously avoided him while Lainey twisted a glossy strand of dark hair around her finger. The silence stretched a moment, then she tucked the strand behind one ear and pulled a small notebook from her purse. "I guess we should start the interview now."

"All right. What would you like to know?"

"Well, let's see..." She fumbled through her bag and found a pen. With the ballpoint poised over the pad, she took a deep breath. "I suppose I should ask what you've been doing since you left Scarlet."

He smiled. "Considering the twenty-year time span, would you care to narrow that down a bit?"

She blushed prettily, lowered the notebook and sighed. "Obviously I'm not an experienced reporter."

"Everyone has to start somewhere." He laid an encouraging hand on her shoulder and felt her tremble under his touch. Although nearly imperceptible, the tiny movement jolted him to the core. When she took a startled step back, he slid both hands into his pockets and tried not to look shaken. "You're doing fine."

"No, I'm not." She stared down at the blank notepad. "I wish Broddie had given someone else this assignment."

Clay touched his chest as though wounded. "Why? Has my deodorant failed?"

She smiled and shook her head. "It's just that a front-page article touting your success could go a long way toward easing the town's hostility. It should be written by a seasoned professional, not a neophyte who's never even had a byline."

"Perhaps McFerson thought you could bring a unique perspective to the piece."

"Perhaps," she murmured, although a skeptical frown conveyed she didn't believe that for a minute. With her full, pink lips set in a determined line, she lifted her pen. "Where did you and your mother go after the tri—" She coughed away the indiscretion and made an admirable recovery. "After leaving Scarlet?"

"You can say the word 'trial,' Lainey. There's no reason to tap-dance around an incident that changed the course of both our lives."

Since discussing that particular event was vital to his plans, Clay carefully gauged her reaction and was disappointed when she stared at the notebook without reply. He remembered McFerson's warning that Lainey wouldn't be pleased to learn of the project that had brought him back to South Carolina. That, too, had been a disappointing discovery. Clay had believed that the reason for his return would be as critical to Lainey as to Clay himself. Still, he decided to honor her silent request by avoiding all mention of his father's trial. For the moment, anyway.

Pasting on a pleasant smile, he casually answered her original question. "After leaving Scarlet, Mother and I went to Atlanta."

Her taut shoulders relaxed slightly. "And you stayed there all these years?"

"Yes. It's a beautiful city, with ample employment opportunities. That was important, since my mother worked two jobs to keep a roof over our heads and food on the table."

Lainey's eyes softened sympathetically. "That must have been very difficult for her."

Clay shrugged. "Life was never easy for my mother, but she rarely complained—except when she learned that I wasn't going to college."

"Why on earth wouldn't you want to further your education?"

"It wasn't a matter of want. It was a matter of money. I'd been counting on a literary scholarship. When it didn't come through, I figured I'd have to work for a couple of years to save enough for tuition."

"I take it your mother wasn't happy about that."

"Not in the least." As Clay's mind rambled back in time, he smiled at the memory of his mother's soft gray eyes flashing with indignation. "She told me that education didn't insure success, but lack of it definitely guaranteed failure. Then she handed me a bank passbook."

Lainey's eyes lit up. "A college fund?"

"Yes. No matter how tough times had been, she'd managed to squirrel away a few dollars every week."

"She sounds like an extraordinary woman."

"She was. I miss her." Clay saw confusion in Lainey's eyes and explained. "Mother died last year."

"Oh." She touched her throat. "I'm so sorry."

The grief in her eyes took his breath away. Clay had expected a polite response—she was much too well-bred to be unkind—but he hadn't expected sincere sorrow for the woman whom many had blamed as the ultimate cause of Gerald Sheridan's tragic death.

"Catherine Cooper was a beautiful woman," Lainey whispered. "I remember how close you and your mother were. You must feel an enormous sense of loss."

After acknowledging her sympathy with a curt nod—his throat was too tight to speak—they walked in silence for a few minutes. As they passed the chain-link fence surrounding the elementary school, Clay slid a glance at the woman beside him, scrutinizing the delicate crease of her arched brows, the pensive pout of her firm pink lips. He briefly wondered if she realized how beautiful she was, but quickly discarded the notion. For some unknown reason, Lainey Sheridan seemed oblivious to her own assets. There was a humility about her, a gratitude for the most minute kindness, that Clay found unsettling.

Lainey spoke suddenly, jarring him from his contemplation. "I remember seeing you and your mother at the courthouse," she said. "You were so protective, and Catherine looked so dazed, obviously heartbroken by what was happening to her husband. I remember wondering why someone so frail and lovely could ever have married such a vicious man."

Clay jerked to a stop and stared down in astonishment. At first he thought she must be joking. When he realized that she was dead serious, the hairs on his nape lifted. Lainey actually believed that his mother shed those tears for her imprisoned husband. Was it possible that Lainey didn't know...?

He shook off the implausible thought. Of course she knew. She had to. It had been the talk of the town, part of the court records, one of the most damning bits of evidence presented at his father's trial.

When he felt a soft pressure on his arm, Clay turned and saw the most incredible sadness reflected in Lainey's lovely eyes. "That was unforgivably insensitive of me," she whispered. "Of course Catherine loved her husband. No matter what mistakes your father made, I never meant to imply that he wasn't worthy of being loved."

Clay felt like he'd swallowed a brick. *Worthy of being loved?* Now she really must be kidding. Ben Cooper had been as mean as a snake. As far as Clay was concerned, the brutal bastard had gotten exactly what he'd deserved, albeit for the wrong reasons.

Now he anxiously studied Lainey's guileless eyes and realized that she hadn't been kidding at all. The poor woman evidently had no clue about what had really happened twenty years ago. That was one hell of a shock to his system, not to mention a mortal blow to his carefully laid plans.

Lainey's distressed voice broke into his thoughts. "I've hurt you. I'm so sorry."

"No... it's all right. Listen, there's something you really need to understa—"

The squeal of tires cut off his words. A Scarlet police car hung a sloppy U-turn, gunned toward them and screeched to a stop at the curb. The driver pushed back his cap, slowly pulled off his mirrored sunglasses and regarded Clay scornfully. "Well, well," drawled the uniformed man. "Lookie what we got here. A six-foot heap of walking garbage."

Although Lainey was astounded by the verbal abuse, she was well aware that Aldrich Clark had always been a vulgar man, too lazy to be considered ruthless and had no ambition beyond his own comfort. Without the good fortune of having Lloyd Reeves as a brother-in-law, he'd have probably spent life with a beer in one hand and a disability check in the other. Instead, he'd managed to wrangle an appointment as chief of police.

Now Clark propped a fat elbow out the car window, scratched his pendulous jowls and gave Lainey a slitty-eyed stare. "Does your uncle know you're slumming, girl?"

Before she could utter a response, Clay laid a warm palm on her shoulder. "Since your problem is apparently with me, there's no reason to insult Miss Sheridan."

The chief's fleshy lips quivered. "You always were an uppity bastard." Glowering, the chief spit out the window and wiped his mouth with the back of his hand. "Them fancy clothes don't change what you are, boy. You was born trash and you'll die trash, just like that good-for-nothing pappy of yours. Weren't a Cooper ever lived had a right to be with decent folks. You'd best be moving on real soon, y'hear?" Yanking his arm inside, Clark tipped his hat to Lainey and murmured, "Y'all have a nice day." With that, he jammed the car into gear and drove away.

Too stunned to move, Lainey watched the police car speed down the block and disappear. Her chest ached and she realized that she'd been holding her breath. She exhaled slowly and slid a worried glance at Clay. To her surprise, he seemed remarkably calm and except for a convulsive grip on her shoulder, appeared unaffected by Clark's verbal abuse. "Are you all right?"

A muscle below his jaw twitched. He managed a thin smile. "Sure."

"He had no right to say those horrible things to you."

"I've heard worse."

Unfortunately, that was probably true. In spite of his stoic demeanor, Lainey suspected that Clay was more deeply hurt than he cared to admit. Her heart ached for him, and as she studied his stern profile, she was struck by a compelling urge to touch him, to trace his rigid jaw with her fingertips and smooth away the strain lines bracketing his firm mouth.

The image was so powerful, so deliciously intriguing, that her heart leapt in anticipation. Suddenly a hand that looked much like her own was pressed gently against his cheek. As a satisfying warmth penetrated her palm, she was vaguely aware that his fingers had left her shoulder to lightly encircle her wrist. Making no attempt to remove her hand, Clay turned slightly and gazed down, his moonlight eyes wide with wonder.

The impact was stunning. For two decades Lainey had dreamed of a warrior's eyes, fierce and protective. But these weren't the eyes of a warrior; these were the eyes of a loving man, a man filled with hope and promise and a sensual hunger that shook her to the soles of her feet.

She yanked away as if singed and was appalled by having taken such liberties with a man she'd just met. Clearing her throat, she forced herself to meet his baffled gaze. "You're a good man, Clay Cooper. You didn't deserve the terrible things that happened to you."

His own hand was poised in midair, empty fingers still curved to the shape of her wrist. "That's a generous assumption, considering that you barely know me."

"I know you've been treated unfairly."

He absently brushed a knuckle over his own cheek as though savoring the remnant of her caress. "If life was fair, you wouldn't have grown up without a father."

The reminder of her own loss was sobering. An image flashed in her mind, the memory of the laughing man who'd spend hours pushing his daughter's swing on a lazy summer afternoon. Since Lainey's mother had been a frail woman, frequently taking to bed for weeks at a time, Gerald Sheridan had assumed primary parenting duties with enthusiasm and surprising proficiency. He'd doted on his daughter, and she in turn had adored him with the intense reverence that only a hero-worshipping six-year-old could muster.

When he'd died, little Lainey had knelt in prayer and somberly asked God if it she could please go to Heaven, too, so her daddy wouldn't get lonely. Apparently God had had other plans because she'd awakened the following morning, heartbroken and very much alive.

"You're right," Lainey murmured, embarrassed by the sudden sting of tears. "Life isn't fair." Turning away, she continued down the sidewalk.

Clay fell into step beside her, and they walked silently. When they reached the corner, he suddenly took her arm. She balked as he tried to guide her across the street. "Where are you going?"

"To your house." The reply was casual enough, but a determined glint in his eye gave her pause. "If we're in luck, your mother might have a pot of coffee brewing."

Lainey's protest faded into a hushed gasp. The old house loomed like a faded gray ghost. Her nape tingled. Her stomach turned. In her mind she heard the long-ago echo of childish giggles, the melancholy squeak of the old porch swing, the playful rustle of a kitten scampering through the overgrown bushes flanking the stoop.

Pulling from his insistent grasp, Lainey spun around and retreated back across the street. Her heart was still racing as Clay followed her onto the curb. When he questioned her silently, she managed a halting—and not completely accurate—explanation of her behavior. "That house hasn't been my home for a very long time."

"Doesn't your mother still live there?"

"No." A cold mist beaded her upper lip. "My mother left Scarlet years ago."

Clay caught himself before the profanity slipped off his tongue. It had never occurred to him that MaryBeth Sheridan, who held the key to his investigation, would have ever left the town in which she'd been born and raised. He flexed his fists, took a deep breath and tried not to sound desperate. "Where is she living now?" As Lainey issued a vague shrug, her discomfort did not escape his notice. "Don't you know where your own mother is?"

"She, uh, isn't very good at writing."

"What is that supposed to mean?" Clay demanded, suddenly unable to control a mounting sense of panic.

Lainey shrugged again and gazed back toward the center of town. "I really should be getting back—"

He stepped forward to block her path. "Exactly when did your mother leave town?"

She fidgeted with the cuff of her sweater. "A long time ago."

"How long?" When she ignored the question, his heart sank to the pit of his stomach. One of the answers he needed from MaryBeth was an explanation of why she'd hadn't told the truth at—or even attended—the trial of her husband's alleged killer. Now a chilling theory formed in Clay's mind. "Your mother left Scarlet twenty years ago, didn't she? She just took off and left you alone."

"I was never alone," Lainey said defensively. She folded her arms and studied the sidewalk. "I had my aunt and uncle."

The imprecise vision of a limping, tight-lipped crone popped into Clay's mind. He recalled having disliked the scowling woman because during the trial she'd kept such a merciless grip on her tiny niece's arm. "Where is your mother now?"

"It's, uh—" Lainey wiped her damp forehead "—hard to say. She travels."

After a concerted effort to unwind his balled fingers, Clay took a deep breath. He tried not to sound desperate, but this was a complication he hadn't expected. "Okay. So she travels and she doesn't write. Still, you must have some way to get in touch with her...a post office box, a forwarding service of some kind?"

She poked a bent weed with her toe. "Not really."

"But—"

"Gracious, it really is getting late!" Straightening, Lainey gave her watch a halfhearted glance then looked up brightly. "If this story is going to make deadline, I'd better get back to the office and write it up."

"Lainey, wait." Clay snagged her arm as she turned. "You don't have the real story yet."

A perplexed frown creased her brow. "What do you mean?"

Reluctantly releasing her, he folded his arms and rocked back on his heels. Obviously Lainey was lying. Clay didn't have a doubt in his mind that she was well aware of her mother's whereabouts. Apparently, however, she didn't trust Clay enough to share that information.

After a brief inner struggle, Clay decided the only way to gain that trust was to reveal the truth about his return to Scarlet. He blew out a breath and met her quizzical gaze with one of staunch determination. "This article you're writing... I'd like it to include the fact that I'm researching a new book."

She brightened. "Really? What kind of book? Will you use Scarlet as the setting—" Her excited glow faded. "Wait a minute. I thought you only wrote nonfiction." When he confirmed that with a nod, she stepped back, eyeing him warily. "Exactly what kind of book are we talking about?"

He hesitated, massaged his eyelids, then took a deep breath and blurted the truth. "A factual analysis of how my father was framed for a murder he didn't commit."

Lainey went white. "You can't be serious."

"I've never been more serious in my life." Clay raked his hair, stung by her horrified expression. "Look, Lainey, I've done my homework on this. I've studied court transcripts, police and coroner reports and depositions. You could drive a tank through the holes in the prosecutor's case."

"Stop it!" Lainey spun and strode away.

Clay caught up with her.

"Please, hear me out. Exposing the truth will be as crucial to your peace of mind as to my own. You need to know who killed your father."

Jerking to a stop, she stared straight ahead. "Ben Cooper killed my father."

"Why, Lainey? What was his motive?"

Lainey felt the blood drain from her face. She didn't want to talk about this. "I... don't know."

"You know what the prosecutor said, don't you?"

"He..." Lainey licked her lips. "Ben Cooper was demented. He didn't need a reason."

After a pause, Clay spoke softly. "But he had a reason, didn't he? And that reason was the only truth that came out of that trial. My mother and your father were in love."

"No!" Lainey shook her head violently. "It's a lie. Daddy would never have been unfaithful to my mother."

"It happened," he said gently. "I have proof—"

"You have nothing! *It's not true!*"

When Clay extended his hand in a pleading gesture, Lainey covered her ears and turned away. She couldn't stand to hear another word. Gerald Sheridan had been the only stable person in her life. He'd died a hero, trying to protect the family he'd adored. Now Clay was threatening to dredge up old hurts and give credence to that vile rumor about her father having an affair with Catherine Cooper.

Lainey had been a teenager the first time she'd heard the awful gossip. She hadn't believed it then, and she didn't believe it now. As far as she was concerned, Ben Cooper had destroyed her father. All she had left was his memory, and it seemed as if Cooper's son was out to destroy that.

But what frightened her most were Clay's insistent questions about her mother. She swallowed a lump of panic. Dear God, what would happen if he somehow managed to find MaryBeth? Then everyone would know. They'd all look at Lainey with revulsion and pity, and the cruel whispers would start all over again. She wouldn't be able to bear the shame.

Squaring her shoulders, she turned to face the man who had betrayed her trust and her kindness. "I won't allow you to smear my family's name."

Clay stiffened. "I'm not going to smear anyone, Lainey, but I am planning to write the truth."

"You're planning to write slanderous lies, and I won't have it, do you hear?" She ripped her notes from the pad and threw the wadded papers in the gutter. "It's disgusting. I won't have any part of it."

As she spun around, Clay took hold of her arm, stopping her. His eyes were as cold as frozen ponds. "If you don't write the article, McFerson will."

It took a moment for that to sink in. When it did, she was outraged. "I don't believe Broddie would ever be part of such a vile scheme."

"McFerson is interested in exposing the truth."

"Great. That's just great." She angrily shook off Clay's restraining hand, feeling doubly betrayed. "Well, you can both go straight to the devil because I'm going to stop you, Clay Cooper. That book will be published over my dead body!"

With that, she spun and stalked away.

Stunned and furious, Clay watched her disappear around the corner and tried to grasp the consequence of what had just happened. Since he'd assumed that Lainey would naturally want to know the truth about her father's death, her threat to interfere had taken him completely by surprise. Obviously she was frightened about something. Clay didn't have a clue as to what it was and, at the moment, was too angry to care.

He was also deeply disappointed. Throughout the years he'd kept an image of Lainey Sheridan as a six-year-old child standing on the courthouse steps with huge brown eyes and a dazed expression. Their gazes had met once, a mind-link of two innocents embroiled in an adult rage that was far beyond their comprehension. In a single, bewildered glance, the two of them had connected to share loss, pain and confusion over a world gone mad, a world they could neither understand nor control. At that moment Lainey Sheridan had been his soul mate. Now she was his enemy, and they were locked in mortal combat. Clay took no solace in knowing that it was a battle she was destined to lose.

Lainey strode into Broddie's office without knocking and slammed both hands on his desk. "How could you do this to me?"

To his credit, Broddie didn't bother to feign ignorance. Instead he screwed the top back on the whiskey flask that had been a constant companion since the death of his wife eight years ago. "Cooper's story is news, Lainey, lass."

"It's not news, it's *history*." Hating the hysterical edge to her voice, Lainey straightened, pressed a palm against her forehead and took a calming breath. "There's nothing to be gained by dredging up the past."

Broddie absently scratched his stubbled chin. "There's truth."

She balled her fists and tried to sound reasonable. "Twenty years ago there was a trial. You covered that trial yourself and reported that Ben Cooper murdered my father."

"No, darlin'. I reported that Cooper was *convicted* of murder—"

"It's the same thing." She cut off his protest with an impatient gesture. "Please, Broddie. Arguing semantics won't change the facts."

"'Tis right you are." Leaning forward, the old man propped his elbows on his desk and steepled his hands. "Facts are facts, so why should you be concerning yourself with Clay's investigation?"

She steadied herself on a file cabinet, refusing to look at him. "Because he wants to find Mother."

After a long, silent moment, she glanced over her shoulder and saw Broddie staring thoughtfully at the top of his cluttered desk. "That's something he'll not be needing to know," he said finally.

Closing her eyes, Lainey exhaled in relief. "So you agree that Clay's book has to be stopped?" Hearing only a pained sigh, she looked up warily.

Broddie pushed his chair back and stood. "'Tis a free country. If the man doesn't believe his father was guilty, he's got every right in the world to say so."

"Not if it's libelous!" Panic surged like bile into her throat. "Do you know what kind of garbage he's going to write? He plans to tell the entire world that my father was having an . . . an— " She nearly choked on the word. "Affair."

Broddie moved around his desk and reached for her hand. "Lainey—"

"No!" She pulled away. "I can't let Clay publish those lies!"

"If lies are written, you can sue for the truth."

"What good will that do? The damage will have already been done." Fear made her irrational, unable to control the flow of hurtful words. "My God, Broddie, you were my father's best friend. I can't believe you'd help destroy his reputation just to sell a few newspapers."

Broddie stiffened as though slapped. "So that's what you think of me, is it?"

Lainey put one hand on her hip and covered her eyes with the other. She honestly didn't know what to think. Before storming into Broddie's office a few minutes earlier, she'd been shocked to see proofs of his most recent editorial. The column was a scathing reminder of the town's abysmal behavior two decades ago along with a stern warning about Christian tolerance. Even worse, the editorial reiterated how ChemCorp executives had fueled town hysteria by publicly indicting Ben Cooper and unjustly firing his innocent wife. And there was more. Much more.

Since the *Banner*'s editorials were usually conservative and judicious to the point of being bland, the vehement attack had shocked Lainey to the core. She hadn't been alone. The newsroom was in chaos. Marge Slattery had walked out in protest and taken half a dozen people with her. The remaining staff members were locked in verbal combat, either staunchly defending or hotly opposing the editorial content. The only thing on which everyone agreed was that there'd be hell to pay when the afternoon edition hit the streets.

"I'm concerned about you," Lainey said. "Your editorial is going to ruffle a lot of important feathers."

"Probably." Broddie snatched the flask from his desk, opened it and took a healthy swallow.

"What if this whole thing backfires?" After skimming a glance at her dear friend, she winced at the pain in his eyes and quickly looked away. "I mean, you've managed to insult just about everyone in town. The *Banner* isn't exactly rolling in excess revenues. If people start canceling subscriptions and ChemCorp pulls its advertising, we could be in real trouble."

Broddie tipped the flask once more, then wiped his mouth with the back of his hand. He regarded her coolly. "I'll not be turning this paper into a public relations brochure. *Banner* policy is not for sale."

"But we're not talking about *Banner* policy, we're talking about *your* policy, *your* opinions—"

"Yes, by God." He slammed down the flask, snatched the engraved nameplate from his desk and held it in front of her startled face. "As long as this says Editor In Chief, my policy *is Banner* policy."

Fear loosened her tongue and numbed her brain. "Policy can be changed," she snapped. "And editors can be replaced."

As the light faded from Broddie's eyes, Lainey gasped and covered her mouth, horrified that she'd done the unthinkable by pulling rank and threatening to fire the man she dearly loved.

"So that's how it's to be, is it?" Broddie's wizened complexion was nearly as white as his hair. Before she could extend a conciliatory hand, the grizzled newsman turned his back. "Do what you have to," he said quietly. "And close the door on your way out."

Chapter 3

At night, the old house seemed even more frightening. Rubbing the chill from her bare arms, Lainey stood on the corner where she and Clay had been that morning. Moonlight filtered through a maple tree in the front yard, throwing eerie, dappled shadows on the weathered gray clapboards. The leaves swayed with the breeze; the building appeared to move with the shadows, expanding and contracting as though it were alive and breathing.

Never once since her father's death had Lainey returned to the home she'd shared with her parents—now she'd come twice in one day. The first visit had frightened her, awakening long-repressed emotions. Then the memories had come, and with them, a compelling urge that had drawn her here once again.

She vaguely wondered if she was reacting to a subconscious need for parental solace, rather like a kneading cat trying to rekindle the comfort of its mother's breast. At the moment she could empathize with the weaned kittens of the world. She, too, felt alone, cast adrift in a world without softness or love. She'd experienced these feelings of inner isolation when her father died. Now the rift between her and Broddie brought those feelings back to the surface.

Broddie had been so hurt, so desperately, deeply wounded. If she lived a thousand years, she'd never forget the pain in his eyes or the stoic quiver of his mouth. She didn't understand how she could have ever said such terrible things. There'd been a panic inside her, a burgeoning hysteria that had swelled beyond control and burst through an emotional dam that had stood for decades.

Since childhood Lainey had struggled to suppress many fears—anxiety about the recurring nightmare, a quiet terror born of her mother's haunting secret, and an ambivalence about her own aimless future. Clay Cooper's return had solidified those fears and added a new dimension, an instinctive perception that for better or worse, her life would never be the same.

Lainey leaned against a lamp pole and gazed across at the place where everything she'd loved had been cruelly taken away. Because the memories were so bitter, she'd tucked them into a secret part of her mind. Now, however, she remembered that there had been joy, too, days filled with the only true happiness of her life.

As she gazed at the house, her mind replaced the dappled shadows with a brilliant wash of sunlight. Colorful blooms spilled from carefully tended flower beds surrounding the freshly cut lawn and the maple limbs were alive with songbirds.

It had been a warm day—summer, she thought. Lainey recalled picking shasta daisies while her father had raked grass clippings. When he'd finished scooping the thick green pile into a lawn bag, she'd run to him clutching a ragged bouquet. "Daddy, daddy! Look what I picked for Mommy."

Grinning, Gerald had lifted his excited daughter and cradled her in his strong arms. "They're beautiful, Peaches."

Lainey had wrapped a chubby arm around her daddy's neck. "Do you think Mommy will like them?"

"I'm sure she will."

She giggled when Daddy blew a love-bubble on her neck. "I wanna give Mommy my flowers."

"Mommy's resting now." Gerald's smile faded slightly as he lowered his daughter to the ground. "Let's wait awhile, okay?"

"Okay." Deeply disappointed, Lainey chewed her lower lip, eyes downcast to hide the gathering tears. Daddy hated to see her cry because it made him feel bad. "Can I go watch TV?"

"It's such a pretty day. Wouldn't you rather stay outside and help me with the yard?"

She stared at his denim-clad knees and shrugged. "I don't care."

A warm hand cupped her shoulder. He knelt, urged her chin up, then smiled sadly and wiped her wet cheeks with his thumb. "Mommy loves you very much, Peaches. You know that, don't you?"

"Yes." In truth, Lainey knew no such thing. Deep down, she feared that her mother didn't like her at all. Mommy had never been mean or anything, but she was always feeling sick or tired or under the weather, whatever that meant. Lainey found it all very confusing.

"I have an idea," Gerald said suddenly. "Let's put your flowers in a big vase of water, then you can help me bake an apple pie for dessert tonight. How does that sound?"

A husky, feminine voice floated from the front door. "That sounds lovely." The porch screen squeaked as MaryBeth Cooper took a rare step into daylight.

Lainey was beside herself with excitement. "Mommy!" she squealed. "Look at the pretty flowers!" Dashing up the wooden stoop, she held out the bedraggled clump of daisies. "They're for you."

Smiling graciously, MaryBeth accepted her daughter's gift. "Well, aren't these just the prettiest things? Thank you."

"I picked them all by myself," Lainey announced.

MaryBeth delicately seated herself on the porch swing. "Did you now? I declare, you're such a clever girl."

The praise made Lainey proud enough to burst. Without thinking, she clambered onto the swing and gave her mother a fierce hug. The woman stiffened. Lainey instantly backed away, ashamed to have forgotten that Mommy didn't like to be touched.

"Sorry," Lainey mumbled, staring miserably at her own knees. From the corner of her eye, she saw her mother's thin hand reach out and hover uncertainly. She was disappointed although not surprised when Mommy drew back and folded both hands neatly in her lap.

Gerald, too, seemed disappointed. He leaned casually against the whitewashed railing and spoke gently to his wife. "Are you feeling better, MaryBeth?"

Her dark eyes softened. "Yes, thank you. I'm quite well."

"You look lovely," Gerald murmured, and was rewarded by her radiant smile.

When Mommy smiled—*really* smiled—Lainey thought her the most beautiful woman on earth. People always said Lainey was the spitting image of her mother because they shared the same liquid fudge eyes and perky, upturned nose. But instead of MaryBeth's shining, sun blond tresses or even Gerald's thick chestnut mane, Lainey had a headful of coarse, dirt brown hair that didn't seem to match anyone in the family. Except maybe Great-gramma Hildebrand, whose hair had supposedly been the color of river mud and as kinky as a horse's tail. People said Great-gramma was real ugly. That meant that Lainey was ugly, too, and that's probably why Mommy didn't like her very much. If she'd been born with blond hair and sky blue eyes, Mommy might have even hugged her sometimes.

But Daddy never seemed to care what Lainey looked like. He always pretended his daughter was the prettiest little girl in the world and when he looked at her, his eyes smiled the same way as they did when he looked at Mommy.

Lainey scooted against swing's armrest, hugged her knees and studied the silent interaction between her parents. Anyone could tell that they loved each other. Every time Daddy came into a room, Mommy's eyes would turn all dark and misty. And Daddy treated Mommy as if she were the most special person in the whole wide world. But sometimes, when he didn't think anyone was looking, Daddy's expression would turn all sad and wistful, as if he wanted something he'd couldn't ever have. That always bothered Lainey. Sometimes it even scared her.

But at the moment, Lainey wasn't scared at all. Everything was just wonderful because Mommy had come out of the bedroom and Lainey was going to help Daddy bake an apple pie. It was going to be a really happy day....

As the sunny scene faded into darkness, Lainey shivered and turned away from the memories. Odd, she thought, that she'd forgotten those happy times, choosing instead to brood about having had her childish affections rebuffed. In retrospect, she realized that although her mother had had difficulty with physical expression, she'd always treated Lainey kindly and with gentle compassion.

Lainey recalled overhearing various discussions about her mother—few of which had been flattering. Most people conceded that MaryBeth had been fond of her daughter even though she'd been undeniably devoid of maternal instinct. Some said the poor woman had never recovered from the pain of childbirth, which also explained why she'd never returned to her husband's bed; others theorized that she'd been traumatized by some unspeakable past abuse. No one knew for sure, of course, but that didn't stop the idle speculation that had always been Scarlet's favorite pastime.

On one thing, however, the entire town agreed: MaryBeth Sheridan had been the epitome of a genteel Southern lady, sweet as a julep, fragile as a magnolia and deeply in love with her husband.

If only they'd known—

A sharp pain pierced Lainey's skull. She gasped, pressing her palms to her temples. Squeezing her eyelids shut, she turned away from the house across the street, away from the agony that always struck when her thoughts ventured too far into the past. She had to clear her mind, erase the tormenting memories. The pain would stop then. It always did.

Lainey cried out as someone took hold of her shoulders. Pushing against her anonymous captor, she struggled until a familiar voice penetrated her blind terror.

"Lainey... what is it?"

She squinted at the blurred face. "Clay?"

"Are you all right?" His warm palms gently framed her skull. "Do you need a doctor?"

"No," she croaked, wincing at another stabbing pain. "Headache."

"Take a deep breath and hold it," Clay commanded. When she complied, he cupped the back of her head with his fingers and pressed his thumbs on a pressure point between her eyes. "That's good," he murmured. "Now exhale slowly... slowly... good. Take another breath... hold it..."

After Clay had guided her through several cycles, her muscles had softened and the pain had eased to a gentle throb. She briefly considered stepping away, but dismissed the thought because his touch was so soothing. She was comforted by the warmth of his nearness, intoxicated by his masculine scent.

Aware that a strange heat was penetrating her palms, Lainey realized that her hands were intimately pressed against his chest. Of course she should remove them immediately. Familiar contact in a public place was highly inappropriate. If she'd been observed in such a compromising position, particularly with Clay Cooper, everyone in town would know by morning and the reputation she protected so fiercely would be permanently tarnished. In Scarlet, popular perception had always held more value than truth.

Despite that knowledge, Lainey's tingling fingertips continued to absorb the strength hidden beneath the smooth fabric, the hard muscle and warm flesh radiating a palpable aura of raw sexuality into her quivering palms. She wanted to forget where they were—*who* they were—and step into the circle of his sheltering embrace. She couldn't, of course. But God knew how much she wanted to.

With some effort, she peeled her palms from his chest and took a shaky step back.

He regarded her with concern. "Are you feeling better?"

"Yes. Thank you." She clasped her hands together and lifted her chin. "What are you doing here?"

At the curt question, she noted a shift in his demeanor. His shoulders lifted, his jaw tightened, and there was an unsettled wariness in his eyes. After a long moment, during which he seemed to be weighing response options, he said simply, "I wanted to talk to you."

"How did you know I was here?" Lainey watched his gaze flicker and was instantly incensed to realize that she must have been under surveillance. "You followed me?"

He didn't bother to deny it. "Like I said, I wanted to talk to you."

"Have you ever heard of the telephone?"

"I thought you might hang up on me."

"You thought right." Outraged, Lainey roughly raked her shoulder-length hair, then spun around and strode angrily away.

She'd traveled less than twenty feet when Clay fell into step beside her. "The truth is that I did go to the Clemmonses' house tonight. Unfortunately, I arrived just as you were putting supper on the table. I didn't want to disturb you."

Since the kitchen window faced the front yard, activity in that room was clearly visible from the street, so Lainey didn't find Clay's observation to be particularly startling. She was, however, disturbed by the notion of how long he'd stood there and what else he might have witnessed. "So you just sat and watched?"

"It's a public street."

"Have you always been a peeper or is this a relatively new perversion?"

To her surprise, he responded with an amused smile. "Your family did provide a certain amount of entertainment."

Her face flamed, remembering the bitter argument that had raged through the supper hour. "I hope you enjoyed yourself."

"Not particularly, although I must admit to having been impressed. I've never seen anyone cook, wash clothes and do the ironing all at the same time." His smile faded. "Someone should inform your aunt and uncle that slavery is against the law."

"That's a ridiculous thing to say."

"Is it?" The sharp edge to his voice startled her. "From what I saw, Russ and Hallie make Cinderella's stepfamily look like saints."

She slid him a guarded glance. "Then whatever you saw, or think you saw, was obviously interpreted out of context."

Clay suddenly pivoted around, forcing Lainey to either stop or bump into him. She stopped. "So you like waiting on them hand and foot?" he asked roughly.

A weak protest died on her lips. Lainey *did* wait on her aunt and uncle, but she'd never really minded. Actually, she was nurturing by nature and rather enjoyed the details of homemaking. Sometimes she'd pretend to be tending her own home and would imagine the house filled with boisterous children and happy laughter. Occasionally she'd even catch herself smiling wistfully before reality destroyed the lovely image. Lainey could never have those beautiful children, never be part of a loving family. Her future was clouded by uncertainty and fear, a secret burden that she must carry alone.

A lump rose in her throat and her heart ached as though squeezed. Crossing her arms like a shield, Lainey avoided both Clay's probing question and intense gaze by stepping around him. She walked briskly, aware that he was right beside her.

After a moment he spoke. "The meal didn't seem to be a particularly pleasant one."

She managed not to flinch. In truth, supper had been absolutely miserable. Despite repeated assurance that Lainey had had nothing to do with the *Banner* article, her uncle had been furious. And while Russ had ranted, Hallie had confirmed Lainey's deepest fears by lamenting that unless Cooper was stopped, MaryBeth's secret shame would be exposed to the world. When Russ's furious diatribe had been interrupted by a phone call, Lainey had slipped out the back door and rushed blindly into the night.

Apparently Clay Cooper had been right behind her.

"My van is right here," he said suddenly. "I'll drive you home."

"I'd rather walk."

He briefly touched her arm. "There are some things we should discuss."

"We have nothing to talk about."

"I think we do."

"Your thoughts are of no concern to me."

"Do facts concern you?" This time he took hold of her arm and held it firmly. "Does the truth concern you? I have evidence, Lainey, proof that my father was nowhere near your parents' house the night your father died."

She stared at his restrictive hand. "Let go of me, Mr. Cooper."

"If you don't care about justice, aren't you at least a bit curious about who murdered your father?"

Her nerves snapped. She yanked out of his grasp and faced him angrily. "I *know* who murdered my father, and the fact that Ben Cooper took his last breath in a stinking jail cell is all the justice I need."

"I see." Clay's expression was as dark as a thunderstorm and just as dangerous. "It seems I've misjudged you, Miss Sheridan."

"Yes, it seems that you have." With that, she spun on her heel and walked briskly away. She half expected to hear his muffled footsteps behind her; instead she heard only the thrum of a car engine. In a moment the van whizzed by and disappeared into the night.

Lainey exhaled all at once and slowed her pace. In spite of feigned bravado, she was conflicted and deeply upset by Clay's assertion that the truth about her father's death had never been exposed. She'd always been convinced that Ben Cooper was guilty. Now she was beginning to wonder if Clay really did have evidence to the contrary. The thought that an innocent man might have died in prison was horrifying. And if that was true, where was the real killer? The disturbing question made Lainey's head throb violently.

Massaging her aching temples, she reminded herself that Ben Cooper had been convicted in a court of law. If a jury had found the man guilty, then he was guilty. Period. Clay's crusade was obviously a case of misplaced loyalty by an emotionally wounded son. He was probably so desperate to clear his father's name that he actually accepted his own lies. Yes, that pathetic theory was both rational and reasonable. Unfortunately, Lainey didn't believe it.

Clay slammed the motel room door, flipped on the glaring overhead light and flopped angrily on the bed. So far his carefully constructed mission had been a roaring disaster. During the weeks since he'd first established confidential communications with Broddie McFerson, Clay had made every attempt to anticipate problems and devise options to deal with them. Unfortunately, he hadn't seriously considered the old newsman's worry that Lainey might be one of those problems. It had seemed inconceivable to Clay that she wouldn't leap at the chance to expose her father's killer.

Well, she'd been given that chance and she damn well hadn't leapt and Clay didn't have a clue what to do about that.

Frustrated, he sat up far enough to beat a pillow into submission, then propped it behind his back. He laced his fingers, cupped his hands behind his neck and brooded about the past.

During the trial, his mother had testified under oath, swearing that her husband had been home at the time of the murder. Since that hadn't been what the town had wanted to hear, Catherine Cooper had been verbally crucified, labeled every kind of liar and slut. She'd been telling the truth, of course, but then, truth didn't matter much in Scarlet. That was going to change. Clay was going to shove those filthy accusations down the collective throat of this self-righteous town, with or without Lainey Sheridan's help.

Although proving Ben Cooper's innocence would restore his mother's good name, Clay didn't give a damn that his father's name would also be cleared. Ben Cooper had been a monster when drunk and not much to brag about when he was sober. Even though Ben hadn't killed Gerald Sheridan, Clay knew perfectly well that his father had been capable of murder. Years ago a convenience store clerk had been stabbed to death during a robbery; later Ben had staggered home with a bloody shirt and a pocket full of cash. And one night a bar patron had shown off a solid gold watch hours before being found slumped in his car with a naked wrist and a bullet in his brain. The next morning, Clay caught his father flushing a pawn shop receipt down the commode.

Clay didn't think his mother had known about either incident. For some odd reason, Ben had liked bragging about violent encounters to his son while carefully concealing such dubious activities from his wife. Wisely, Ben had never forced Catherine to choose between loyalty and conscience. He was, in fact, an expert at gaining his wife's sympathy and support, portraying himself as a misunderstood man whose efforts to earn a better life for his family had constantly been thwarted by rotten luck and an elitist society.

And the ploy had worked. Or at least, Clay had thought it had, although he'd often wondered how his bright, intelligent mother could have been so blind to her husband's faults. After Catherine's death, she'd answered that question—and so many others.

Suddenly restless, Clay went to the desk where the bulging briefcase sat beside his laptop computer. He unfastened the leather buckle, dug through the mass of papers and files until he found the thick notebook that had been his mother's personal journal. Beneath the worn cover was the essence of his mother's thoughts, emotions and shattered dreams. Because Clay couldn't help himself, he turned to the first entry and traced the first line of delicate script with his fingertip.

Yesterday was my seventeenth birthday.

He smiled and although he'd long ago memorized the passage, continued to read.

Today I received the most blessed gift. My son was born at three minutes after midnight, the most brilliant and beautiful child this world has ever seen. Clayton Charles Cooper—isn't that distinguished? Just writing it gives me goose bumps! Ben thinks it's a sissy name—says real men are called Joe or Bill or Bubba. Fortunately, my husband also believes that naming offspring is a mother's prerogative. Since Ben will be forty next year, he never expected to be a father in the first place and was terribly upset by my pregnancy. I've been so worried about what will happen when the baby arrived, but now that his son is here, Ben is strutting around like any other proud Papa. Maybe things will work out after all—

Clay was startled by a sharp knock on the door. Frowning, he slid the journal back into his briefcase, wondered if Lainey'd had a change of heart and decided to hear him out. The thought lifted his spirits until he realized that the forceful pounding was more likely caused by a man's fist than a woman's delicate hand.

After putting the briefcase in the closet, Clay glanced through the peephole. There stood Lloyd Reeves and a scrawny, ferret-faced man with a nasal inhalant stuffed up one nostril. Both looked grim as death.

Clay set his jaw, opened the door and greeted his visitors with cold eyes and a hard smile. "It's about time I had a proper welcome," he drawled. "Where's the marching band?"

The smaller man dropped the atomizer into his pocket and sneered like a snappish terrier. "Cut the crap, Cooper."

Reeves laid a gloved hand on his companion's shoulder and favored Clay with a politic smile. "I wonder if we might have a moment of your time."

"Gee, I don't know. I planned to wash my hair tonight."

"How commendable." Although Reeves's smile never wavered, his thin eyes narrowed into icy slits. "Since there are matters of some urgency to discuss, perhaps you'd be good enough to postpone your personal toilette."

"Urgent, is it? Well, hell, now I'm really intrigued." Clay stepped back, inviting them inside with an effusive sweep of his hand.

With an acknowledging nod, Reeves entered and glanced acutely around the dreary room. He meticulously released each finger from the formfitting leather before removing the gloves and tucking them into the pocket of his overcoat.

Although in his mid-sixties, Lloyd Reeves was still an impressive man, physically powerful and ethically ruthless. As ChemCorp's CEO for more than three decades, he'd ruled the company and the town itself with an iron fist. Despite having officially retired last year, few believed Reeves had completely released the reins of power, particularly to a snippish prig like Sandborne Hunicutt, who was now slinking into the motel room.

After pasting himself beside the exit, Hunicutt pulled out a monogrammed handkerchief and noisily blew his nose. The pinched little fellow was a blur of nervous motion—eyes darting, fingers plucking, feet shuffling. Peering over the damp linen cloth, he seemed a pathetic creature, bearing more resemblance to cornered prey than the chief executive of a powerful conglomerate.

"Do you remember Mr. Hunicutt?" Reeves asked politely.

"Yeah." Clay spared the odious little man a disdainful glance. "How'd you get him to heel without a leash?"

Hunicutt emitted a strangled snarl and nearly tripped over his own fidgeting feet. "You rotten—"

Reeves froze him with a look, then turned a cool gaze on Clay. "You always did have a smart mouth. I was hoping you'd changed."

"I have. I'm taller and I wear better clothes." Crossing his arms, Clay propped a hip against the desk. "So, is there a reason for this unexpected visit or were you just taking Fido for a walk?"

Since Reeves purposely ignored the insult, Hunicutt could do nothing more than twitch furiously, twist his earlobe and glare at the floor. The tall man's shrewd gaze slid across the cluttered desk, lingering on a copy of the evening *Banner* folded beside the laptop computer. "I hear you're a writer now," Reeves said. "A laudable achievement. Your mother must be very proud, although I imagine she must find your current project rather distressing."

Clay lifted a brow but said nothing.

Clasping manicured hands behind his back, Reeves rocked back on his heels and feigned interest in a poorly framed watercolor pinioned on the faded plaster. "But perhaps you and your mother aren't as close as you once were. Perhaps she isn't even aware that you plan to publicize a very private, very painful time in her life." When there was no response, Reeves stiffly glanced over his shoulder. "I'd hate to see your mother suffer the consequences of her son's indiscretion."

Clay nodded somberly. "Your concern is touching."

"Catherine is a bright, sensible woman," Reeves murmured. He meticulously straightened the picture, then turned to face Clay. "I've always held her in the highest regard."

"She'd be surprised to hear that, considering that you fired her for refusing to perjure herself."

A irritable rhythm drew Reeves's attention to the corner where Hunicutt was obsessively tapping his foot. When Hunicutt's darting eyes caught Reeves's annoyed glance, his vibrating trouser leg stilled and the maddening sound stopped.

Reeves returned his attention to Clay. "I'm not surprised that certain facts have been distorted over time. The truth is, that once it became obvious Catherine had lied to the authorities, she could no longer be entrusted with the sensitive industry information to which she had access. I had a duty to my stockholders to terminate her employment."

"And did that dubious duty include inflammatory speeches and televised interviews portraying my mother as the town harlot?"

It took less than a moment for Reeves to expertly arrange his expression into one of sincere regret. "An unfortunate response to a highly emotional situation. My cousin, for whom I had enormous affection, had just suffered the tragic loss of her husband. I was understandably outraged. In retrospect, however, I realize that my reaction should probably have been more restrained."

"Ah, yes. I'm sure Cousin MaryBeth appreciated having such stalwart vocal support since she wasn't willing to speak for herself." Clay thoughtfully rubbed his chin. "When family is involved, emotions do get hot, don't they?"

"Indeed." Reeves issued an agreeable nod, but the wariness in his eyes didn't escape notice. "And since we agree that protecting one's family is a paramount concern, I'm certain we can come to terms that will adequately suit both of our needs."

A movement caught Clay's eye. Hunicutt was fiddling with the sleeve of his suit coat, compulsively pinching and rubbing the expensive fabric between his thumb and forefinger. Perspiration misted his creased brow and settled in wet droplets along his upper lip. Unlike Reeves, Hunicutt had yet to master the subtle art of practiced dispassion. His body language was easier to read than a kindergarten cookbook and confirmed that the meat of this impromptu visit was about to be sliced and set on the table.

Clay regarded Reeves lazily. "What 'terms' did you have in mind?"

The executive lips curved ever so slightly. "The job of a professional writer is to produce books in return for financial consideration. I understand that. In fact, I applaud it and am prepared to ensure you receive every cent to which you are entitled."

Clay got the message. "In other words, you'll pay me for not writing the book."

"It's eminently logical. Instead of waiting years for royalties to dribble in, you'll receive all your money up front and still have time to work on other projects."

"I assume there would be conditions."

"A few." Reeves flicked his hand as though shooing a pesky moth. "Hardly worth mentioning."

"Mention them anyway."

He shrugged. "Naturally, it would be best if you left Scarlet."

"Anything else?"

"Just the standard contract clauses. My lawyer can explain the details." Reeves glanced casually at his watch. "I'll have accounting prepare a cashier's check for fifty thousand—"

"Forget it."

Reeves's head snapped up. "Excuse me?"

"You heard me. No deal."

For a brief moment Reeves's veneer of confidence cracked, revealing bewilderment and a delicious hint of fear. "Of course, the exact amount is subject to negotiation."

"You don't get it, do you?" Clay laughed unpleasantly. "Let me lay it out in words that even a pompous jerk like you can understand. I don't give a fat flying fig about money."

"I see." Reeves's pupils contracted into pinpoints. "Then it's vengeance you want."

"Justice," Clay replied calmly. "Although you probably aren't aware that there's a difference."

For a moment Clay thought—hoped—that Reeves would take a swing at him. Instead he suddenly snapped his fingers, which caused Hunicutt to leap from his corner and yank open the door.

Tilting his head haughtily, Reeves moved toward the exit. "Obviously this has been a waste of time."

"Not at all." With a quick step, Clay blocked the tall man's path. "And since you're so concerned about the accuracy of my research, perhaps you'd like to clear up a few facts for me. On the record, of course."

The hatred in Reeves's eyes would have silenced most men. But then, Clayton Charles Cooper wasn't most men. He tossed a chummy arm around the stiff man's shoulders. "Here's the thing...Gerald Sheridan was supposedly shot on his own front lawn not ten feet below your cousin's bedroom window. But she wasn't called to testify at the trial and—see, this is the really weird part—the police never even bothered to take her statement." Stepping away, Clay clicked his heels and dramatically spread his hands. "I can't believe those good ol' boys would forget to have a chat with someone who might have witnessed a murder, particularly with your brother-in-law being the police chief. Of course, I'm just a simple country boy, but that's just a real puzzlement, don't you think?"

Reeves spoke through clenched teeth. "What I think, Mr. Cooper, is that my lawyers should have a chat with your publishers."

With a raucous whoop, Clay slapped his knee and drawled, "You have 'em do that, Lloyd-boy. I'd consider it a personal favor. Why, the scandal of a juicy lawsuit will guarantee a slot on the bestseller list." Ignoring the fact that Reeves was stiff as a broomstick, Clay grinned happily. "By the way, whatever happened to MaryBeth? Any truth to the rumor that she packed everything but her little girl and ran off with a computer salesman before poor old Gerald's bones had been put to rest?"

Clay had heard no such thing, of course, but thoroughly enjoyed provoking them. Hunicutt choked on a snort as his squinty gaze flipped frantically around the room and settled on the furious flush oozing up Reeves's throat.

"I certainly hope this kind of libelous speculation doesn't find its way into print," Reeves snapped. "Your publishers may survive the unpleasant publicity, but I guarantee that your mother won't."

"Gee, I forgot that you didn't know. My mother died last year. You can't hurt her any more." Clay suddenly grabbed Reeves's perfectly tailored lapels and hauled him forward until the startled man was teetering on the balls of his imported Italian shoes. "Did you hear me, you sanctimonious bastard? I've lost everything I ever cared about. By the time I'm through with you, you're going to know exactly how that feels."

With a rough shove, Clay turned him loose and bounced him off the wall.

Hunicutt was rooted with his pinched jaw drooping like a sprung clothespin. After a moment he leapt forward and frantically brushed his boss's rumpled overcoat until Reeves unceremoniously swatted him away.

Straightening his lapels, Reeves gave Clay a look cold enough to freeze meat. "We'll meet again," he said ominously. "Soon." Then he pivoted smartly and strode out the door with his weasel-faced lapdog at his heels.

Clay sauntered to the open doorway. "Y'all come back now, hear?" He flipped the door shut, sat on the bed and smiled. The first part of his plan had worked like a charm. The smug bastards were nervous. Soon they'd be drowning in their own sweat. Then Clay would have his revenge.

Chapter 4

Lainey guided the hissing iron around the collar's curve, ducking a puff of squirting steam that vaporized in the cool morning air. She set the hot iron on end, expertly flipped the shirt, then pressed the cuffs until they were crisp enough to stand alone. A few minutes later she hung the freshly ironed garment on a wire rack above the laundry area and snatched another shirt out of the dryer.

The morning routine was running well ahead of schedule, an unexpected turn of events that allowed her to get an early start on her evening chores. Although the sun was barely up, breakfast had already been served, the dishwasher was loaded and the kitchen floor had been swept. Despite the accelerated schedule, Lainey was tense and edgy. She'd had the dream again.

But last night it had been different. The clowns' voices had been raised in anger and the polka-dotted legs had been surrounding something inert. At first she'd believed the object to be a stuffed feed bag or even a pile of wadded canvas. Then she'd realized that the pile had feet. And arms.

Then there'd been a scream, an anguished lament that had jolted her from the nightmare. She'd awakened with tears streaming down her face, a throbbing migraine and the horrifying realization that the dream was evolving, exposing more and more details—details that Lainey didn't understand. And didn't want to understand.

Arms. Feet. A body.

Lainey's knees wobbled as renewed terror boiled in the pit of her stomach. She steadied herself on the ironing board. Her heart was racing; her hands trembled. She closed her eyes for a moment, waiting for the palpitations to ease while she silently scolded herself for being such a cowardly fool.

It was only a dream, a silly nightmare. Everyone had nightmares once in a while; most people woke up and forgot about them. Why couldn't she? Why did she suddenly see polka-dot trousers in the middle of the day? The haunting image was as frightening as the dream itself. Even more frightening because it exploded in her brain without warning. But she couldn't tell anyone. They'd think she was crazy. And maybe she was.

With a soft whimper, Lainey squeezed her eyes shut and was immediately startled by a harsh buzz. She jumped as though shot, realized it was the doorbell, and sagged against the washer. In another moment, she heard quiet voices in the living room. The hairs on her neck lifted as she recognized Sandborne Hunicutt's high-pitched nasal whine.

In truth, the company's pinch-faced executive had never said or done anything offensive, so Lainey couldn't pinpoint why she was so bothered by him. Perhaps it was his sniveling voice that grated on her nerves, or his irksome fidgeting. Perhaps it was the fact that his beady eyes and twitchy, pointed nose reminded her of a sewer rat. Rodents were repulsive enough, but a human rodent— She shuddered.

Regardless of the reasons, Lainey could barely stand being in the same room with Hunicutt and found his predecessor even more unsettling. Lloyd Reeves was arrogant and deceitful, slick enough to float on water. And he had mean eyes. She hated the way he looked at her. There was something sinister in his gaze, a ruthlessness that sliced to the core. Reeves scared her. At least Hunicutt wasn't particularly frightening; just repugnant.

Sighing, Lainey unplugged the iron and dropped the unpressed shirt back into the dryer. Annoying or not, Hunicutt was a guest. In the Clemmonses' house, guests were entitled to fresh coffee and a cheerful smile. Lainey figured she could handle the coffee part. The smile was doubtful.

After filling Aunt Hallie's fluted silver coffee carafe, she loaded an ornate tray with sugar bowl, creamer and a cup and saucer from the good china. Then she hoisted the tray and carefully backed through the swinging door. Forcing a practiced smile, she turned toward the living room and froze in her tracks. Sandborne Hunicutt wasn't their only guest.

Lloyd Reeves stood politely. "Good morning, Lainey. You look lovely, as always."

She set the tray on the coffee table. "I'll just get another cup."

"You needn't bother." Reeves touched her arm as she started to turn. "Please, have a seat."

Something in the tone of his voice put her on guard. She angled a wary glance toward the sofa, where Russ was bent forward, hands clasped between his knees, staring at the carpet as though expecting it to rise up and fly. Beside him, Hunicutt squirmed uncomfortably, repeatedly crossing and uncrossing his scrawny legs, and in the corner Aunt Hallie sat in Granny's wooden rocker cradling both canes in her lap. Their somber expressions made Lainey feel as if she'd stumbled into a mortuary slumber room. At that moment, all she wanted was out.

"I, uh—" she licked her lips and gestured weakly toward the kitchen "—have work to do."

Russ cleared his throat and leaned back against the faded paisley cushions. "It can wait. Sit yourself, girl."

Her heart sank as Reeves solicitously guided her toward two crushed-velour wing chairs. Because she had no choice, she perched on the closest one. Reeves settled into the other.

Wasting neither time nor words, he opened with a blunt command. "Tell us everything you know about the book Clayton Cooper is writing."

She blinked. "I don't know anything about it."

Reeves hoisted a haughty brow. "You were with him yesterday morning."

Rankled by the accusatory tone, Lainey lifted her chin and met the man's cool eyes. "Yes, I was."

"What was discussed?"

She glanced at her uncle, who was still staring at the floor. "We... talked about a lot of things."

"Such as?"

Dismissing an uncharitable urge to offer Reeves succinct directions to an extremely warm locale, Lainey rubbed her hands together and tried to gather her thoughts. Although Reeves could have gotten information on her movements from any one of a dozen places, Lainey figured the police chief was the most likely source. Not that the method mattered. Lloyd Reeves had informants all over town.

As far as Lainey was concerned, her conversation with Clay Cooper had been personal and none of Lloyd Reeves's business. She deeply wished she had the chutzpah to tell him so. Since she didn't, she offered a prim smile and did the next best thing. "I'm so sorry. Except for what was printed in the *Banner,* the rest of our conversation was off the record." From the corner of her eye, she saw her uncle's head snap up.

"Off the *what?*" Russ's eyes bulged in disbelief. "Good Lord, girl, answer the man's question!"

"I can't. It would be unethical." Thankfully she sounded more confident that she felt.

Reeves straightened, nostrils flaring. "I'm disappointed to hear that."

When Hallie emitted a frantic gurgle, Lainey was pricked by guilt. Since Lloyd Reeves was the most powerful man in town, the entire family would pay the price for offending him. Much as Lainey despised the imperious fool, she had no right to do anything that would endanger her uncle's job.

Suppressing a sigh of regret, she forced a conciliatory tone. "What I can tell you, Mr. Reeves, is that everything I know about Clay's book was in last night's paper."

"I see." He regarded her sharply. "May I ask if you approve of this shameless attempt to exploit your family's tragedy?"

"Certainly not!" Her voice rose as indignation overcame prudence. "I made my objections abundantly clear to Mr. Cooper and assured him most vehemently that I'd do everything in my power to stop him."

"Of course you did, dear." Obviously pleased, Reeves patted her arm as though she were an obedient pet, then leaned back and crossed his legs loosely. "We all empathize with your distress over this disgraceful violation of privacy." He encompassed his relieved disciples with the casual sweep of his hand.

She cast a skeptical eye on the group. As suspected, no one seemed the least bit interested in Lainey's "distress." Or in Lainey herself, for that matter.

After closing his eyes and crossing himself, Uncle Russ pulled out a handkerchief to wipe his sweaty face. Aunt Hallie's head drooped forward until her chin touched her chest, and Hunicutt was obsessively tapping the crystal face of his Rolex with a smug grin that made Lainey want to gag. An unnerving atmosphere of deception and secrecy permeated the entire room. Although Reeves and Hunicutt were undeniably pleased with themselves, Lainey had never seen her aunt and uncle so jittery.

"You will, of course, file an injunction," Reeves announced suddenly.

Lainey frowned. "Excuse me?"

"An injunction," he repeated impatiently. "In cases such as this, the victim's next of kin has the best legal grounds to stop publication."

"A lawsuit? I don't know..." The concept made her dizzy. She realized that legal action might be a viable option, of course, but hadn't given up on other less drastic alternatives. Unfortunately she didn't yet have a clue what those less drastic alternatives could be. "I've never needed a lawyer before. I wouldn't even know who to call."

"ChemCorp has a large staff of attorneys, each of whom will be at your disposal until this matter is resolved."

"That would be rather expensive."

"Nonsense. The company will absorb the cost."

Startled by the idea that a corporate entity would finance a personal lawsuit of questionable merit, Lainey blurted, "Why?"

Reeves blinked as though unaccustomed to the word. "I beg your pardon?"

She moistened her lips, took a deep breath and tried again. "Why would you want to do that? I mean, thousands of corporate dollars spent for noncompany purposes... How could you possibly explain that to the stockholders?"

Russ muffled a groan and covered his face.

Reeves, seemingly astounded by the question, took a moment to compose himself by adjusting his tie and examining the shiny orbs on his cuffs. "As chairman of the board, I am not required to explain my decisions."

"Lainey, for God's sake—" Russ's croaking plea was cut off by the subtle lift of Reeves's outstretched palm.

Then the self-proclaimed chairman turned to Lainey and spoke in a voice lithe with silky persuasion. "Obviously Cooper's book will generate a certain amount of unpleasant publicity and since many of Scarlet's leading citizens are also ChemCorp executives, the company has a duty to protect them from undue embarrassment. You understand that—" he leaned forward with a sly smile and took her hand "—don't you, my dear?"

Reeves's touch made her flesh crawl. Withdrawing her hand without comment, Lainey absently wiped her palm on her linen skirt. Besides the fact that his explanation, slick as it was, didn't quite ring true, she was perplexed by the breathless intensity with which he and the rest of the group awaited her reply. Since no one in the room except Lainey herself had a personal stake in the matter, their peculiar desperation was all the more troubling. Every eye in the room was focused on her, every ear attuned to her slightest utterance.

Suddenly she couldn't breathe. Panic swelled from the pit of her stomach, clogging her throat and squeezing her lungs dry. She had to get out. Dear God, she had to get out of that room.

Lainey stood so quickly that her knee hit the coffee table. "I have to go. I'm late."

Looking dazed, Reeves rose slowly. "May I tell the legal department when to expect you?"

"No. I mean, I'll let you know." Her frantic gaze darted to her uncle, who was staring in openmouthed astonishment. "I have to think about it."

Before the words were out of her mouth, Russ was on his feet. "What'n hell needs thinking about?"

"I just want a little time to sort things out, that's all." Lainey nearly tripped over the magazine rack beside the chair. "We'll talk about this later, okay? I have to get to work."

Before anyone could stop her, Lainey whirled around and disappeared through the swinging kitchen door. In a moment, the back door slammed.

Lloyd Reeves returned to his seat, impassive except for a telltale ache along his jawline. He consciously relaxed the muscle, a concealing habit honed by years of corporate deception. The girl's reaction had startled him. Lloyd didn't like to be startled. He hadn't clawed his way to power by allowing himself to be taken by surprise.

Beyond the partitioning coffee table, Hunicutt twisted a wrapped button on his coat sleeve and glared at Russ. "You said you could handle her."

The burly redhead tugged at his collar. "Lainey's always been kind of high-strung. She'll come around."

"What if she doesn't?" As Hunicutt released the button and dug an inhalant out of his coat, his foot tapped an irritable rhythm on the wooden floor. "If Cooper publishes that book, we'll all be ruined."

Lloyd pinched the bridge of his nose. "Not necessarily. If Cooper had any evidence, he'd have already notified the authorities."

Russ considered that. "So you think he's fishing?"

"Perhaps. It's possible that he's counting on renewed public interest to unearth some diabolically damning morsel that will serve his personal vendetta. Of course, we won't allow that to happen." Lloyd nodded at the coffeepot, then leaned casually back in his chair.

Reacting to the silent command, Hunicutt leapt up and filled the china cup with steaming coffee. "I still don't like it. If Cooper figures his father was convicted with tampered evidence, he'll start sniffing around other things that don't concern him."

"But there's nothing to find, right?" Russ hunched forward like a huddled linebacker. "All the documentation on that tainted batch was destroyed twenty years ago... wasn't it?"

"It was." Lloyd took the cup Hunicutt offered and aristocratically balanced the saucer on his knee. He sipped the hot liquid, uneasy with the direction of their discussion. Over the years he'd learned that walls do indeed have ears; and occasionally, they have eyes, as well. He was also painfully aware that in certain situations, suspicion and speculation can be as damaging as hard evidence.

A manufacturing accident twenty years earlier had been just such a situation. The clandestine investigation Reeves had ordered revealed that hundreds of heads of livestock had died. And perhaps a few people, although no one knew for certain. It had been a tragic mishap that, had it not been for his own brilliant leadership, would certainly have destroyed the company. No one had ever discovered the contamination source because no one had known where to look. Lloyd had seen to that.

After a few months the mystery deaths ceased and eventually people forgot about them. Unfortunately there had been a few loose ends to tidy up; Lloyd had tended to them. If Clayton Cooper tried to unravel what had been so carefully concealed, Lloyd would tend to him, as well.

An unpleasant sound broke into Lloyd's thoughts.

Holding one nostril shut, Hunicutt snorted noisily. He changed sides, repeated the procedure, then screwed the cap back on the inhaler. "I still don't like it," he mumbled. "If Cooper keeps poking around, he might stumble over the truth about Gerald."

Russ was white as death. "That isn't possible, is it? I mean, there's no way anyone could find out, is there?" As he spoke, his wife's rocking chair creaked faster.

Carefully masking his annoyance, Lloyd set the coffee cup on the table, silently bemoaning the day fate had tethered him to these blithering imbeciles. "Must you repeatedly be reminded that there was no one outside this room who knew what really happened that night?"

The creaking stopped. Hallie whispered, "MaryBeth knew."

Lloyd wished Southern decorum allowed the slow strangulation of such bothersome old biddies. Since it didn't, he settled for a cold stare. "MaryBeth is in no position to talk about it, is she?"

The woman rewarded Lloyd with a flash of fear before lowering her gaze. When Russ started to speak, Lloyd silenced the redheaded cracker with a stern look, then steepled his fingers and was lost in thought. As he considered options to alleviate their current dilemma, an idea formed in his brilliant mind. Lloyd smiled. It was another masterful strategy, one guaranteed to end this distasteful matter by eliminating Cooper's credibility—and perhaps Cooper himself.

Lloyd glanced at his watch to confirm that there was sufficient time for the rumor to sweep Wall Street before the opening bell. If Lloyd played his hand well—and he always did—nervous investors would be convinced that the famous C. C. Cooper was planning a hit piece on ChemCorp and company stock would drop six points by noon. By the time corporate brass in Cincinnati was able to squash the false report and stabilize holdings, furious townsfolk would have either driven Cooper out of town on a rail or dumped his dead body in Tupaloosa Slough. Either way, the problem would be resolved.

Lloyd abruptly stood. "Where's the telephone?"

"Over there." Russ weakly gestured toward a small stand beside the window. "Uh . . . will this be a toll call?"

"As a matter of fact, it is." Lloyd lifted the receiver and dialed his stockbroker's number. "Think of it as an investment in your future."

Broddie McFerson parted the yellowed sheers and eyed the surly group gathered in the motel parking lot. "'Tis getting ugly out there."

Raking his hair in frustration, Clay pushed away from the desk, crossed the room and peered over McFerson's shoulder. An hour ago there'd been a couple of sullen ChemCorp workers kicking stones and glaring at the motel room window. Now there were more than a dozen people, and the mood was growing testier by the minute. This was a problem he didn't need.

McFerson released the sheers and scratched his fuzzy white head. "Like sharks on a blood trail, they are. Damn fools."

"They're scared." Clay rolled his head until his stiff neck gave a satisfying pop. "Nearly everyone in Scarlet owns a piece of ChemCorp. By nightfall half the town might be out there."

"Humph. By nightfall they'll be back in their homes, ashamed of themselves for acting like common thugs."

Clay wasn't so sure. He was, however, certain that the unprecedented drop in ChemCorp stock had been no accident. Fortunately, McFerson's years in the news business had given him access to a wide variety of confidential contacts. The surly old goat had been on the phone all morning, polling media and questioning brokerage house informants. No one could verify the source of the rumor that had turned ChemCorp stock into a panic sell.

Word on The Street blamed Clay's publisher for the leak. Shortly after noon, chagrined executives of ChemCorp's parent company had united with the publishing house in a mad scramble to effect damage control. Later this evening, the *Banner* would carry front-page coverage of the joint press release. Maybe then the town's hanging mood would soften; maybe not.

But at the moment the situation was touchy enough that Clay was concerned about McFerson's safety. He laid a hand on the old man's shoulder. "Listen, Mac, I appreciate your help, but you've got a newspaper to run. I can take it from here."

"Are you daft, lad?" McFerson lifted one droopy eyelid and pointed a bony finger at the heaped desk. "We've barely started. The prosecution files alone are thick as man's arm and we've not so much as scanned a page of court transcript."

"Believe me, I've been over every word a dozen times, and all I've come up with are questions. Thanks to you, I have Gerald's personal files. Maybe there are some answers in there."

"Now y'know what they say about two heads." McFerson slid a worried glance toward the window. "But the fact is, this dinky room's enough to cramp a man's brain. Now I know of a place, not a castle, mind you, but large enough for two sets of rattling bones."

Clay smiled. "Thanks, but I'm not about to lead that motley crew to your house. You've done more than enough already, and besides, this isn't your problem."

An expression of pure misery clouded the old man's eyes. "That's what I've been telling myself all these years. Trouble is, I'm not believing it anymore."

"What are you talking about?" When McFerson shrugged and turned away, Clay was instantly concerned. "Are you all right, Mac?"

Ignoring the question, McFerson cupped a gnarled hand behind his neck and eyed the desk drawers. "You wouldn't have a wee bottle of liquid comfort tucked in there, would you now?"

"No, I'm sorry." Clay hesitated. "Do you want to talk about what's bothering you?"

"No sense burdening you with my troubles, lad. You've enough of your own."

Clay played a hunch. "Why do you blame yourself for Gerald Sheridan's death?"

McFerson's stoic expression crumpled. His bloodshot eyes brightened with unshed tears. The stooped shoulders curled forward until it seemed the poor fellow would collapse in on himself and disappear entirely. Before Clay could offer assistance, the trembling man dropped onto a nearby chair and whispered, "So you know, do you?"

Clay pulled up a second chair. "After studying old library copies of news reports, I realized that there wasn't a single issue of the *Banner* that contained an original story on Sheridan's death. There was only one logical conclusion as to why the local newspaper relied on UPI reprints to report a murder that was the biggest news story in town history."

McFerson couldn't meet Clay's eyes. "And what conclusion might that be?"

"That the story was too painful for local reporters to deal with."

"There were those who'd have done the stories and done them well. Truth is, I wouldn't allow it." With what seemed to be a great effort, McFerson squared his gaunt shoulders. "I took the coward's way."

Clay didn't understand and said so.

"My reporters were good lads and would've beat bushes until the truth fell out."

"You didn't want that truth to fall out, did you? You were afraid someone else might be hurt."

"Aye." The word cracked in his throat. He looked away, composed himself and continued. "But 'twas deeper than that. Gerald Sheridan was a good man. Like a brother, he was, though we didn't always see eye to eye on the running of the business. It was like that, you see . . . on his last day."

Something in the old man's eyes sent a chill down Clay's spine. Because McFerson and Gerald Sheridan had been so close, Clay had figured the cranky codger would be the last person to help clear Ben Cooper's name. As it had turned out, McFerson had been the only one willing to seek the truth. Although grateful, Clay had wondered why. Now he was going to find out.

And as Clay's teeth grinded in a nervous habit that had plagued him since childhood, he wasn't at all certain he was going to like it. Nonetheless, he encouraged McFerson to continue. "What was the argument about?"

Sighing, the old man rubbed his eyelid with a swollen knuckle. "It was about what it was always about. Gerald figured the *Banner* should do hard-hitting investigative pieces—'twas a *news*paper, after all—while I was a'worrying about the bottom line."

"And you figured that irritating the wrong people would affect profits?"

"That I did." McFerson glumly shook his fuzzy head. "So when Gerald wanted to follow up on a tip about some kind of hush-hush trouble at the plant, I knew there'd be hell to pay when Lloyd Reeves got wind of it. 'Course, Gerald never cared much about politics, but I did. ChemCorp's advertising dollars were about the only things keeping the *Banner* afloat in those days." He scratched his chin. "Still is. The company owns the newspaper just like it owns about everything else in Scarlet."

Clay tried to stifle his impatience. "You said that something happened at the plant?"

"Hmm?" McFerson blinked. "Aye. Some kind of manufacturing problem, I'm thinking."

"Some kind of—" Clay swallowed the rising anxiety, balled his fists and forced a calm tone. "Am I to assume that you won the argument and no investigation was ever done?"

McFerson issued an embarrassed shrug. "Since there wasn't hard evidence of wrongdoing, there seemed no need to assign a reporter. We argued like always. Gerald said if 'twas evidence I wanted, he'd just trot off and get some..." The words trailed away.

Clay's heart sank. "So when Gerald died, whatever he'd found out died with him."

"I don't know." McFerson gestured toward several coffee-stained folders on the desk. "There might be something useful in his personal files."

"*Might* be? Are you saying that you haven't read them?" The thought was astonishing. "A man dies after digging up dirt on the most powerful entity in town and it never even occurs to you to follow up on the lead?"

"There seemed no connection at the time, lad. The evidence against your father seemed clear." McFerson coughed uncomfortably as he glanced anxiously around the room. "If there was something to wash this damnable dryness from my throat—"

"I don't believe this!" Clay leapt to his feet, raking his hair in frustration. "You knew all the time that Gerald's death was connected to his investigation—"

McFerson rose indignantly. "Now wait a minute, lad. I knew no such thing."

"Because you didn't want to know. Hell, you couldn't even be bothered to read your partner's notes." Furious, Clay spun around and took a wild swipe at the file folders. "While my father was being hung out to dry, you stuck your head in a whiskey bottle and let it happen."

McFerson flinched as though struck.

Instantly regretting his harsh words, Clay extended an acquiescent hand. "I'm sorry. I didn't mean that."

Squaring his bony shoulders, McFerson faced him directly. "Aye, you did, and it's right you are. I can't be making up for my cowardly ways, but I'm here now and it's here I'll stay until the truth be known to all." He pulled a chair to the desk, sat down and glanced over his shoulder. "Best we start, lad, before them outside forget whatever manners their mums taught 'em."

Clay hesitated only a moment before accepting the file McFerson held out. He pushed the laptop computer aside, sat down and went to work.

Over the next half hour, the two men isolated several discrepancies surrounding Ben Cooper's arrest and subsequent trial. Although the murder weapon—Gerald Sheridan's own gun—had been conveniently found in Ben's truck, it had been wiped clean. None of the official reports questioned why a man would carefully remove his fingerprints, then leave the incriminating evidence lying in full view on the seat of his own vehicle.

Among the old police records was also a startling tidbit of information that hadn't found its way into the court transcripts. It seems a neighbor had initially reported hearing loud voices and seeing several men in Sheridan's yard just before the shot rang out. Like MaryBeth Sheridan, however, that witness had left town without testimony or deposition.

No one had ever asked why, certainly not Ben Cooper's defense attorney, a public defender whose father and uncle both served as ChemCorp legal consultants. During the trial, Ben's attorney hadn't even mentioned the witness's initial statement, and the handwritten police report prepared the night of the crime had never even been entered into evidence. Instead, a typed version omitting any reference to the neighbor's original declaration had been presented to the court.

The more Clay learned about the trial, the sicker he became. He'd always believed that his father had been falsely convicted. Clay hadn't realized he'd been framed so blatantly that everyone from investigating officers to the presiding judge had to have known what was going on.

Disgusted, Clay pushed away from the desk. "It was a setup, pure and simple."

"Don't be jumping to conclusions, now." McFerson leaned back and absently tapped a pencil eraser against his forehead. "All we have here is evidence of a sloppy investigation and incompetent attorneys. Grounds for appeal, to be sure, but 'tisn't a crime that I know of."

"Are you saying that my father wasn't framed?"

"No, lad. I'm saying we can't prove it."

The frustration was too much. With a bitter curse, Clay stood and started to pace the small room. "Then I'll get proof. First I'll find that neighbor . . . what was her name?"

"Gebloski, Emma Gebloski."

"Right." Clay's teeth vibrated until his jaw throbbed. He scoured the back of his neck with his fingers. "I want to know exactly what she saw and why she took off like a scared rabbit."

"That might not be such an easy task. It's been twenty years, you know."

"I'll find her," Clay said grimly. "And I'll get answers."

McFerson shrugged a fat brow. "Has it occurred to you that she might not be with us anymore, if you know what I mean?"

Unfortunately Clay knew exactly what he meant. If the Gebloski woman had died, getting the needed information would be difficult. But not impossible. "Then I'll have to get my answers from the other witness."

"There were no witnesses."

"There was Sheridan's wife."

McFerson went white. "You must be joking."

"I've never been more serious in my life. MaryBeth was in the house when Sheridan was killed. By the time the cops got there, she was on the front lawn holding her dead husband on her lap."

The old man turned away. "The police questioned her. She didn't hear anything and she didn't see anything."

"I don't believe it." Clay sat back down and gripped McFerson's arm. "Think about it, Mac. Sheridan was killed right below the open window of his wife's bedroom. She has to know something."

"She doesn't," McFerson insisted.

"I want to hear that from her. And while I'm at it, I want to know how any woman could abandon her daughter to the likes of Russ and Hallie Clemmons."

Had Clay not been so focused on his own thoughts, he might have noticed McFerson's sudden tremor and the fear in the old man's eyes. Instead, he saw only a bullheaded obstructionist.

McFerson shook off Clay's hand and hunched over the paper mound. "We've no time to waste chasing phantoms. Now let's get back to work."

Clay watched silently for a moment. "You know where MaryBeth is, don't you?" When there was no response, he added, "Perhaps Lainey will be more cooperative about divulging her mother's whereabouts."

McFerson stiffened and spoke without looking up. "Leave the lass out of this."

The quiet statement issued a loud warning, one that piqued Clay's suspicions and made him even more determined to find out exactly what Lainey's elusive mother knew—or didn't know—about the night her husband was killed.

Although Clay had no intention of dropping the subject of MaryBeth Sheridan, he was well aware that continued pressure on McFerson could result in alienating his only ally. As he contemplated taking that risk, a crude expletive resonated from the parking lot.

McFerson looked up, his forehead furrowed in concern. "Getting a bit testy, are they?"

Standing just beyond the glass, Clay parted the sheers enough to offer a view of the swelling crowd. Protest signs sprouted from the clumps of angry people congregating around the lot. Clay eyed the crudely painted messages. Some were rather mundane requests that he leave town with all due speed; others were a bit more intimidating, particularly one portraying a bloody hangman's noose—personalized, of course. Clay thought that was a bit melodramatic. His personal favorite was the sign with his name inside a slashed circle. No Coopers, huh? Clay grinned. Simple, tasteful, clever without being gauche. Definitely a ten-plus.

McFerson uttered a sharp oath. "Come here, lad!"

As Clay returned to the desk, the old man held out a torn scrap of paper. Clay took it, read the cryptic message and smiled. It looked like they'd finally gotten lucky.

Chapter 5

Clay studied the obscure note. Beside an inked abstract doodle, Gerald Sheridan had boldly scrawled, "Batch #74-38692,10/3/74."

"This could be a quality control lot number," Clay said, noticing that October third was approximately six weeks before Sheridan's death. "I wonder if this was the date of manufacture or the date he received this information."

"I wouldn't be guessing the latter. Gerry wouldn't have let any grass grow under his feet on this one." McFerson took the scrap and held it at arm's length. "There's a lady I know—handsome woman, she is—works in the company records vault. With a wee bit of persuasion, she might be agreeable to checking out the old manufacturing logs. 'Course if it's what I'm thinking—" McFerson ended with a snort and laid the torn scrap on the desk.

"Yeah, I know," Clay muttered. Neither man had to speak aloud what both understood all too well. If the company wanted to cover up a manufacturing problem, the batch logs certainly would have been altered and incriminating evidence long since destroyed. "I can't figure what could be serious enough to warrant that kind of cover-up."

McFerson shrugged. "Could be a lot of things, all of them coming down to the pocketing of the green."

"Money?"

"'Tis all that matters to the likes of Lloyd Reeves." The newsman propped a scrawny hip against the desk and thoughtfully scratched his chin. "As I recall it, Gerry was rattling on about something big enough to close the company's doors. Scared me spitless, it did."

Clay didn't have to ask why McFerson had been worried about the prospect of ChemCorp going belly-up. In one way or another, everyone in town was economically dependent on the plant. Without it, Scarlet would be nothing more than a historical relic, just another crumbling Appalachian ghost town. As far as Clay was concerned, that would be a just fate for the town that had destroyed his family.

Then he reminded himself that he hadn't returned for vengeance. Not that it wouldn't have tasted sweet, but his mother never would have approved. Despite the snubs and insults, Catherine had always loved this place. Clay had never shared her feelings, but he'd always respected them.

A commotion outside caught his attention. Loud voices. Shouts. Shattering glass, like a bottle smashed against asphalt.

McFerson dropped the file he was perusing. "What in God's name..."

Clay silenced him with an upturned palm, sidled to the window and couldn't believe what he saw. There in the parking lot was Lainey Sheridan surrounded by half a dozen screaming men. The foolish woman actually seemed to be negotiating with the burly thugs. Or at least, she was trying to. As she extended her hands, a barrel-chested jock in red suspenders stepped forward and spit at her feet. She went rigid, then spun around and strode briskly toward the motel room.

Clay swore bitterly and headed for the door, yanking it open just as Lainey arrived. He reached out, hauled her inside and slammed the door. "Are you all right?" he demanded.

Her delicate hands trembled as she smoothed her disheveled bangs. "Yes... I'm fine."

But Clay saw the fear in her eyes, and a murderous rage swelled in his chest. Clenching his jaw, he whirled around and grabbed for the doorknob.

"No!" Lainey clutched at his wrist. "Don't go out there!"

In spite of her death grip on his arm, he wrestled the door open. "Those cowardly bastards need a lesson in manners."

"There's too many of them." Lainey moved in front of him, slamming the door by throwing her weight against it. "They'll kill you."

"She's right, lad." A surprisingly firm hand gripped his shoulder. "Those rowdy hooligans were sent to stop you from doing what you're doing. Now I ask you, what sense is there in giving them what they want?"

Clay's fist tightened around the doorknob. Logically, he understood that McFerson's assessment was accurate. Emotionally, however, all he wanted to do was get his hands on the spitter and twist those red suspenders around the guy's hairy neck until his plebeian eyes bulged.

A tender warmth permeated his heart. When he saw Lainey's sweet hand pressed against his chest, something inside him melted. "Please," she whispered. "I don't want you to be hurt."

Clay looked into those liquid fudge eyes and was instantly lost. The emotional connection between them was still there, as deep and strong as it had been twenty years ago when they'd first bonded with a look, a tear, an ethereal touch. Now he wanted to tell her how beautiful she was and how precious, but a sudden lump in his throat rendered him mute. He could barely breathe, let alone speak.

As the pressure on his shoulder eased, Clay noticed that McFerson had moved to the window. "Them nasty-looking lads belong to the company's loading dock crew," he said. "The enforcers, they are."

With some effort, Clay managed to pull himself away from Lainey's fathomless gaze. He swallowed hard and stepped back, digesting this new information. "So, Reeves choreographed this mob?"

"Likely as not." McFerson sauntered back toward the desk. "Not much occurs around here without his say-so. Besides, there's no better way to rile folks than by threatening their pocketbooks."

Lainey seemed shocked by the implication. "Are you saying that Mr. Reeves deliberately started that rumor about Clay's book just to create panic?"

"Can't say what can't be proved," Broddie said flatly, glancing at his watch before eyeing her with evident disapproval. "And you, lass, should be working the final pasteup, so why is it you're here?"

"I, uh..." Allowing the words to dissipate, she clasped her hands and tried to gather her thoughts. It wasn't an easy task with Clay Cooper standing so close she could feel the masculine heat radiating from his body. She was dizzied by his scent, a musky maleness that engulfed her like an erotic caress, while the rhythm of his heartbeat was etched on her tingling palm.

When she didn't answer immediately, Broddie's weathered face creased with renewed concerned. "Did Roger send you?"

"Who's Roger?" Clay asked.

"Roger Elkert, our managing editor," Broddie explained, casting a pointed glance at Lainey. "The only one who knew where I'd be."

Hoping a little distance would clear her fuzzy brain, Lainey moved toward the window and tested her voice. "Don't blame Roger. I begged him to tell." When she saw Broddie's worried expression, she rushed to reassure him. "Nothing's wrong, really. It's just that you left the office so suddenly this morning and I—I needed to say how sorry I am—" She swallowed hard. "About what happened yesterday. I had no right to say such awful things to you."

Broddie's eyes softened. "We both said things, lass, things best put behind us."

A humiliating moisture seeped into her eyes. "I was afraid you wouldn't forgive me."

"Now, you know better than that."

"Yes," she whispered, discreetly wiping her face. Broddie McFerson couldn't carry a grudge in a bucket. He was the dearest man in the world. Lainey loved him fiercely.

"Well, then." Broddie, whose own eyes had reddened considerably, made an exaggerated point of clearing his throat. "You'd best be getting back to the newsroom."

Clay pointed at the shuffling mob outside. "She is *not* going out there alone."

Startled by his vehement pronouncement, Lainey stated, "My car is just outside—"

"I said *no!*"

She blinked. "Excuse me, but that sounded very much like an order."

He had the grace to look embarrassed. "I didn't mean it that way."

"I'm happy to hear that."

Sighing, Clay tugged his earlobe and slid her a look that made her pulse leap. "Look Lainey, those goons had you surrounded. Obviously I'm—" he slid a sheepish glance at Broddie "—I mean, *we're* concerned about you."

"I appreciate that, but what happened in the parking lot was...well, it was my fault." Feeling foolish, Lainey avoided Clay's gaze by plucking invisible lint from the sleeve of her knitted tunic. "I attempted to enlighten the demonstrators by explaining the false rumors."

"But they weren't interested, right?"

"I don't know. The dockworkers kept shouting me down and wouldn't allow me near the main group." Lainey couldn't even look at him. As the hateful mood escalated outside, she couldn't deny her own part in stirring up what had become an ugly, frightening situation. "The point is that my safety isn't at risk, Clay. Yours is. Please, you have to leave Scarlet before something awful happens." Although Clay folded his arms without response, Lainey recognized the stubborn set of his jaw. Frustrated, she turned to Broddie. "You know he's in danger. Can't you do something?"

Avoiding her gaze, Broddie made a production of inspecting the chewed pencil he'd pulled out of his shirt pocket. "He's a man fully growed, lass. It's his own conscience he'll be listening to, not the dictates of a weathered old man."

Lainey followed Broddie's gaze to the mounded desk. Beside the miniature computer and atop an untidy scattering of loose papers were several folders, one of which was encoded with a familiar red-and-white Confidential sticker. An image flashed through her mind, the memory of that folder lying open on the kitchen table while her father studied the contents. "Are...those are my father's private papers?"

Broddie still didn't look up. "Aye."

A sudden surge of resentment stiffened her spine. "How could you violate his privacy like this?"

"It's what he'd have wanted, Lainey, lass."

"Am I supposed to believe that my father would have wanted his killer's son to have access to his personal notes?

This is an outrage." She turned on Clay. "You're determined to destroy my father's memory, aren't you? Mr. Reeves was right. You have to be stopped, no matter what—" Realizing what she'd said, Lainey pressed her hands to her lips. "Oh, my God."

Clay stared in stunned disbelief. "You...and Reeves...?"

Closing her eyes, she sagged against the window wall and gestured limply outside. "I had no idea he was going to do something like this."

Broddie propped one hip on the corner of the desk, crammed the dull pencil into his overloaded pocket protector and crossed his knobby arms. "What is it you've been up to, Lainey?"

She shook her head miserably. "They just showed up at the house this morning—"

"They, who?" Clay asked sharply.

"Mr. Reeves and Mr. Hunicutt." Lainey massaged her eyelids, wishing the ground would open up and swallow her whole. "They wanted to know how I felt about this...book of yours."

A tiny muscle below Clay's ear twitched. "And what did you tell them?"

"I told them the truth, that I wasn't happy about it."

Clay jammed one hand into the pocket of his double-pleated slacks as he roughly massaged the back of his neck. "So now there's a price on my head, right?"

"Don't be ridiculous."

"Are you pooling resources for the reward or is Reeves enough of a gentleman to pick up the full tab?"

"Clay—"

"I mean, hell, an experienced hit man won't come cheap. And you'll have to pay for the best, honey, because I'm not going down easy."

"Oh, for crying out loud." Frustrated, Lainey tossed up her hands and turned in front of the window. "You know, you've really missed your calling, Clayton Cooper. Put that wild imagination to work and you could make a fortune writing fiction."

Across the room Broddie cleared his throat. "Now, children, let's play nice, shall we?"

Clay flashed him a look hot enough to melt concrete. "You think this is funny?"

"What I think is that Lainey deserves a chance to explain herself." Broddie turned expectantly. "Well, lass?"

She rubbed a sudden chill from her bare arms and tried to sound nonchalant. "Mr. Reeves simply suggested that I file an injunction to stop you from publishing the book."

Clay's face reddened. "No damned way—"

Broddie silenced him with a look, then turned back to Lainey. "On what grounds?"

"Invasion of privacy, emotional distress...whatever it takes, I suppose." She shrugged miserably. "I only promised to think about it."

Turning his back, Clay balled his fists and glowered at the floor. Lainey felt sick, realizing that he had every right to be angry at her. By publicly acknowledging disapproval of the project, she'd given Clay's enemies more ammunition with which to fuel the town's fury. Now his safety had been jeopardized, and she couldn't shake the feeling that she was at least partially to blame for the dangerous mob in the parking lot.

Although she'd never meant Clay any harm, Lainey was still committed to stopping his book. There was simply too much at stake. It was bad enough that he planned to portray her father as an adulterer, but if he discovered what had really happened to her mother—

Even the possibility made her stomach churn and her head ache. Absently clutching her midsection, she shook off the unpleasant thought and stepped forward. "Clay..." The words evaporated when she saw the powerful back muscles rippling beneath his crisp white shirt. Suddenly she was struck by an overwhelming urge to slip her arms around his waist and feel his strength against her cheek. The image was so vivid, so sensual, it took her breath away.

As she stood gawking like a moonstruck adolescent, he suddenly turned. The anger had drained from his eyes and in its place was an expression of such sorrow that her heart nearly broke on the spot. "I never believed that this project would hurt you, Lainey. I didn't realize—" Clay's gaze flickered, as though caught by a movement outside the window. His eyes widened.

Shouting a warning, he dived forward and knocked Lainey to the ground, rolling protectively on top of her just as a fist-size rock shattered the window. During the next chaotic moments Clay gathered Lainey in his arms and lifted her as though she weighed no more than a feather. After moving across the room, he crouched in the corner, hugging Lainey against his firm chest.

Broddie was on the floor beside the desk, cussing a blue streak. A din of angry shouts rushed through the broken windowpane as the old man rolled onto his side and glared at the billowing sheers. "Why those rotten, good-for-nothing—I've half a mind to take that blasted rock out there and shove it down their foul-mouthed throats!"

Ignoring Broddie's bluster, Clay frantically brushed splintered glass from Lainey's clothing. "Are you all right?"

She opened her mouth, planning to assure him that she was fine. But no sound passed through her loosely parted lips. Her throat was paralyzed. Clay's hands gently framed her face, each fingertip tenderly inspecting her lips, eyelids, brows, mesmerizing her with a touch so loving, so infinitely sweet that she nearly cried out in wonder.

When he stroked her forehead, his eyes reflected utter terror. "My God," he whispered, withdrawing his hand. "You're hurt."

She stared stupidly at the tiny red smear on his thumb. "It's nothing, really."

But Clay would not be consoled and shouted at poor Broddie. "Get a washcloth, dammit. Can't you see she's bleeding?"

"I'm not deaf, lad." Broddie sat up and peered over Clay's shoulder. "'Tis only a prick."

Clay's eyes narrowed. "Get the damned cloth."

"Aye, don't get your shorts in a knot." Before Broddie ducked into the bathroom, Lainey could have sworn the old goat was smiling.

Clay solicitously caressed her temple. "Does it hurt much?"

"I, uh..." Actually, she couldn't feel anything but his gentle fingers. "Really, it's nothing."

"If anything had happened to you—" He glanced away as Broddie crawled back with the damp cloth and plopped it in Clay's outstretched hand.

Clay delicately dabbed Lainey's forehead, leaning so close she could feel his breath against her cheek. Her hands were shaking and her heart was ready to climb up her ribs. So affected was she by his nearness that it was amazing the moist cloth didn't steam against her fevered brow.

Finally Clay seemed satisfied with his ministrations. He sat back on his heels. "How does that feel?"

Her breath escaped all at once. "Fine, thank you."

"'Tis sorry I am to interrupt a healing moment," Broddie said, jerking a bent thumb toward the window. "But we have a wee bit of a problem."

Clay never took his eyes off Lainey's face. "The bathroom window opens into an alley. You and Lainey can get away without being seen."

She stiffened. "And leave you here? Absolutely not!"

Ignoring her protest, Clay reached up and plucked the red-stickered file off the desk top. He handed it to Broddie. "Take Gerald's notes. Put them somewhere safe." The two men exchanged a significant look before Broddie accepted the file with a grim nod.

Lainey was beside herself, horrified by the belief that Clay would be left to the mercy of the mob. "Either we all go out that window or I'm not moving."

"I don't want you involved," Clay said kindly. "Besides, those good ol' boys obviously want to have a chat. Sooner or later, I'm going to have to oblige them."

"You'll do no such thing." Lainey grabbed the phone cord and hauled the instrument down from the desk.

Broddie took the receiver out of her hand. "Now it wouldn't be the police you're thinking to call."

Moaning, she sagged against the wall. What a fool Clay must think her. If Scarlet's esteemed police chief had wanted the mob scene stopped, he had the resources to have resolved the situation hours ago. Evidently, Chief Clark condoned what was going on. He may have even orchestrated it. In either case, they were quite obviously on their own.

"Okay. Fine." Lainey crossed her arms. "I'm still staying."

To her surprise, Broddie agreed. "The lass is right. You'll have to come with us. Alone, you haven't a prayer."

"I won't leave my research materials, and there's too much to carry. Besides, I've no place to go." He silenced Broddie's protest before it was issued. "I'm *not* going to put you at risk, Mac, no matter how damn big your house is."

"Then you'll have to leave town," Lainey stated. "There's no other choice."

An odd light flickered in Clay's eyes. "There's one other option," he murmured. "But I'd need help."

Ignoring his sly expression, Lainey anxiously blurted, "I'll do anything you want."

"Anything?" A slow smile spread across his face. "Now there's an offer no man could refuse."

With the tires bouncing, Lainey struggled to steer her reluctant vehicle over the unpaved ruts and forest debris of the winding mountain road. When she swerved around a fallen branch, the front fender brushed the steep embankment jutting up on her left. She muttered peevishly, straightened the wheel and shot an irritable look at her passenger. "Is it much farther?"

"I'm not sure." Clay glanced impassively at the wooded ravine on his right, then held up a small sheet of paper and studied the penciled directions Broddie had dictated a half hour earlier. "The turnoff is supposed to be five miles up this road. How far have we gone?"

She braked lightly and steered around a sharp downhill curve before chancing a quick look at the odometer. "About three miles." And three incredibly long miles at that.

Moistening her lips, she flexed her stiff fingers around the padded wheel. Her poor little compact, unaccustomed to such primitive conditions, shuddered at every turn. They were heading toward a small nameless lake about twelve miles outside of town. As a child, Lainey had been there once or twice, although it had been so long ago she'd forgotten how steep the terrain was. And how lovely.

She did recall that there'd been a few dilapidated rowboats strewn along the shore beside a partially submerged dock area and boarded-up cabin. Evidently the privately owned reservoir had been used as a fishing retreat by a wealthy industrialist with a taste for deep-water bass. After spending a small fortune stocking the lake with his fish of choice, the water had later been contaminated by chemical leachate from nearby coal mining operations. The bass died; the industrialist, unable to resell the worthless parcel, had abandoned it sometime in the 1930s.

Modern locals were still afraid to swim in the clear waters or consume the native catfish that had thrived undisturbed for decades. Most townsfolk had forgotten about the place. Lainey's father, however, had loved it. Sometimes he'd taken her there just to enjoy its natural beauty. They'd hike through the lovely woods, then spread a cloth on the shore to share a picnic lunch and talk. Those had been such special times; and until this morning, Lainey had completely forgotten them.

"Hey! Slow down!"

Startled from her reverie, Lainey realized they were careening down an exceptionally steep area and instantly hit the brake. She angled an embarrassed glance at her pale passenger and offered a meek apology.

"No problem," he murmured without taking his eyes off the road ahead or releasing his white-knuckled grip on the dashboard.

"It's been such a long time since I've been here." Wincing at the lame explanation, Lainey decided that conversation, no matter how mundane, would keep her mind from wandering into the past. She tried for a bright smile. "You, too, huh?"

"Hmm?" He was staring out the windshield as though his life depended on it.

Lainey couldn't blame him. "I said, it's probably been a long time since you've been to the lake."

"Oh. Actually, I've never been there."

That was a surprise. While plotting their escape from the motel, Clay had specifically mentioned the lake's fishing cabin as a perfect hideaway. Because he'd requested directions from Broddie, Lainey assumed that Clay, like herself, had simply forgotten the way. If he'd never been to the lake, she couldn't figure out how he'd known about it or the cabin.

When she questioned him, he appeared more uncomfortable with the innocent query than with their wild ride around the mountain. "I heard about it," he muttered. "People talk."

Lainey smiled. "They certainly do, particularly in Scarlet. In fact, the entire town is probably buzzing about your daring escape. It was a very clever plan."

Clay responded with disdainful grunt and an annoyed frown. "I'm nothing if not clever."

"Why are you being sarcastic? It really *was* clever."

Sighing, Clay rubbed his eyelids. "I don't mean to be ungracious, but I'm not particularly proud of what happened at the motel."

"None of that was your fault." Lainey angled him a perplexed look. "Besides, everything worked out fine."

Clay chose not to argue the point. The plan had worked well enough, but he couldn't help thinking about all the things that could have gone wrong. The worst part was watching helplessly while Lainey had crossed the parking lot toward her car. In spite of McFerson's insistence that Reeves's men wouldn't bother her, Clay's initial misgivings had turned into stark terror the moment she'd stepped foot outside the room.

As it turned out, the old coot had been right. After the longest ten seconds of Clay's life, Lainey had strolled across the parking lot, gotten into her car and driven away. By the time she'd pulled into the alley behind the motel, Clay had been waiting and McFerson had been handing files and suitcases out the bathroom window. Clay had loaded his possessions into Lainey's car, tossed the van keys to Mac, then he and Lainey had driven away unmolested.

Now Clay could only pray that McFerson's part of the plan had gone as smoothly. The gutsy old guy was supposed to wait fifteen minutes, then saunter out to Clay's van and drive off, leaving Reeves's dimwitted goon squad to rush an empty motel room. And in case any of the thugs tried to follow the van, Mac had telephoned Roger at the newsroom and worked out an intricate hide-and-seek plan. Clay hoped it hadn't been necessary to implement the elaborate stunt, although he wouldn't know for sure until later this afternoon when McFerson was scheduled to bring the minivan up to the lake.

Even if everything had gone smooth as glass, Clay was still disgusted by the entire scene. Lainey and Broddie had both been endangered by the confrontation with Reeves's men, a confrontation that never would have happened if Clay hadn't been there in the first place. He was beginning to wonder if there was some truth to his father's grim prognostication that trouble flocked to a Cooper like fleas on a hound.

"I think this is it," Lainey said suddenly.

Realizing that the car was idling, Clay glanced out and saw a dirt path snaking through the forest. "The turnoff?" He reread McFerson's directions. "All it says is five miles, first road on the right. I suppose this could be it."

"Well, there's only one way to find out." Lainey turned the wheel sharply and inched along the overgrown entrance. They'd traveled about three hundred yards when the road opened into a clearing. She stopped the car in front of a small structure at the far side of the area and cast a skeptical eye on the weather-beaten shack. "It seemed a lot bigger when I was a kid. Are you sure you want to stay here?"

"I don't need much room." Clay pushed the car door open and stepped onto a thick mat of dried leaves. "And you certainly can't beat the view."

Beyond the thick curtain of fall color, the shimmering water reflected rippled hues of crimson and gold cast by the surrounding forest. The lake itself was rather small, probably a half mile across and two miles around, but Clay could see a few pocket beaches dotting the tree-encrusted shore. It was difficult to believe that a place so clean and pristine had once been polluted to the point of sterility. Fortunately, nature was forgiving; if left undisturbed, she'd do her best to clean up mankind's mistakes. At this nameless little lake, she'd done a hell of a good job.

Lainey came up beside him. "It is lovely, isn't it?" Closing her eyes, she inhaled deeply. "Ah. Everything smells so fresh and leafy."

Clay smiled. She was even more beautiful now, with her cheeks all flushed and her eyes glistening like precious stones. The breezed lifted a few strands of glossy sable hair. She absently brushed them from her face, then turned away from the wind and saw him looking at her. For a brief moment their gazes locked and like the time so long ago, Clay's heart leapt at the intangible contact.

Her eyelids fluttered. She nervously moistened her lips and gestured toward the cabin. "I guess we'd better unload your things. If you're sure you want to stay, that is."

"I'm sure."

"It's only a two-hour drive to Greenville. You'd be a lot more comfortable there." She slid her hands down the front of her skirt as though automatically searching for pockets. Finding none, she absently hugged herself. "I'd still keep my promise, you know."

The reminder hit him like a fist. While in the hotel room, Clay had agreed to leave town only if Lainey promised to read his book notes and review the evidence he'd gathered. Since the mob outside had been circling like starving vultures, she'd had little choice in the matter.

At the time Clay had felt a sense of victory. Now he just felt like a bully. Lainey had obviously been concerned for his safety; he'd taken advantage of that to get what he wanted. It was the kind of thing Ben Cooper would have done.

Clay wanted to release her from the coerced promise but couldn't seem to spit out the words. Although the method had been despicable, he was nonetheless desperate to achieve the result. If he could only break through Lainey's stubborn denial, Clay was certain she'd understand why revealing the truth was vital to both of them. Of course, that still didn't excuse his methods.

Disgusted with himself, Clay turned away and started hauling his belongings from the back seat. After setting his suitcase on the ground, he started to reach for his briefcase and caught a reflection in the car window. He froze, sickened to the core by the shadowy image of Ben Cooper's face superimposed on his own.

"Clay?" A soothing warmth touched his shoulder. "Are you all right?"

He jerked out the briefcase. "I'm fine."

"Are you sure? You look like you've seen a ghost."

The briefcase slipped from his hand, bouncing roughly onto the ground. Clay closed his eyes, wiped the dampness from his forehead and growled, "I'm fine, dammit."

The warmth instantly left his shoulder as she stepped away. After a moment she broke the thick silence. "I'll, ah, just go check out the cabin."

Without responding, he listened to her footsteps crunch across the carpet of dried leaves. When he heard the soft thud of sneakers on the wooden porch, he sagged against the open car door. A ghost, she'd said. God, he wished to hell it had been that simple. He could have handled that. A specter from another dimension would have been less frightening than the bitter reality Clay had so diligently concealed all these years. The truth was that Ben Cooper would never die because part of him lurked inside the heart and soul of his living son. That was Clay's secret. And it terrified him.

Chapter 6

The bloodcurdling shriek sliced Clay like a blade. He dropped a file box in the dirt. "Lainey?" Another piercing scream emanated from the cabin. Before the horrifying echo had died, Clay was sprinting across the clearing. He hit the rotting porch like a human tank and burst through the door. "My God, what is it?"

With her hands pressed against her mouth, Lainey was staring at a vintage 1920s icebox as though expecting it to rear up and attack. Her eyes were enormous. She wiggled a finger toward the dark opening beneath the antiquated appliance. "There! It's under there!"

Clay followed her frantic gesture. "What's under there?"

She took a wheezing breath. "It *looked* at me!"

Since she was obviously too distraught to offer further information, Clay crossed the living area to the corner of the room that served as a food preparation area. He didn't have a clue what "It" was, but figured that as long as the damned thing had eyeballs, he could handle it. Kneeling down, he peered into the darkness. A baseball-size shadow scurried into the corner. "It looks like a squirrel. Or it could be a—"

"Rat!" Lainey screamed as the shadow shot out from between the chipped enamel legs. She dove onto a nearby din-

ing table and scrambled to her feet. "Oh, God! Get rid of it! Make it go away!"

Clay bit back a smile and spoke to the confused creature circling the room. "Go away, rat," he said pleasantly. The fat rodent paused, looked straight at Clay, then spun around and dashed out the open doorway. Clay stood, spread his hands and grinned smugly. "Any other dragons you'd like me to slay, m'lady?"

Lainey was not amused. Shuddering with revulsion, she wrapped her arms around herself and refused to step down from the table. Her frightened gaze scanned the floor. "There could be more of them."

"I doubt it. He looked pretty lonely to me."

She skewed him with a furious stare. "You find this amusing?"

"Yes, actually."

"But it was a *rat,*" she sputtered, so angry she nearly fell off her perch. "Everyone knows what disgusting creatures they are. They spread disease and filth and...and they've got *teeth,* for God's sake! Nobody likes rats...*nobody!*"

"I didn't say that I particularly liked them." Clay slid his hands into his pockets and rocked back on his heels. "It's just that I'm not compelled by the mere sight of one to toe-dance on a table and belt out operatic high notes that any diva would envy."

A crimson flush crept up her throat. "Go ahead. Have your fun. But I'm not coming down until you've looked under every piece of furniture in the entire place."

Still smiling, Clay glanced around the sparsely furnished room. "That shouldn't take long." Besides the icebox, the kitchenette contained a wood stove, a faded tile counter and a huge, single-basin sink fed by an old hand pump. He opened one of the two lower cupboards. "Here, rat. Hee-eere, rat." He closed the cupboard and glanced over his shoulder. "No rats there," he announced.

Her eyes narrowed into angry brown slits.

Enjoying himself immensely, Clay made a production of rat-checking every rodent-size cranny in the kitchen, then sauntered into the living area. A few beer and soda cans littered the floor, along with crumpled potato chip bags, candy wrappers and other evidence that the cabin had occasionally been used as a party place.

Ignoring the clutter, Clay investigated the massive stone fireplace, the dusty upholstered sofa and the broken-down rocking chair in the corner. From there he moved to the small bedroom, which contained a hardwood armoire and two narrow cots with thin mattresses jelly-rolled at the foot of the rusting wire frame.

In the bathroom, Clay found an old claw-foot tub and a rust-stained porcelain water closet. There was no sink, although Clay assumed that a bowl and pitcher on the corner vanity was meant to serve that function.

Upon emerging from the bathroom, Clay brushed his hands together and officially proclaimed the tiny cabin a rat-free zone. Lainey clutched her stomach, took a shaky breath and eased down from the table. Anxiously eyeing the floor, she sidled along the wall and kicked the front door shut. She folded her arms and glumly glanced around. "This place isn't fit for human habitation."

"Sure it is." To prove it, Clay plopped comfortably onto the sofa. A dust plume rose up from the misshapen cushions. "There are cooking uten—" he coughed "—sils in the kitchen and I found—" cough, cough "—bed linens bagged in plastic—" His throat went into spasms. He leapt up, eyes watering, and frantically fanned the rising dust cloud with his hand.

Lainey sauntered across the room, snickering. "Yes, I can see that you'll be quite comfortable." She reached out and haphazardly brushed his shoulder. "Although I doubt that your Brooks Brothers wardrobe is accustomed to such rustic accommodations."

Blinking madly, Clay wiped his stinging eyes. "I'll, uh, just sweep up a bit before I unpack."

"Good choice," she murmured, flicking at his sleeve. "Now hold still for a minute."

Clay frowned. "Why?"

Lainey scanned the folds of his white dress shirt. "There's a spider on your—"

"A *what?*" Horrified, Clay uttered a succinct oath and blindly whacked at himself. "Where is it? Is it gone?"

"Good grief, if you'll just be still for a minute—".

Clay bellowed when something tickled his chest. Cussing under his breath, he ripped the shirt open and frantically clawed his bare skin. "Get it off me!" he hollered, spinning in a frenetic circle. "Get the damned thing *off!*"

"Oh, for crying out loud—"

"*Argh!*"

Lainey pinched his chest, then dropped something on the floor and covered it with her shoe. "It's okay now," she crooned sweetly. "The big bad bug is all gone."

With his skin still crawling, Clay spun his head from side to side in a futile effort to inspect his back. "I still feel something..."

"Trust me. Your little buddy has gone to arachnid heaven." She lifted her foot to reveal the squashed remnants.

Clay nearly gagged at the sight, then squinted up and cringed at the profusion of silken webs clustered along the peaked beam ceiling. He cursed again. "There must be a whole nest of them up there."

"Do you think so?" Barely able to keep a straight face, Lainey cupped her mouth and called upward, "Here, spider. Hee-eere, spider." She glanced over her shoulder, eyes sparkling. "Nope. No spiders there."

He managed a thin smile. "Okay, I admit it. When it comes to eight-legged dragons, m'lady is on her own."

"So my gallant knight has a chink in his armor."

"I'm afraid so. Are you disappointed?"

The amusement drained from her eyes. "Everyone is afraid of something," she whispered. "But not everyone has the courage to admit it."

As she looked up, their eyes met. Clay was aware of a strange sensation, a shimmering aura of engulfing energy separating them from the world. For those brief seconds Clay was drawn into a fathomless vortex in which nothing else existed except this precious woman and the indefinable emotion swelling at the core of his being.

Then she lowered her gaze, shattering the fragile link to eternity. Clay felt empty, as though an intrinsic part of him had been suddenly sliced away. He took a shuddering breath. When she responded with a tiny gasp, he glanced down and saw her gaze riveted on his exposed chest.

She nervously fluffed her feathered bangs and turned stiffly away. "I'll, uh, start in the kitchen."

Still shaken by the ethereal experience they'd shared, Clay struggled to rebutton his shirt. "Start... what?"

"Cleaning." Her shoulders lifted as she took another deep breath. "This place is a health hazard. It really needs a good vacuuming but without electricity, I guess we'll have to do it the old-fashioned way. Did you happen to see a broom?"

"In that tall cupboard," Clay replied absently before adding, "But this isn't your problem. I'll do it."

"I don't mind." After removing a rag mop and straw broom from the cupboard, she began rooting through the remaining drawers and cupboards. "Besides, it'll be hours before Broddie gets here, so I might as well make myself useful."

"You don't have to stay," he told her, although he desperately hoped that she would.

"I wouldn't feel comfortable leaving you here without food or transportation.... Ah! Rags... detergent... lamp oil, all kinds of good stuff." She blew dust off a can of cleanser and tossed it to Clay. "You can do the bathroom."

"Thanks," he murmured, but she was too busy inspecting the antique hand pump to respond. After a moment a stream of rusty water sputtered from the spout and she gurgled with childlike delight.

Entranced, Clay watched while she puttered in the tiny kitchen, humming happily. She was so giving and guileless, an innocent heart too trusting to recognize that she was surrounded by duplicity and deceit. Now Clay had to expose the lies, shatter the illusions on which she'd built her life. Then he'd simply walk away and leave her to sweep up the splintered remains of all she'd held dear.

His father would have been proud.

Lloyd Reeves swiveled in his plush lambskin executive chair, reached across the gleaming onyx desk and answered the ringing telephone. A raspy female voice responded. "Mr. McFerson and Mr. Elkert have returned to the newsroom."

After leaning back and propping a foot on his knee, he wiped a speck from his imported Italian loafer. "Thank you, Marge. What's the status of today's edition?"

"They're holding the front page."

Not surprised by that information, Lloyd absently gazed out the bay window overlooking his immaculate estate. "No doubt they plan to headline the motel incident."

"Mr. McFerson called it a riot," Marge said indignantly. "Can you believe it? A group of decent, God-fearing folks just wanting to rid their town of murdering trash like Clayton Cooper. It's a travesty, that's what. A travesty." She lowered her voice to a conspiratorial whisper. "Say the word and we'll stop it."

"Hmm?" Lloyd frowned. "Stop what, Marge?"

"Why, that disgusting story, of course. Anyway, Billy Jim says— You know my nephew, don't you?"

Lloyd impatiently tapped his knee. "Yes, Marge, I know your nephew."

"Thing is, Billy Jim works over in machine maintenance, and he says all he has to do is poke a screwdriver through the lens of that big ol' camera and poof! No paper."

Lloyd could almost feel the woman's triumphant grin. He swallowed an exasperated sigh. Such sabotage would do little more than add to McFerson's aggravation since there were any number of presses available in Greenville. The *Banner* had made frequent use of such services during power outages, equipment failures and other emergencies. Marge Slattery, who'd worked for the newspaper most of her adult life, should certainly be aware of that fact, but Lloyd couldn't be bothered to enlighten her. The clucking old woman was an annoying imbecile, but she'd also been a reliable source of information over the years. Some of that information had actually been useful.

Deciding that alienating the idiotic busybody would serve no useful purpose, Lloyd added a touch of gratitude. "I appreciate the suggestion, but I doubt that will be necessary. Do keep me informed."

After a silent moment, a less-confident voice filtered over the line. "Um, well, sure—"

Lloyd cradled the receiver, gazed thoughtfully out the window for a moment, then returned his attention to the man in red suspenders who was seated on the other side of the massive polished desk. "So you weren't able to retrieve any documents from the motel room?"

The man squirmed uncomfortably. "He musta took 'em out the john window."

Steepling his hands, Lloyd nodded sagely. Although he would have been interested in reviewing the information Cooper had gathered thus far, there were bound to be other copies of the documents. Besides, the fact that Cooper had returned to Scarlet confirmed that he hadn't yet found what he was seeking.

Still, the entire confrontation had gone badly. Lloyd was not pleased. "Is there a reason you chose not to have your men surveil the back alley?"

"Uh, do what to it?"

Lloyd closed his eyes, issuing a silent request for deliverance from ignorant fools. He took a calming breath and fixed the man with a penetrating gaze. "Why wasn't someone watching the back alley?"

"Oh." Red Suspenders mopped his soggy forehead. "Well, y'know, I didn't figure on that Sheridan gal helpin' the enemy like she done."

"Perhaps the young woman was annoyed by having been spit upon," Lloyd suggested calmly. "May I remind you that I requested only a small protest to emphasize resentment at Cooper's attempt to sully the town's good name. I did not request, nor did I wish for the sympathy backlash provided when your mob of unchivalrous ruffians molested the virtuous daughter of Scarlet's martyred hero." Leaning forward, Lloyd spoke through carefully clenched teeth. "Do I make myself clear?"

"Yessir, sure do, Mr. Reeves." The man's Adam's apple bobbed frantically. "But don't ya worry none. Cooper's gone fer sure, running like a three-legged dog with a bobcat on his butt. Prob'ly back in Atlanta by now, picking himself a sweet Georgia peach." With a wily wink and a smug grin, Red Suspenders settled comfortably back in the plush guest chair.

Shaking his head, Lloyd looked away in disgust. It was possible that Cooper had given up, of course, although Lloyd seriously doubted it. But he'd know soon enough. Nothing happened around here that wasn't brought to his attention sooner or later. Scarlet was, after all, Lloyd's town; he made the rules; he enforced them. Unfortunately, Clayton Cooper had chosen to ignore those rules. It was a choice the unfortunate young man would live to regret.

Working together, it took Clay and Lainey less than two hours to scrape away the top layer of grime so the cabin was somewhat presentable, although certainly not up to Lainey's strict standards of cleanliness. She placed a bud vase of red and orange maple leaves on the Formica-topped dinette, glanced around the now-tidy living area and decided that under such primitive circumstances, there was little more she could do.

Besides, she doubted Clay would be staying here more than a day or so. Although this evening's *Banner* should effectively dismiss the rumor that had whipped the town into such a hanging frenzy, Clay must realize that returning to Scarlet had been a bad idea. Now Lainey had to convince him that his book was also a bad idea. She didn't have a clue how to do that but was nonetheless determined.

Not that she wanted Clay to go. In fact, she desperately wanted him to stay. There was something enduring about Clayton Cooper that made her feel secure. She admired his accomplishments and his dedication in overcoming obstacles that would have thwarted all but the most obstinate soul. Compared to her own life's aimless ramble, Clay's ambition and unwavering sense of purpose seemed even more commendable. In Atlanta he'd conquered the tainted past that Scarlet could neither forget nor forgive. Lainey knew Clay could never build a life here; and she could never build one anywhere else.

A thump on the front porch interrupted her sad contemplation. Clay backed through the door balancing a cardboard box of files and clutching the plastic handle of his folded computer with his free hand. He turned and kicked the door shut behind him. "This is the last of it."

As he unloaded the box's contents onto the table, Lainey came up beside him. She watched quietly as he arranged the file folders and loose papers in some kind of order understood only by him. He reached back into the box, extracted a large leather album and laid it carefully beside the tiny computer. Lainey eyed the worn cover. "Is that where you keep your book notes?"

"No." Clay didn't look up. He hesitated before adding, "It's my mother's journal."

"Oh." Without knowing why she was compelled to do so, Lainey absently touched the supple leather. "It must mean a lot to you."

He started to speak, apparently thought better of it and responded with a curt nod.

"Tell me about your mother," Lainey said suddenly, startling herself. "I mean, if you want to."

Clay regarded her for a moment, then gazed down at the journal as though considering the request. After a moment he spoke quietly, in a voice that hardly shook at all. "My mother was a very special woman. Life wasn't kind to her, but she never complained. Little things excited her, like spring wildflowers or a cracked mirror decorated with moss and acorns."

Lainey smiled. "A gift from her son, perhaps?"

He returned her smile. "I was only five at the time, too young to be embarrassed by a Mother's Day gift that was nothing more than a gussied-up throwaway."

"But she adored it, didn't she?"

"Evidently so. She hardly ever used the silver vanity set I gave her later."

Since Lainey was a sucker for heartwarming tales, she encouraged Clay to expand on the mirror story. At first he seemed reluctant, relaying the story only to please her. Eventually, he appeared caught up in reminiscence of the past.

Lainey was fascinated by his description of how Catherine had graciously accepted her grown son's gift and had laid the gleaming hairbrush and hand mirror on her dresser so she could admire them daily. Clay went on to describe that every week without fail, his mother had lovingly polished the ornate baroque handles and cleaned the sparkling mirrored face, then repositioned the set between the cut-crystal atomizers that he'd also given her. Afterward, she'd pick up the cracked mirror and use a dime-store brush on her sleek ebony hair.

Clay sat across from Lainey, who'd pulled up a chair and was leaning across the table in rapt fascination. "I gave her the new set hoping she'd throw that miserable piece of junk away. But she just kept regluing acorns and when the moss wore off the edges, she gathered more from the woods to replace it."

"A child's love is pure and innocent," Lainey said. "Each time she looked into that mirror, she probably reexperienced that very special love. Nothing, not silver, not gold, could ever replace it."

Perhaps it was Lainey's tender compassion causing the tingling sensation along Clay's spine; or perhaps it was the alluring, breathless quality of her voice. All he knew was that he hadn't felt so exposed, so emotionally vulnerable, since the night his mother had died. It wasn't a comfortable feeling.

Turning sideways in the ladder-back chair, he forced a casual shrug. "Mom deserved nice things. I wanted her to have them. God knows she'd done without most of her life."

"A lot of people are poor. It's nothing to be ashamed of."

"That's easy to say with a full belly and decent clothes on your back." Clay instantly regretted the harsh words and the bitterness with which they were issued.

Lainey studied a scratch in the Formica tabletop. "You're right, of course. I've always been very fortunate."

Clay's stomach sank like a rock. Fortunate? First her father was murdered, then she had the sterling good fortune to be abandoned by her mother and raised by a pair of jackals who treated her like chattel. The way Clay saw it, Lainey's luck to date had been mostly bad and only her wistful expression kept him from saying so.

"I guess I really don't know much about your family," she said suddenly. "Were your parents born here in Scarlet?"

"No, they were both raised in West Virginia. After my mother's pa died of black lung, she had to take a job and help support her nine brothers and sisters."

"How awful," Lainey murmured sympathetically. "How old was she?"

"About sixteen, I think. I know she always regretted having to quit high school because she'd once hoped to be a teacher." Clay's gaze slid to the journal where the secrets of Catherine's heart had been exposed. Anger bubbled up again, along with burning resentment of how his mother had been coerced into marrying a man she'd never loved.

A gentle hand covered his. "Clay?"

"Hmm?" He looked up and gazed into the softest eyes he'd ever seen.

"What were you thinking about?"

"Why?" The warmth of her palm radiated from his wrist to his elbow.

"You suddenly looked...I don't know...angry, I guess."

He exhaled slowly, wondering how to explain what he himself couldn't understand. Finally he decided to start at the beginning, explaining how Ben Cooper had promised Catherine that if she'd marry him, he'd put her through college so she could earn a teaching certificate. Although Ben had been a coal miner more than twenty years her senior, the possibility of actually achieving her dream had been irresistible, particularly when Ben had thrown in the added bonus of promising to take her away from the poverty-stricken town she'd grown to despise.

That had been the only promise Ben Cooper ever kept. After hearing that ChemCorp was building a new manufacturing plant, Ben had packed up his bride and headed for South Carolina. He'd even gotten a position in the company's shipping department—the job had lasted less than a year.

"What happened?" Lainey asked.

Clay used his finger to draw an invisible circle on the tabletop. "My father had always been a heavy drinker. When it started affecting his work, he was fired."

"And your mother was never able to return to school?"

"No. I came along and that was that." Clay stretched lazily, then draped an arm over the back of his chair. "For the next ten years, my mother was subjected to conditions even worse than those she'd tried to escape. At least in West Virginia being poor wasn't a crime. Here in Scarlet, she was snubbed, insulted and treated like trash."

Chewing her lip, Lainey avoided her gaze. "Why did she stay?"

"Because for some reason unfathomable to me, my mother loved this town."

Lainey's head snapped up. "How could she? I mean, it's difficult to believe that the people I grew up with could be so cruel . . . but if they were, if they really treated your family so badly, I'd think this would be the last place she'd want to live."

He shrugged. "Some people were kind to her. Unfortunately, my father wasn't one of them, but because she'd had so little in her life, even one friend was more than she'd ever had before. But during the trial—" Clay saw Lainey's eyes cloud at the word "—my mother discovered how shallow those friendships were. Suddenly she was totally, completely alone. It broke her heart."

Clay abruptly stood and walked to the window. He heard a chair scrape. In a moment he felt Lainey's presence behind him, offering silent encouragement. He took a shuddering breath, leaned against the windowsill and whispered, "My mother died during that trial. It just took twenty years for her to stop breathing."

While Clay stared out at the glimmering lake, Lainey slid her hand beneath his folded arm and rested her head against his shoulder. Through the kinship of shared pain, she felt an affinity with Clay Cooper that she'd never experienced before. Now she understood him. She recognized his guilt, his anger, the turmoil he must have endured watching the person he loved most in the world suffer a torment he was helpless to heal.

Lainey recognized those feelings because she'd shared them. Although she couldn't tell Clay, she, too, had suffered the wretched agony of seeing a loved one slowly destroyed by grief and the devastation of a terminally shattered heart. But while she'd tried to escape her silent suffering, Clay had faced his own demons with courage and a steadfast conviction that made her own efforts seem even more futile. She was awed by his strength and shamed by her own cowardice in refusing to acknowledge her own painful past. Instead she'd circled life like a lost soul with no objective beyond surviving another night, another terrifying dream.

Both of their lives had been shattered by the same tragic truth, a truth Clay was striving to understand. All he asked was that Lainey do the same. It seemed a small price to pay compared to all that he had suffered.

Stepping away, she released his arm and clasped her hands nervously. "I'd like to read your book outline now...if you still want me to."

When Clay turned toward her, she was humbled by the gratitude and relief in his eyes. "You have no idea how much that would mean to me."

Deep down, Lainey knew exactly how much it meant to him. That's why she couldn't meet his gaze. Instead she went to the table and waited for him to join her.

"Let's see...I think it's in this stack... Ah!" He pulled out a neatly clipped bundle, then hesitated. "At the moment it's just a chronological outline. The book structure itself may be arranged differently, depending on..." The words evaporated as Lainey took the thin manuscript.

She finished his thought aloud. "Depending on what you find out over the next few days."

"Yes." He puffed his cheeks and blew out a breath. "I, uh, think I'll take a walk down to the lake."

She nodded, grateful that he'd been perceptive enough to realize that she'd prefer to review the notes in private. After a hesitant moment, Clay offered a thin smile and left.

Lainey glanced down at the title page and was immediately startled. She'd expected a clandestine title like *A Scandal In Scarlet* or *Blind Justice* or something shamelessly designed to announce a potboiler exposé of tantalizing dark secrets.

But the book was simply entitled *Catherine*.

Taking a deep breath, Lainey flipped the first page and started to read.

The cabin door cracked open. "Do you need more time?" Clay asked. "There must be a few miles of trails I haven't covered yet."

Licking her lips, Lainey clipped the pages together and laid them aside. "I'm through."

A shaft of light flooded the table. Clay stepped inside. The sunlight thinned, then disappeared as he closed the door. He stood there for a moment, studying her. "What do you think?"

Lainey swallowed hard. "It... wasn't what I expected."

"You don't like it," he said flatly.

She wanted to dispute that, but a sudden lump in her throat threatened to choke her. If she tried to speak, if she even looked up at him, she'd humiliate herself by bursting into tears.

To say that the book wasn't what she'd expected had been an understatement. The more she'd read, the more astounded she'd been to realize that Clay was trying to prove his father's innocence only because Catherine had served as her husband's alibi during the trial. By dismissing her sworn testimony, the town had labeled her a liar. That was what Clay planned to refute. The focus, and indeed the book itself, would be an ode to Clay's mother, a loving tribute to a courageous woman's life.

Lainey had been touched to the core. In spite of her effort, a single tear slid down her cheek.

That tear affected Clay like a body blow. "Lainey," he whispered. "I never meant to hurt you. I thought if you read it, if you knew—" He raked his hair helplessly. "God, I'm so sorry. I thought you'd understand."

She looked up, her eyes shimmering. "I do understand. It's just so... so moving."

He sat warily beside her, wanting to comfort yet afraid that if he embraced her, he'd never let her go. "Then you'll support publication?"

"I—" She shook her head miserably. "I can't."

Taken aback, Clay straightened. "Why not?"

She laid her palm on the manuscript. "Please understand, most of what you've written is incredibly beautiful and touching. But there are... mistakes, inaccuracies that I simply can't allow."

"Errors can be easily corrected. Just point them out and I'll take care of them."

A glimmer of hope flickered through her guarded gaze. "It's the part about my father."

He frowned. "Which part?"

"The, uh—" she cleared her throat "—part about his relationship with your mother."

Although Clay's stomach nearly dropped to his toes, he managed an impassive expression. "Why do you feel it's inaccurate?"

Lainey's eyes widened. "Because it never happened, of course."

"How can you be so certain, Lainey? After all, you were only a child—"

She stood so quickly the chair tilted backward and crashed to the floor. "My father *loved* me! He loved my mother. And he would have never, *ever* done anything to hurt either of us."

As she spun away, Clay pushed to his feet and took her arm. "Of course he loved his family, but he loved my mother, too. They never meant to hurt anyone... it just happened."

"No." She pulled away from his restraining grip and vehemently shook her head. "It's nothing but a lousy, rotten lie, and I won't listen to another word about it."

Further discussion was futile. Sighing, Clay opened the leather journal and took a folded sheet from the final page. He hesitated. Still holding the proof in his hands yet fearing Lainey's reaction, he was reluctant to offer it. Denial was her shield, a way of blocking out that which was too painful to acknowledge. Clay had the power to destroy that shield; but did he have the right to use it?

As he silently pondered the dilemma, Lainey made the choice for him.

"What's that?" she asked.

Clay blinked, looked up and saw that she was staring at the paper he held. "It's a letter."

Her gaze narrowed, but she said nothing.

He sucked air between clenched teeth. "The truth is in there, Lainey. You can read it or not. It's up to you."

"I already know the truth."

"Then there's nothing to be afraid of, is there?" Despite the defiant tilt of her chin, he saw fear in her eyes.

Then she extended her hand.

Chapter 7

Clay laid the creased stationery on Lainey's open palm.

She paused a moment, then unfolded the sheet and immediately turned pale. "This is my father's writing."

No response was necessary and none was given. Every word of that letter was indelibly etched in Clay's memory.

> Catherine, my beloved,
> Every moment we're apart is a moment of darkness. You are the light of my soul, the joy of my heart...

Lainey emitted a tiny cry and touched her throat. The paper fluttered to the floor. "No," she whispered. Her devastated expression nearly tore Clay's heart out. "It's not true. It...can't be true." Covering her eyes, she turned away and began to sob. "H-he lied to me. He said he l-loved us."

"Lainey, honey..." Clay moved behind her to wrap his arms around her quivering shoulders. "He did love you and he loved your mother—"

She whirled and pushed him away. "Then how could he betray us? How could he cheat on my mother and...and—"

"Shh, it's all right." He reached out, wincing as she slapped his hand away.

"It's *not* all right." She gazed up with wet, imploring eyes. "Don't you understand? Nothing will ever be all right again."

"This doesn't change anything, Lainey. Gerald was still your father, still the man you loved and who loved you with all his heart."

"If he'd loved us, he wouldn't have wanted *her!*" She swept an angry hand at the worn leather journal on the table. "The man I knew—the man I *thought* I knew—wasn't a . . . a philandering adulterer!"

Clay wanted to hold her so bad his teeth ached. "I know how you feel, honey, but it's not what you think."

"You can't know how I feel," she snapped. "No one knows how I feel."

"I do," he said quietly.

Lainey's furious expression crumpled. "Oh, God. Of course you do. I'm so sorry . . ." As the words evaporated, he opened his arms and she fell into his embrace. "I know she was your mother. Forgive me."

"There's nothing to forgive." He pressed her cheek against his chest and stroked her soft hair, overcome by a sudden surge of protectiveness. At that moment he'd have fought a six-foot spider to take away the pain he'd just caused her. "You know, honey, the human heart is a magnificent thing, no bigger than a man's fist yet it has an endless capacity for love."

She quivered against him. "What are you trying to say?"

Good question, Clay thought. Too bad he didn't have an answer. At least, not an answer that Lainey would willingly accept. But he'd opened the door; now he had to make an attempt, however lame, to get through it. "Think about all the people you've loved in your life. Have you ever had to stop loving one person so you'd have enough room to love another?"

"Of course not." She wiggled to free the hand that was trapped between their bodies, then used it to wipe her wet face. "But that's not the same thing and you know it."

"Actually, it is the same thing. My mother and your father fell in love. They didn't plan it. They didn't even want it to happen, but when it did, neither of them stopped loving the other people in their lives. They simply added each other to the list."

Lainey shivered and took a step back, forcing Clay to release his hold on her. Although she was only inches away, to Clay it seemed like a mile. Air rushed into the space between them, chilling away her warmth. His arms felt empty.

Sniffing, she wiped her face with the back of her hand. "All those awful things that were said at the trial were true."

"Some things were true. My mother never lied about the aff—" He caught the indiscretion and coughed it away. "She, uh, openly admitted that she and Gerald cared about each other."

Lainey stared numbly across the room. "That's why Ben Cooper killed him."

"No." Clay slid his thumb under her chin, urging her to look at him. "I'm not defending my father. If he'd sobered up long enough to figure out what was going on, he very well might have done it. The point is that he didn't know until the trial. The night your father died, my father was at home, passed out on the living room sofa."

Clay scrutinized her closely, hoping to see some spark of comprehension in her dull eyes. All he saw was despair. "My father abandoned us," she repeated softly. "No wonder my mother went—" Suddenly biting off the words, Lainey closed her eyes so tightly that fresh tears were squeezed from beneath the dark fringe of lashes.

Her exquisite sorrow touched Clay to the quick. Over the years he'd frequently remembered the suffering reflected in her little-girl gaze and had equated the simultaneous twist of his heart as nothing more than empathy for a child in pain. Now, as she looked up and allowed him to gaze deeply into her soulful dark eyes, Clay realized that he felt a great deal more for Lainey Sheridan than mere sympathy.

. . . The light of my soul, the joy of my heart . . .

Suddenly Clay understood those tender words, absorbed them into the very core of his being. Lainey Sheridan had illuminated the darkness in his own soul. Her guileless heart couldn't perceive the hidden evil, the unseen demons lurking deep within him. Reflected in those innocent eyes, Clay saw himself as she saw him, a man of truth and goodness and strength. For one brief and shining moment, he basked in the glow of that reflection and became that man.

When he framed her face with his hands, her eyes widened in surprise, then suddenly darkened with sensual promise. She laid her palms against his chest as though to push him away; instead, her fingers caressed him, tracing muscle and bone with such erotic delicacy that his knees nearly gave way.

His thumb rolled a lazy circle around her temple as he whispered huskily, "I don't think you know how very special you are." They were close now, so close that his breath lifted the fine hairs feathered across her forehead. "I've never known anyone like you."

Her tongue darted nervously. "Are... you going to kiss me?"

He blinked. "Would you like me to?"

"Yes, I think so." She took a deep breath, closed her eyes and raised her parted lips.

Clay didn't need a second invitation. He brushed her mouth gently. A tingling sensation glided down his spine. When their lips touched again, his tongue grazed the cushiony softness, and she uttered a tiny cry that he felt all the way to his toes. Caution dissipated. With a growl of pure passion, he took her lips in a deep, throbbing kiss that ignited his blood into a river of pure passion flowing through his veins.

The first moment he'd laid eyes on Lainey Sheridan, he'd wanted to hold her, to gently kiss away her pain. They'd both been children, yet he'd been overwhelmed by a desperate desire to protect her and offer comfort. He still felt those things, but his desires had deepened, become more complex, more intimate. He wanted her as a man wants a woman—with passion and fire, with tenderness and joy—he wanted to fill the room with moans of pleasure and tiny sounds of sexual delight. He wanted to make mad, passionate love to her—right here, right now—and bury himself in her pulsing softness, absorbing her sweet innocence into his own frayed, cynical soul.

Clay went rigid. Dear God, what was wrong with him? Stepping back roughly, he steadied Lainey's shoulders while her frantic fingers tangled in the fabric of his shirt. She took a shaking breath while her dark eyes questioned him silently.

Releasing her, Clay folded his arms and turned away. Lainey Sheridan was the embodiment of all that was pure and selfless and good. She couldn't understand the tainted blood coursing through his veins. Ben Cooper had, in his own perverted way, loved his wife deeply; yet he'd abused her psychologically, emotionally and physically. Clay was his father's son. His worst fear was that he, too, might be capable of such crushing betrayal.

It was a chance he couldn't take with any woman, let alone this woman, this precious soul who'd touched a place inside him where no one had been before. She deserved better. And the realization was shattering.

While Lainey watched from the porch, Broddie pulled a cardboard box of supplies out of the sleek gray minivan and related the thrill of outfoxing his pursuers. "Burning rubber, I was, careening around them curves like a leprechaun was perched on my shoulder." He handed the box to Clay, then reached inside the vehicle and brought out two stuffed grocery bags. "I don't mind admitting to being just a wee bit nervous, having those hooligans smooching with my bumper."

Clay shifted the box under his arm and took one of the grocery bags. "How'd you managed to lose them?"

"Well now, that's the sweet part, y'see." Chuckling happily, Broddie yanked another bag from the van and started toward the cabin. "There's this old train hole up by the reservoir—"

"The tunnel that runs through Skunk Mountain?"

"The very one." Broddie issued a triumphant snort. "Jumped the tracks, I did, zipped into that hole, then coasted to the shoulder so the damn fools passed me by. Probably chased themselves all the way to Greenville." The old man was still grinning as he mounted the porch and winked at Lainey. "Haven't had this much fun since Maddie Magellan drained a bottle of port and came to mass in her bloomers."

Lainey managed a thin smile, acutely aware that Clay, having crossed the porch without so much as a glance in her direction, was already inside the cabin. "I'm just glad you're back," she told Broddie. "I've been worried about you."

"Were you now?" Tilting his head, the sly old fellow regarded her for a moment, then glanced through the open door into the cabin where Clay was roughly unloading supplies onto the compact counter. "No white flags a'waving, so I'm guessing no truce has been declared."

Since her lips still tingled from Clay's kiss, Lainey felt a slow heat crawl up her throat. "Mr. Cooper and I are not at war, Broddie. We simply have a difference of opinion."

"Aye." He shifted his parcels and emitted an exaggerated sigh. "Pity you can't get along, seeing as how you're both on the same side."

With her face flaming, Lainey leaned on the porch rail. She was angry with Clay for having touched emotions that she didn't want to explore; with herself for not having the strength to maintain the emotional distance so vital to her psychological survival; and angry with Broddie because he obviously recognized and was amused by what was happening between her and Clay.

"We get along just fine," she announced tightly. "We are *not,* however, on the same side of anything."

"Is that a fact?" Broddie pursed his pruney lips. "But isn't it the truth you're both wanting?"

"The truth?" She straightened and glared furiously over her shoulder. "What would you know about the truth, Broddie? You've been lying to me since I was six."

The sparkle faded from his eyes. "I've never lied to you, lass, not once."

"Lies of omission are still lies." She turned to face him directly. "You knew about my father and Catherine Cooper."

Broddie went pale, but his steady gaze never wavered. "Aye. I knew."

With three words, Broddie had dashed the unlikely hope that Gerald's letter might have been written as a joke or at the very least, a tasteless exercise in creative writing. Lainey bit her lip and stared at the splintering porch planks. "Well, thank you for sharing. After all these years of believing my father a hero, I really enjoyed discovering that he was just another adulterous cad."

"That's not how it was—"

The strenuous protest was cut off as Lainey lost control of the terrifying rage that was swelling up from a dark place deep inside. "That's *exactly* how it was. And of course, hearing it directly from the son of my father's *mistress* was such a special experience." Fingernails cut her fisted palms. "How could you keep such a secret, Broddie? Why didn't you tell me?"

Bending slowly, the old man set the bags on the porch. When he straightened, his shoulders folded forward as though strained by the weight of an invisible burden. "There was no need to tell what you already knew."

Lainey's heart thudded once, then fell silent for an eternal moment. When the palpitations started again, the beat was rapid and irregular. "What...are you saying?" The question nearly choked her.

The answer was even more terrifying. "You've always known, lass, though you chose not to believe."

Suddenly an image flashed through her mind: an undulating shadow cast by a ceiling fan in the stifling courtroom. She remembered the sickening smell of stale sweat and cigar smoke, and how she'd squirmed restlessly on the wooden bench because her bottom was numb. Aunt Hallie had jerked her wrist and told her to sit still.

Across the room, a stern man wearing a black bathrobe sat behind a big square desk. Lainey hadn't liked him very much, because he'd seemed really mad at everyone and sometimes he'd even banged a big hammer on the desk. The first time he'd done it, Lainey had been so scared she'd wet her panties. After that, she'd kept a real close eye on the hammer and covered her ears when the robed man reached for it.

There was a chair beside the square desk, too. Sometimes people sat in it and answered questions. A pretty lady with black hair had been sitting there while a mean man wearing a brown suit shouted at her. The man had said nasty things about the lady and about Daddy. The lady had started to cry. So had Lainey.

Afterward Lainey had asked who the pretty lady was. Aunt Hallie's chin got all puckery, like she'd squished a lemon with her teeth. "She's your father's whore."

Lainey didn't know what a whore was, but she'd been hearing a lot of strange words lately, most of them in the courtroom. Since her aunt had seemed kind of upset about this whore thing, she'd decided to ask about sexual intercourse instead. Aunt Hallie had slapped Lainey's face so hard that she'd fallen down the courthouse steps and skinned both of her knees.

One minute she was crumpled in a sobbing heap on the concrete, the next, she was gently lifted to her feet and soft hands were wiping away her tears. "Shh," said the pretty, black-haired lady. "Everything will be all right, sweetheart."

Lainey sniffed, looked into loving eyes the color of her mommy's favorite opal broach, and blurted, "Are you really my daddy's whore?"

The woman smiled sadly. "I loved your daddy very much."

Lainey considered that. "Did he love you, too?"

"Your daddy was a wonderful man. He loved a lot of people, but most of all, he loved you." The lady looked behind Lainey. Her pretty face grew solemn as she took a step back.

Aunt Hallie's bruising fingers suddenly encircled Lainey's wrist. She hissed mean words at the pretty lady, then jerked Lainey's arm and half dragged her away. Stumbling, she managed to twist around and look back. The lady was standing on the sidewalk with her arm around a boy who looked just like her.

As the memory faded, Lainey could still feel the gentle fingers brushing away her tears, still hear the hushed reassurance. "Shh, honey. Everything will be all right."

But now it was a man's voice.

Lainey gazed up into the pale, loving eyes that were so like his mother's. "Oh, God, Clay. I *did* know." Wincing at a stabbing pain in her temple, she shaded her eyes and squinted at Broddie, who was still standing beside the open cabin door. "You were right. I always knew. Catherine told me herself."

"Aye, lass."

Clay laid a tender palm against her cheek. "You've remembered what happened on the courthouse steps?"

All at once, the fear hit, a black terror rising up from an empty pit in the center of her soul. Trembling, she backed away from Clay, away from the comfort he offered. "How could I have forgotten something like that? It doesn't make any sense. It's crazy...it's—" Her throat contracted as though squeezed by an invisible hand when she saw her own horror reflected in Broddie's eyes. "No," she whimpered, shaking her head. "Please, no."

"Lainey?" Clay's voice cracked with panic. "My God, what is it?"

When he reached out, Lainey raised her arms and pulled back to evade his grasp. Her brain throbbed, a blinding agony of jumbled thought and physical pain. *It was crazy to have forgotten....*

She felt fingers on her wrist and fought the confining grip.

"Stop it, lass. Are you hearing me, now?"

Realizing that Broddie had pushed in front of Clay and had hold of her, she instantly stopped struggling. His somber expression scared her to death. "Oh, Broddie," she whispered. "What's wrong with me?"

"Not a bloody thing." After having given the denial too much emphasis, Broddie slid a surprisingly strong arm around her shoulders. "At least, not anything that cannot be cured by a wee bit of rest."

Lainey closed her eyes. As she took a deep, cleansing breath, the pain inside her skull eased, then dissipated as quickly as it had begun.

She sagged gratefully against the dear man's bony frame, realizing that she really was exhausted. Between the stress of the past two days and a lack of sleep resulting from the resurgent nightmare, she was little more than a walking zombie, which also served as a convenient excuse for having fallen into Clay's arms like a love-struck adolescent.

Clay hesitated before taking a step closer. He reached out as though to stroke her hair, but only flexed his fingers. His arm dropped limply to his side. When he spoke, his voice trembled slightly. "Come inside. You'll feel better if you lie down for a while."

Going back into that cabin was the last thing Lainey wanted to do. She reluctantly stepped away from Broddie's fatherly embrace and massaged her forehead to rub away the final traces of the violent headache. All Lainey wanted now was simply to be left alone. There was too much confusion, too many jumbled emotions that she had to sort out and absorb. "I really have to get home. It's almost time to start supper."

Clay's brows lowered in concern. "You're too tired to make the trip alone. I'll go with you."

"Thank you, but it's only a few miles. I'll be fine. Besides, the whole idea here was to keep you *out* of town, remember?"

"She's right, lad. Even with corporate damage control and media coverage, folks won't be calming down until the company stock stabilizes. What with the market being closed over the weekend, it'll be taking a few days for that to happen."

Clay was insistent. "Then you go with her, Mac. You need a ride back to town, anyway."

With a perplexed scowl, Broddie said, "What about the work we've yet to do? If we're to be poking holes in the prosecutor's case, we've pages of testimony to analyze."

Lainey needed no reminder of the original plan. After spending this evening documenting evidence, Clay was to drive Broddie back to Scarlet under cover of darkness. Now both men were treating Lainey like glass, as though her fragile psyche could shatter at the slightest touch.

Deep down, she feared they might be right. Although that possibility terrified her, she concealed her turmoil with a confident smile. "Really, gentlemen, I appreciate your concern, but there's no reason to scrap the original plan. And I'm feeling much better," she added, hoping her nose wouldn't grow. Inside she was as jumpy as a treed cat, unable to erase those disturbing courtroom images from her mind.

In the end it didn't matter. Despite her protest, Broddie finally agreed to accompany her back to town. With the vote now two to one, Lainey accepted defeat with as much grace as the circumstances would allow. She nervously fluffed her hair with her fingers. "It's getting late. We should be going."

"Aye." Broddie nodded at Clay before descending the porch steps.

Clay stopped Lainey as she turned to follow. "Just a minute." He disappeared into the cabin, emerging a moment later with Catherine's journal. "I'd like you to take this."

Lainey stared at the leather-bound diary. Her palms grew moist. "It's private... I wouldn't feel right."

"Please." He pressed the book into her wavering hands. "My mother would want you to read it."

Lainey fingered the cover, instinctively rubbing the area that had been worn smooth by frequent handling. Sandwiched between the frayed leather were words, those precious, tangible expressions of thought and emotion, hope and fear, secret dreams and private passions. Captured on the tattered pages was the essence of a pretty, dark-haired woman with tender hands and a poignant smile. Although Lainey wanted desperately to explore that essence, a secret part of her mind recoiled at what she might learn about Catherine, about her father... and about herself.

Lainey swallowed hard and spoke without drawing her gaze from the object of her fascination. "I... shouldn't."

"Read it. Please." Clay clasped both of her hands along with his mother's diary between his strong palms. "Afterward, if you're still concerned about the book, I'll honor your wishes."

Stunned, Lainey looked up sharply. "Are you saying that if I read this journal, you won't publish the book?"

"If that's what you want, yes. You have my word."

After reviewing Clay's outline, Lainey couldn't believe he would willingly give up a project that obviously meant the world to him. Her resolve faltered, then cracked. Clutching the journal to her breast, she agreed to the terms and hurried across the clearing to her car.

Clay watched her drive away in a cloud of churning leaves and road dust. He stood there a long time, staring at the treed opening where her car had disappeared into the forest. A crimson glow spread over the western sky as if the setting sun was fastened to her bumper. He thought about the journal's final entry, penned the day after Gerald Sheridan's death. *The light has gone out of my life,* Catherine had written. Clay had always understood what his mother had meant by the haunting prose; now his heart experienced that poignant loss.

A chill wind slid in from the north. The woods rustled restlessly. Clay had never felt so alone.

Russ Clemmons roared off the sofa before Lainey had closed the front door. "Where'n hell you been, girl?"

Lainey was so started by his unexpected vehemence that she nearly dropped the newspaper bundled under her arm. Carefully concealed in the paper folds was the leather-bound journal. Since the last thing she wanted was an interrogation about how she'd come into possession of Catherine Cooper's private diary, she tightened her grip on the parcel. "I know I'm a little late. I'm sorry."

The rocker squeaked as Hallie leaned forward, lips tight, eyes worried. "I've been calling the newsroom all afternoon. They said you'd been gone for hours."

"I had, uh, an errand to run for Broddie." That certainly wasn't a lie considering she'd just dropped him off a few minutes earlier. She smiled weakly and sidled toward the kitchen. "How about pork chops for supper?"

"Lloyd's been looking for you," Hallie blurted. "He called three times."

Lainey took a sharp breath. For a frantic moment she wondered if Reeves had somehow discovered the part she'd played in Clay Cooper's escape from the motel. The only word she could manage was "Why?"

Scowling fiercely, Russ muttered under his breath. "You got mush for brains, girl? He wants to know when you're going to meet with the lawyers."

She didn't know whether to sigh in relief or stiffen with indignation. She did both and to everyone's surprise, including her own, added a cool rebuke. "There's no need to be insulting, Uncle Russ. And since I've been an adult for many years, I don't appreciate being referred to as 'girl.'"

Hallie gasped in shock. Russ's jaw dropped like an open drawer, which might have been comical had his thick red brows not been drawn together in such a fierce scowl. With a horned headpiece, he'd have resembled a furious Viking warrior. As it was, he simply looked like a bewildered bulldog with a bad toupee.

Feeling oddly liberated, Lainey barely suppressed an uncharacteristic giggle. She cleared her throat, bit her lower lip and pasted a respectful expression on her face. "Would you like baked yams or mashed potatoes with the pork chops?"

Russ finally closed his mouth and stared at his niece in shocked disbelief.

Lainey's pleasant smile faded. "I'll, uh, return Mr. Reeves's call after supper and let him know that legal action won't be necessary."

A glint of fear glimmered in her uncle's eyes and a frantic crack in his voice chilled Lainey to the bone. "If *Lloyd Reeves* says something is necessary, then it's damn well necessary!"

Absently wiping her palms together, she tried to sound calmer than she felt. "Mr. Cooper has assured me that nothing will be published without my approval."

"Mr. Cooper...*Mr.* Cooper?" With each word, Russ moved closer and his face turned a deeper shade of red. "You've actually been talking to that...that riffraff?"

"Clayton Cooper is not riffraff," Lainey shot back, instantly infuriated. "He's a respected novelist with more class and integrity than half the upstanding citizens in this town.

Now, if you want to talk about riffraff, let's discuss the mob of thugs that attacked him at the motel."

With a derisive gesture and a disgusted snort, Russ waved that away as irrelevant. "You'd defend the son of your father's killer against your own flesh and blood?"

Hallie rocked forward, lamenting, "Have you no shame?"

"Clay has never done anything to harm me or anyone else. He doesn't deserve to be hounded for something his father might—" she lifted her chin "—or might not have done."

Hallie issued a sharp cry and clutched her chest.

Russ wobbled as though he'd been struck. He steadied himself on one of the cheesy velour chairs. "Exactly what is it you're trying to say?"

Tightening her grip on the paper-wrapped journal, Lainey studied her shoes and asked herself the same question. She had no answer, not for her uncle, not for herself. Although Clay Cooper had doubts about his father's innocence, Lainey had none whatsoever. Ben Cooper was guilty of murder. She was convinced of that and had no clue as to why she'd deliberately baited her aunt and uncle by insinuating otherwise.

Now she hoped to defuse what was fast becoming an explosive situation. "I simply meant that Clay is concerned about some, uh, inconsistencies in the evidence presented at his father's trial. He's looking for explanations, that's all. Once his questions have been answered, he'll be able to let go of the past and move on." She hoped her aunt and uncle would be placated by the reasonable explanation.

They weren't. Hallie swooned in her chair, and the crimson flush drained from Russ's face until he was white as a biscuit. "Cooper's got no business nosing around things that don't concern him."

Taken aback, Lainey pointed out the obvious. "Since Clay believes his father was unjustly convicted, he has every right to be concerned."

"He's got no rights!" Russ shouted. "He's a damn Cooper!" Before Lainey could move, her uncle crossed the room and grabbed her arm. "Stay away from him, hear? *Stay away!*"

"Turn me loose!" Lainey pulled away and tucked the slipping parcel back under her arm. She stepped back, frightened, confused and angrier than she'd ever been in her life.

"How dare you speak to me that way? I'm not a child, I'm not a puppy and I'm not an indentured servant." Breathing heavily, she raked her fingers through her hair and softened her tone. "Please understand that I love you both, but I'm grown-up now. I have every right to do as I wish and see whomever I please."

The veins in her uncle's temple pulsated madly. "This is *my* house and you'll do what I say." His hand shot toward her wrist.

With a startled gasp, Lainey spun around, dodging the attempt. "Please...don't—"

"Leave her alone!" Hallie unhooked her canes from the rocker arm and struggled to her feet. There were tears in her eyes. "Look at yourself, Russell. What has happened to you?"

Russ stared at his wife, then down at the fist he'd been shaking at his niece. In an instant, the rage drained from his eyes. "My God," he murmured. Lifting his gaze, he looked at Lainey with an expression of utter despair. The raised fist became an extended palm, a silent plea for which there were no words. Then his arm dropped to his side and he turned away.

Trembling, Lainey struggled to catch her breath. For a brief, horrifying moment, she'd believed he was going hit her. The incomprehensible thought left her numb with shock. Although her uncle's temper was legendary, Lainey had never feared him. She'd had no reason to. Uncle Russ had never so much as raised a hand to her. Until now.

"I don't understand," Lainey whispered. "None of this makes any sense at all."

Russ rubbed his forehead with the back of his hand. It was Hallie who finally spoke. "We're concerned about you. Unless Cooper is stopped, he might...he might..." Obviously distraught, she leaned on her canes and avoided her niece's gaze.

Lainey prodded for an answer. "He might what?"

Shifting her weight, Hallie propped herself upright. "He might find out about your mother."

Lainey felt the blood drain from her face. "What Clay is looking for has nothing to do with that."

"It has everything to do with it!" Hallie cried. "You don't understand—" Cringing under her husband's fierce stare, she bit off the words. Shaking her head in misery, the fragile woman reseated herself in the rocking chair and stared into space with a dazed expression that shook Lainey to her toes.

"Aunt Hallie?" Lainey took a tenuous step forward. "What is it that I don't understand?"

Hallie responded by closing her eyes, turning her head and allowing her husband to answer. "You don't understand that once the door's been opened, anything hiding behind it is bound to come running out," Russ said ominously.

A cold mist settled on Lainey's skin. She felt sick. Rationally, she realized there was no way that an investigation of evidence from Ben Cooper's trial could possibly lead back to MaryBeth Sheridan. If there had been even the remotest chance of that happening, Broddie would have never have agreed to help Clay. Broddie had promised to keep the secret; it was a sacred trust, one her old friend would never betray.

And yet...

Unable to complete the horrible thought, Lainey turned and walked out of the room.

Rubbing his face, Russ sat heavily on the sofa and spoke into his hands. "You know what's going to happen, don't you?"

The rocker creaked slowly. "Yes."

Russ peered over his fingertips. "We got no choice."

"I know." Hallie stared dully into her lap. The rocker squeaked. A cupboard door closed in the kitchen. The old mantel clock ticked softly.

Russ uttered a graphic oath, then quietly went upstairs to make the most difficult phone call of his life.

Chapter 8

Lying on the narrow cot, Clay laced his fingers behind his head and stared into the darkness. When he closed his eyes, he saw Lainey's face shimmering with the tears of shattered illusion. Clay had caused those tears and yet she had clung to him as though he were the only lifeboat in a turbulent sea.

He never should have kissed her—now his life would never be the same. He'd tasted heaven, held eternity in his arms. It was a taunting whisper of what might have been.

Frustrated, he swung his legs to the floor and felt his way into the dark living room. He lit an oil lamp, smoothed the sheet that had been spread over the dusty sofa and stretched out to watch the lamplight undulate on the beamed ceiling.

He wondered what she was doing now, what she might be thinking. They were so alike, he and Lainey, haunted by the sins of their fathers, silently struggling to escape the confining shadow of their parents' flawed lives.

Since childhood, Clay had feared there was a ticking time bomb in his genes, some kind of genetic booby trap that could explode without warning and transform him into the same monster his father had been. It was a secret terror, one he'd never even shared with his mother.

Eventually Clay had overcome the fear; at least, he'd thought that he had. Now the icy terror had returned, crawling through his belly like an alien parasite and consuming the mirage upon which he'd built his life. Because no matter how far he ran, no matter what mask he wore for the world, Clay was still his father's son. And the ominous ticking continued.

It was 2:00 a.m. Lainey turned the final page in Catherine's journal, set the book aside and took another tissue from the box on her nightstand. As she wiped her red eyes, a fresh flood of tears rendered the gesture useless. She dropped the saturated tissue into the wet heap beside the bed, buried her face in the pillow and sobbed until her throat ached.

Surely no woman on earth had suffered as much grief as had Catherine Elizabeth Cooper. And yet there had also been joy, incredible rapture of the spirit beyond anything Lainey could imagine.

Throughout the early years, Catherine had endured poverty and prejudice and devastating personal hardship, living with a man so embittered by failure that he'd eventually become no more than a cruel stranger. During the final six months of the journal, which had also been the final six months of Gerald Sheridan's life, Catherine had apparently undergone a unique personal metamorphosis.

Lainey sniffed, took another tissue and walked to the window. Outside, a glowing streetlamp reminded her of Catherine's poignant description of a crescent moon glimmering over the lake on a soft summer night. That had been a particularly moving passage, one that had affected Lainey deeply. But then, every page had affected her deeply, raising her consciousness and offering new insights into a past that seemed less distant and, oddly enough, less frightening.

The bittersweet passages had chronicled Catherine and Gerald's relationship from the day they'd met...

> As my birthday gift, Clayton secretly asked the local newspaper to print one of my poems. I was terribly embarrassed. Afterward, Mr. Sheridan encouraged me to submit my work for publication. Naturally, I couldn't. Ben would never approve. Still, it was the first time any-

one other than my beloved son has ever shown interest....

To the passion of their first kiss...

I've never felt such ecstasy. We both know that it's wrong, but something is happening between us, something too powerful to control—and yet, control it we must. God give us strength....

There was pathos, humor, passion and pride, arguments, reconciliations, tears and laughter, all related in Catherine's touching narrative of blossoming romance...

The lake was beautiful this afternoon. We walked in the sunlight, holding hands. Gerald picked wildflowers for me. My heart filled with such astonishing happiness, I feared it might burst from sheer joy. I love him so....

And of exquisite agony...

I cannot burden Gerald with my pain—he endures so much of his own. He is tormented by guilt, for he loves his wife deeply and cherishes the sweet daughter who is the center of his life. He could never leave them, nor would I ask him to. They are a part of his soul, as he is a part of mine....

In those stirring pages, Catherine had exposed her most private moments as though sharing secrets with an intimate friend. Lainey had become that friend and experienced an emotional bonding so intense she was now grief-stricken by the realization that this extraordinary woman was truly gone. Under different circumstances, Lainey realized she and Catherine could have shared a deep, abiding friendship—a concept that a few hours earlier would have seemed inconceivable. But that was before Lainey had opened the journal and glimpsed the purity of Catherine Cooper's radiant soul.

It was, Lainey realized, little wonder that her own dear father had fallen in love with such a remarkable woman, although she still had difficulty accepting that the man she knew as "Daddy" could have been swept up in the exquisite passion so eloquently described in the journal. The person Lainey had molded into her memory bore little resemblance to the man about whom Catherine had written such flourishing details. Catherine had described a complex man, a paradox of indecisive determination, weakened by the love that had also been his greatest strength.

Since Lainey had never admitted—even to herself—that her father had ever been less than perfect, discovering that he had been afflicted by human flaws was most wrenching. Although Gerald Sheridan had been basically kind and decent, he'd also been a troubled man. Lainey had never recognized the depth of her father's anguish. In retrospect, she probably should have. There had been signs, subtle symptoms of a man at war with himself. But Lainey had been a child. Even if she'd had the maturity to identify her father's torment, there'd been no way for her to ease it.

But if the journal had contained disturbing discoveries, it had also offered a certain amount of comfort. Earlier this afternoon, for example, Lainey had been devastated by proof of her father's extramarital relationship and furious that the man she'd believed a hero had been a common adulterer. Now she realized that there had been nothing common about her father's feelings for Catherine. Their relationship had not been a casual affair but a deep, enduring love between star-crossed soul mates who understood that they could never be together—at least, not on a mortal plane.

It seemed a cruel irony that Catherine's son now sought refuge at the lakeside shack that had once been the lovers' secret rendezvous. At least Lainey now understood how Clay had learned about the place.

Gazing out her bedroom window, she wondered what Clay was doing now, what he was thinking. It was a foolish contemplation, of course, considering the hour. The man was probably asleep, as Lainey should be if she expected to be anything more than a walking zombie in the morning. Still, she couldn't help creating an image of Clay in her mind, picturing how he might look in tousled slumber. She wondered if he slept on his back, with his thick hair ruffled untidily around his face. Perhaps he was a restless sleeper, flipping from side to side with arms flailing, legs alternately askew. He might even be one of those who curled into a comatose ball and didn't so much as twitch a whisker until jarred to life by the alarm clock. She considered the last option to be least likely and finally decided that a man with Clay's unwavering intensity must be a flailing-flipper type.

She smiled wistfully, enjoying the fanciful speculation. That fantasy was all she would ever have. Lainey could never share life with Clay or any other man. While her father, it appeared, had had more lovers than he could handle, Lainey was destined to live her life alone. And that was the saddest irony of all.

Clay shifted the cellular phone to his shoulder and poured a cup of coffee. "So what's the mood in town, Mac?"

"Being Saturday, it's hard to tell. Seems quiet, though. Folks on the street are walking fast, counting cracks in the sidewalk." McFerson chuckled softly. "A twinge of collective conscience, I'm thinking. After what happened at the motel yesterday, the town seems a mite ashamed of itself."

Clay set the steel pot on the iron stove grate and sipped the hot liquid. As far as he was concerned, few people in this godforsaken place had shown any indication of even having a conscience, so he figured the town's mood was more likely sincere disappointment at the lack of a public flogging.

The line crackled with the sound of rustling papers and irritable muttering. "What the devil did I do with . . . Ah!"

Clay carried his coffee to the cluttered table. "What have you got?"

"Wait till you hear, lad. I had a lovely chat with my lady friend in the company records room. Such a charming woman, she is. 'Twas more than happy to help an old chum."

"Was she able to track the batch number?"

"Aye. That and more, lad."

Setting the cup down, Clay automatically grabbed a lined legal pad and searched for a pen by patting the various paper piles until he felt an elongated lump.

"Fertilizer," McFerson announced suddenly.

Clay clicked the ballpoint with his thumb. "Is that a commentary or a commodity?"

"A bit of both, I'm thinking." There was another round of rustling papers. "Let's see now . . . Batch #74-38692, according to my lady friend, is a product code for chemical fertilizer."

Clay laid down the pen. Since he already knew ChemCorp manufactured a multitude of agricultural chemicals including crop enhancers and pest control products, the information that they'd also produced fertilizer was hardly a news flash. "That's it? That's all we know?"

"Patience, lad. I'm getting around to it." After a teasing pause, McFerson added, "We also know that the batch in question was manufactured in 1974 during the graveyard shift in Production Area Three."

"All that detail from one batch number? I wonder why."

"Well, that's the thing I wondered my own self." McFerson sounded as if he were about to bust. "It seems that the company expanded its manufacturing facility in the mid-seventies so it could dedicate each production area to a particular product or product line."

Clay considered that. "So before that, they must have used the same equipment for more than one product."

"Exactly," McFerson crowed. "And what's even more interesting is that a month after producing this particular batch, there was some kind of hush-hush shake-up in graveyard shift personnel."

"Could be coincidence, I suppose."

"Aye. And it could be a cover-up."

"For a manufacturing accident?"

"Aye."

Clay rubbed his head. "You think someone was hurt on the job and management concealed the accident from OSHA?"

"Wouldn't put it past those company blokes to be hiding injuries to keep worker's compensation rates down."

Shifting the telephone, Clay leaned back in his chair. "For the sake of argument, let's say that the worst happened. There was an accident on the graveyard shift, some poor slob was pickled in a chemical vat. Let's also say that Gerald got wind of the accident and threatened to blow the whistle. Is that a motive for murder? I mean, the penalty for filing a fraudulent accident report is what, a few thousand dollars in fines?" He paused while McFerson mumbled in agreement. "That's peanuts to a company with gross sales in the millions. They'd just write it off as a business expense."

"Murder would seem a wee overreaction, wouldn't it?"

"Damn right." Clay stood and paced the small room, frustrated by what seemed like yet another dead end. "It doesn't make sense, Mac. Maybe we're on the wrong track here."

After a short pause, McFerson responded thoughtfully. "You may be right, laddie, but I'll keep sniffing around just to make sure. And there's something more I've found, something that may be more to your liking."

"What's that?" Clay glanced out the window as Lainey's car emerged from the forest. His heart racing, he drew apart the frayed curtains, hungrily watching her pull into the clearing. She scanned the area like a nervous doe, then stared briefly at the window where Clay was standing. For a moment he considered dropping the curtain and stepping back so she wouldn't suspect he was anxious to see her. But since he'd already been spotted, he offered a limp wave through the smeared glass.

Her response was to look away. He felt sick, assuming that she hadn't found reading Catherine's journal to be a particularly uplifting experience. Another miscue on his part. So far, Clay was definitely batting a thousand. As far as Lainey was concerned, every choice he'd made had been the wrong one.

A distant voice filtered through his unhappy contemplation. A quick glance outside confirmed that Lainey was walking toward the porch, clutching the familiar leather-bound book. When the faraway voice became more irritable, Clay glanced down and realized that the hand holding the telephone was dangling at his side. He quickly remedied the situation. "Mac?"

"Who'n hell else would it be?" came the peeved reply. "I've been jabbering to myself for ten minutes."

"Sorry." Clay opened the door as Lainey came onto the porch. When she saw the telephone, she hesitated until he mouthed the words "It's Mac." He stepped back, motioned her inside and turned back to the original conversation. "Now, what were you were saying?"

After an exaggerated sigh, McFerson said, "I've found Emma."

That got Clay's attention. "Emma Gebloski?"

"The very one. She's living in Clemson, right by the interstate."

"That's less than thirty miles from here." Clay grabbed a pen, scrawled down the address McFerson dictated, then ripped off the notated portion of the page. "I'll drive down there this morning."

"Don't be getting your hopes up, lad. Could be another wild-goose chase."

"Maybe. But one way or the other, I plan to find out."

Clay flipped off the cellular phone, laid it on the table and tucked the torn note into the breast pocket of his knitted sports shirt.

Across the room Lainey was standing in front of the window, staring out at the clearing. Her spine was as straight as a broomstick and her shoulders were so stiff it made Clay ache just to look at them.

She was dressed casually in loose denim jeans and an oversize hunter green sweater that extended below—but couldn't disguise—the neat curve of her hips. Although the garments obviously hadn't been chosen to enhance feminine allure, the effect was oddly appealing. The floppy clothing made her seem even more fragile and vulnerable. He wanted to cross the room, scoop her up into his arms and carry her somewhere warm and safe and intimate. Like the bedroom.

The image of tangled bodies on a narrow cot made him shiver.

"What did Broddie find out?" Lainey asked suddenly.

"Hmm?" Clay blinked and realized that she was now facing him with the journal pressed against her breast. "Uh... find out?"

She eyed him quizzically. "Weren't you talking to Broddie on the telephone?"

The tangled bodies in his mind were groaning and mewing with passion. He started to sweat. "I... yes. We were... talking." Puffing his cheeks, he blew out a breath and gestured limply toward the stove. "Coffee?"

"No, thank you." Tilting her head, she regarded him for a moment. "Who is Emma Gebloski?"

Clay couldn't take his eyes off that floppy sweater. It had a neckline so wide that the entire garment had slid to one side and partially exposed a creamy white shoulder. The fact that no bra strap marred the view did not escape his notice. "Emma Gebloski," he murmured as though hearing the name for the first time. He took a deep breath and tried again. "She lived down the street from your parents. I take it you don't remember her."

"No, but it was such a long time ago." Lainey frowned. "Why are you going to see her?"

"She noted a disturbance at your house the night of the incident." Since Clay saw no reason to reiterate the grisly details of exactly what Emma might have seen and/or heard, he kept a casual tone. "I just thought I'd check and see what she remembered."

"After all these years, she's probably forgotten more than she remembers. Besides, if she'd seen anything pertinent, I'm sure the police would have taken her statement at the time."

Clay chose not to argue the point. "You're probably right." His gaze slid to the journal she was hugging. "Did you have a chance to read any of it?"

She poked an invisible dust speck with her toe. "I read all of it."

Clay swallowed hard. "What did you think?"

Without looking up, she crossed the room and laid the book gently, almost lovingly, on the table. "I think your mother was an extraordinary woman."

"And..."

She licked her lips. "And I understand why you'd want to share her story with the world."

"So you won't oppose the book?" he asked hopefully.

"I didn't say that."

Hope drained away as Clay tried to swallow his disappointment. "Then you want the project stopped."

She shook her head miserably. "I didn't say that, either."

Frustrated, he raked his hair with his fingers. "So far you haven't said anything at all. Exactly what it is you *do* want, Lainey?"

"I'm not sure." She crossed her arms tightly. "I mean, a biography is supposed to highlight the essence of a person's life rather than day-to-day details, right?"

He was beginning to get the gist of her concern. "You don't want the part about your father included."

She fiddled with a bent paper clip on the table. "They only had a short time together, a few months out of so many years."

"Those few months provided the turning point that completely altered the course of my mother's entire life. That relationship, whether right or wrong, was the core of all that followed—your father's death, my father's imprisonment, everything."

"I know that," Lainey whispered. "But there are other people involved, people who could be hurt—"

"Who?" he interrupted curtly. "Your mother? Do you honestly think that she doesn't know about an affair that was front-page news for months?"

She winced without response.

"Then I'll ask her," Clay said sharply. "Just tell me how to contact MaryBeth and I'll find out exactly how she feels. That's fair, isn't it?"

Lainey paled, started to speak, then shook her head and turned away with an expression that shook Clay to the bone. Her hand quivered as she nervously flicked her tousled bangs. "I do understand, Clay. I know how much this means to you. I just need some time to...sort things out in my mind."

Of course she did. Clay himself had assured her that she'd have that right. Instead of honoring his word, he'd pounced like a verbal predator trying to rattle her with coercive tactics and angry demands.

Groaning, he ground the heel of his hands against his temples. He was disgusted that despite his glowing promise, he'd actually been trying to browbeat a shaken woman into an agreement she obviously didn't want to make.

Clay leaned heavily against the table. "I'm sorry."

She looked over her shoulder in obvious surprise. "Sorry for what?"

"For behaving like a bully, for attempting to force you into something you aren't comfortable with, for breaking my word..." Sighing, he propped one hand on his hip and rubbed the back of his neck with the other. "I don't know what's wrong with me."

"Oh, Clay." Lainey's eyes filled with sympathy. "Nothing is wrong with you. You have a dream, that's all. A dream of showing the world what a remarkable woman Catherine was, how deeply she affected your life. I wish—" she closed her eyes briefly "—I wish things were different," she said finally.

A peculiar fluttering stirred inside his chest. He realized that he'd been wrapped up in his own emotions without considering how disturbing the journal revelations must have been for Lainey. The father she'd worshipped had been exposed as a tormented man who'd denied his own happiness for the sake of his family. Although he could relate to the inner torment Gerald Sheridan must have endured, Clay understood how painful that disclosure must have been for the daughter who'd adored him.

Still, she faced the truth bravely, shoulders straight, chin high, reflecting no outward trace of the turmoil that must be churning inside. Clay was humbled by her courage.

"You're right," he agreed quietly. "Other people *are* involved, people that I was willing to ride roughshod over in my petty quest for vengeance." Feeling small and selfish, he sat heavily on the covered sofa. "Please believe that I never meant to hurt you, Lainey. I thought you'd accepted the fact that our parents were, uh, involved. When I realized that you hadn't, I should have dropped the subject then and there. I never should have forced you to read that damned diary."

Because he couldn't bear to see the pain in her eyes, he avoided her gaze and was startled when the cushion beside him dipped beneath her weight.

"You didn't force me to do anything, Clay. I read Catherine's journal because I wanted to." She took his hand, wanting to describe how much the experience had meant to her yet struggling for the words to express the emotion still swelling inside her breast. How could she explain what she didn't even understand? Lainey been profoundly touched by Catherine's words and had actually shared the woman's secret sorrow, the heartache of forced separation from the man she'd loved.

Her feelings, however, had gone far beyond mere empathy because she realized that if she allowed her own emotions for Clay to intensify, she, too, would experience the same agony, the same heartbreaking loss. Rationally, she understood the imparity of maintaining emotional distance. Unfortunately, the realization had come much too late. Just being in the same room with Clay caused her heart to beat wildly. He could melt her heart with a look, weaken her knees with a touch.

And now she was sitting beside him, holding his hand while he generated enough heat to warm Detroit in December.

She carefully withdrew and laid her clasped hands in her lap. "By allowing me to read the journal, you shared something very personal and very special. The experience affected me more than you'll ever know."

He regarded her for a moment, then twisted to face her and slid his arm along the back of the sofa. "Tell me. Help me to know what you felt when you read it, what you're feeling now."

With the subtle movement, his scent enveloped her like an embrace. She breathed him in, holding him deeply until her lungs ached and she was forced to release him. The effort made her dizzy. A comforting warmth settled onto her thigh as he rested his palm on her leg. The gesture was both soothing and sensuous.

"If you don't want to talk about it, I'll understand," he said.

"It's not that." She moistened her lips. "The truth is that I'm not certain what I'm feeling. It's as if the man I knew as my father never existed. I don't recognize the person described in the journal, and yet I have this completely bizarre sensation that I've known Catherine all of my life, that she's a part of me." Lainey chanced a quick glance at Clay, misread his incredulous expression and instantly lowered her gaze. "I know that sounds outlandish."

"No...really." With an astonished smile, he shook his head. "Actually, my reaction was exactly the opposite. I found myself relating to Gerald so completely it was scary, but I just couldn't believe that the woman I knew as my mother could have written all that flowery, erotic stuff. It was like Mom had become a stranger while Gerald Sheridan was suddenly my closest friend."

Lainey studied his unaffected expression. "You're not joking, are you?"

"No." He shrugged sheepishly. "Although I never thought I'd ever admit having less empathy for my own mother than for the man who became her lover."

At the word "lover," Lainey felt her face heat. She glanced away and murmured, "Maybe it's a gender thing. Women relate to women, men relate to men."

"I hadn't considered that." Absently rubbing his chin, he stared thoughtfully into space. "I don't know why, though. It's such a simple, obvious explanation."

Lainey's foot tapped an irritable rhythm on the hardwood floor. "That's me. Simple and obvious."

The irked response got his attention. "I didn't mean to insult you."

She sighed. "No, of course you didn't. I'm being oversensitive."

"It's a sensitive subject." He smiled kindly, adding, "For both of us."

With a jerky nod, she folded her arms and studied the hand resting on her leg. It was an unremarkable hand, clean, well tended, yet undeniably masculine despite a dearth of hair, greasy fingernails and other trappings of virility of which some men seemed inordinately proud. The hiked sleeve of his designer knit shirt, however, exposed a length of forearm along which was an attractive smattering of black hair. It looked unusually soft and supple, without the whiskery stiffness that frequently characterized masculine body hair. She suppressed an urge to touch it. The awkward silence stretched on.

An odd clicking sound caught her attention. She glanced around before realizing the source was right beside her. Although Clay was staring across the room apparently lost in thought, his jaw vibrated in sync with the muffled beat.

"Look! You're doing it!" she exclaimed.

The clicking stopped. He frowned. "Doing what?"

"Tapping your teeth." She chuckled happily. "It's just like Catherine described, kind of an oral Morse code you send out whenever you feel threatened or confused."

She was so delighted by her discovery that she barely noticed his bewildered expression melt into one of total embarrassment.

"I thought she'd made that part up. I mean, I couldn't picture this pitiful little kid sitting in the corner with big fat tears in his eyes and clicking tunes with his teeth. But you still do it, don't you?"

By this time his jaw was clenched tighter than a fist. "Yes, I still sit in the corner with big fat tears in my eyes."

She sobered instantly. "Have I hurt your feelings? I'm so sorry. I didn't mean to. It's just such an adorable habit—" She flinched under the force of his indignant glare. "Perhaps 'adorable' wasn't the right word."

A cool breeze brushed her thigh as he removed his hand and crossed his arms. "You must have been incredibly thrilled by the passages describing diaper rash and potty training." His offended tone was softened by an amused twinkle.

Lainey relaxed, smiling. "Come to think of it, your mother did create some vivid word pictures of your growing years. It was almost like thumbing through the family album."

"My mother was quite eloquent. Unfortunately, she was also quite thorough. Nothing was sacred." Clay skewed a sideways glance. "Did you read, uh, everything?"

"Hmm." She pulled up her feet and hugged her knees. "Don't worry. Your secrets are safe with me. I won't tell a soul you were in love with your first-grade teacher or that you were the one who batted that baseball through the church's stained-glass window."

"I appreciate that."

Lainey's smile faded as she remembered other passages, dark descriptions of a family in crisis. "And I won't tell that you didn't really break your arm falling out of a tree, either." She watched carefully as Clay's expression hardened. Swallowing a lump, she whispered, "Why didn't you tell your mother the truth about that?"

"It would only have upset her."

"She suspected, you know."

"I do now." After a silent moment he spoke again, his voice heavy with resignation. "You have to understand that my father was very careful to conceal certain parts of his character from my mother. He never wanted her to see what he had become. He was ashamed, I think, and afraid of losing her."

"And yet he had no reservations about revealing his cruelty to you?"

Clay responded slowly, as though choosing each word with extraordinary care. "My father believed in the old adage 'like father, like son.' As his blood clone, I was expected to follow in his footsteps, and he taught me well. By the time I was eight, I could pick pockets, cheat at poker and down two fingers of bourbon without puking."

The unbelievable image left her sputtering. "That's child abuse. I can't believe your mother would have allowed it."

"Did I mention that I was also an expert liar?" Allowing his head to drop backward into the cushion, he massaged his eyelids. "I finally learned how to split my personality. One minute I could be the shining son my mother yearned for and the next, the vicious little beast that my father expected."

"My God," Lainey whispered. "I can't imagine anything more terrible. You must have been so confused and so very, very frightened."

"Confused, yes. For the first ten years of my life, I didn't know whether I was an angel in monster's clothes or vice versa. Sometimes I still wonder..." The words dissipated like so much steam.

When Clay straightened, lips tight, eyes veiled, Lainey was disappointed to realize that whatever he still wondered would not be divulged. At least, not now. Yet his silence, too, was revealing. Although traumatized by circumstance, young Clay had survived by guise and by guile. Despite having overcome enormous adversity and evolving into a successful man, a trace of that divided child lingered in his eyes.

Lainey wanted to console him, to validate what he had endured and what he had become. She didn't know how and ended up blurting, "Even when you were a boy, you had a man's eyes." The statement was so ludicrous she nearly moaned aloud and hastened to explain. "I just meant that I was impressed by the way you tried to protect your mother during the trial."

He was kind enough not to point out how stupid she sounded. Instead, he smiled sadly. "Tried is the operative word, I'm afraid. I was simply a little boy trying to bully a whole bunch of people, any one of whom could have snapped my neck like a dried match if they'd chosen to do so."

"I didn't see it that way," Lainey insisted. "I thought you were the bravest boy I'd ever seen in my whole entire life."

"All six years of it, huh?"

Smiling, Lainey chided him gently. "Now be nice. I was old enough to have a major crush on you."

"You're joking."

"Not at all. In fact, I even dreamed about you—" Her jaw snapped shut a word too late.

He leaned forward enthusiastically. "What kind of dreams?"

"Kid dreams, you know, about circuses and clowns." She shrugged. "Silly stuff like that."

"Did I win you a Kewpie doll?"

"No." In spite of the uncomfortable subject, she was emboldened by his evident interest. "In the dream we're both children again. The clowns frighten me and when I start blubbering like a baby, you gallantly step in to protect me from those dastardly, flop-footed villains." She managed a thin smile. "I guess that sounds pretty twisted, doesn't it?"

"No." He regarded her thoughtfully for what seemed a long time. "I'm proud that you chose me as your champion."

The intensity of his gaze made her squirm. "It's just a silly dream."

"Is it?"

She sighed. "I was just trying to tell you that when I was a child, I saw the same strength in you that your mother saw."

The arm that had lain quietly along the sofa back now slid smoothly around her shoulders. "And as a woman, what do you see in me?"

Searching his eyes, she whispered, "I see a man in terrible pain."

He withdrew slightly. "What do you mean?"

"Before today, I never understood why you seemed so conflicted."

Whatever he'd expected to hear, that obviously hadn't been it. He frowned. "So now you understand me, right?"

"I'm not sure anyone really understands you. You're much too complex. But I think the book you want to write is secondary to what you're really seeking."

He eyed her warily. "And what's that?"

"A sense of completion, of closing the fragmented chapters of your mother's life." She took a deep breath. "And I want to help you do that."

After a moment's hesitation, Clay slid his thumb beneath her chin and urged her to look at him. "You know what that means, don't you?"

Lainey closed her eyes and shivered. She knew all too well what it meant. She'd just given him permission to write Catherine's biography—all of it. To do that, secret layers surrounding her father's death would be peeled away to reveal a pulsing core of absolute truth—a truth that would help Clay find peace of mind. And quite possibly lead to her own destruction.

Chapter 9

Broddie entered the open doorway of Sandborne Hunicutt's plush office and leaned casually against the jamb. "Working on Saturdays now, are you?"

Startled, Hunicutt straightened so forcefully that he nearly fell over. Grabbing the lip of his massive walnut desk, he steadied himself and gaped in disbelief. "How the hell'd you get in here?"

Tucking both hands into the pockets of his twill slacks, Broddie sauntered casually into the expansive room and propped a scrawny hip against the antique Victorian settee. "Ah, Sandy, m'lad, 'tis a sorry sight, the company chief slaving in an ivory tower instead of enjoying such a glorious day. I don't recall Lloyd working weekends, though. There was always some poor sot around to do his bidding." Broddie made a production of scratching his fuzzy head, then feigned a revelation by suddenly snapping his fingers. "Glory! That poor sot was you, wasn't it now?"

A purple flush crawled over Hunicutt's earlobes and his pointy nose started to twitch. Ignoring the man's discomfort, Broddie grinned happily and poked a leather-clad toe into the springy carpet. "But then, you've got yourself a fine, fancy office for your trouble. 'Course, what with Lloyd only letting you use it on weekends—"

"Get out!" Hunicutt slammed a fist on the desk and rose from the chair, nostrils flaring.

When the furious little man snatched up the telephone, Broddie bent forward and casually plucked the receiver from his hand. "Now don't be disturbing the security guard. The poor lad has his hands full because some fool dropped a crate of ball bearings in the lobby."

Pressing his palms on the desktop, Hunicutt leaned forward with hatred in his eyes. "And who do you suppose did that?"

Broddie's grin broadened, but he suppressed an urge to brag about the clever distraction he'd created downstairs. "Thing is, Sandy, m'boy, you haven't been returning my calls."

The weasly eyes narrowed. "That should have given you a clue."

"Aye." Broddie pushed away from the settee, settled himself in the tapestry Queen Anne across from Hunicutt's desk and whipped a small notebook from his breast pocket. "Since you're obviously such a busy man, I'll only be taking a wee moment of your time."

Sighing, Hunicutt seated himself, straightened his tie and fiddled with one of his gemstone cufflinks. "Very well. Let's get this over with."

"There's a good lad." Broddie opened the notebook. "Now, what I'm wondering is—"

Hunicutt interrupted by yanking open a drawer. He pulled out a paper, cleared his throat and began to read in a flat, nasally tone. " 'Corporate headquarters has issued the following statement pursuant to an unfortunate and completely erroneous report of financial—' "

"Now I'm sure 'tis a lovely little letter you have there, but it's my own questions I'd rather be asking."

Hunicutt blinked. "This press release explains the company position on recent vacillation of stock prices."

Broddie waved away the information as irrelevant. "The company position is sugarcoated blarney. Reeves manipulated the market to whip the peons into a hanging frenzy. You know it and I know it, so let's not be planting shamrocks in a dung pile."

"You can't prove that." Hunicutt's nose quivered. He snorted and snatched a tissue from the box on his desk. "If you dare print such vile speculation, we'll sue."

Tsking, Broddie whipped out a pair of rimless reading glasses and was pleased to note beads of sweat lining the little man's brow. "I've no interest in your stock market games, though I can't be saying the same for others. Word is that the Securities and Exchange Commission has been sniffing about. 'Course, you wouldn't be caring about that, since there's no proof and all." He winced as Hunicutt forcefully blew his nose. "Easy, lad. Wouldn't want you to bust a blood vessel until you've answered my questions about 1974."

Two terrified eyes peered over the wadded tissue. "Nineteen seventy—" Hunicutt wiped frantically, then dropped the tissue in a trash can. Leaning forward, he stretched his thin lips into a smile tight enough to curl his chin. "Why, that's ancient history. What questions could you possibly have about that?"

"Well, let's see here." Broddie made a production of scanning his notes. "Seems there was this big ta'doo in the plant—specifically in Production Area Three, which was shut down for near onto a week without so much as a thank-you-kindly to the workers. Can you be telling me why?"

The stretched lips barely moved. "I don't remember such an incident."

"Sure'n you must, lad. Why, the very next week you and Russ Clemmons were both plucked off the production floor and tucked into the executive suite like twin bugs in a cozy rug."

"I don't recall," he insisted, fumbling in his coat pocket.

"Don't recall your first promotion?" Broddie emitted a low whistle. "But then, you've had other promotions haven't you, lad? Climbed right to the top, by jingles. Your sainted mother would be proud, God rest her."

Having extracted an atomizer, the flustered man was barely able to unscrew the plastic lid. "If you wish to write a personality profile, my secretary will forward a copy of my résumé on Monday. I think you'll find my accomplishments to be quite extraordinary."

"Not a doubt in my mind. And would that production renovation have been your work, as well?"

"I, uh..." Hunicutt squeezed the inhalant into one nostril, snorted loudly and repeated the process. "As new technologies become available, ChemCorp continually upgrades its facilities to, um, maintain the highest degree of, uh, modernization." He grabbed another tissue and used this one to mop his sweaty forehead. "Obviously I can't recall the specifics of any particular equipment upgrade."

"Perhaps your memory just needs a bit of a prod. I'm referring to the production changes made after a certain batch of chemical fertilizer...." Adjusting his glasses, he rattled off the batch number, then looked up in time to see Hunicutt claw at his immaculate collar. Broddie smiled pleasantly. "Would that put a jog to your mind?"

"No." Apparently recognizing that he'd been outmaneuvered, Hunicutt dropped all pretense of civility and fixed Broddie with a furious stare. "I am a busy man. This interview is terminated."

Standing, Broddie stretched and rubbed his knuckles on the back of his skull. "This has been an enlightening chat, lad. Have a bonnie day." With that, Broddie removed his spectacles, tucked the notebook back into his shirt and strolled out of the office, closing the door behind him.

Since the secretary's office was deserted, he succumbed to temptation, sidled behind the desk and waited until Hunicutt's private phone line lit up. Broddie lifted the receiver just as a brusque feminine voice answered. "Reeves's residence."

After replacing the phone, Broddie ambled down the carpeted hallway, whistling softly and feeling like a real newsman for the first time in years.

Clay pulled up in front of a small frame house and let the engine idle while he checked a scrap from his pocket. After comparing the inked scrawl to the rusted numbers nailed on the peeling eaves, he flipped off the ignition and turned to his nervous passenger. "Would you rather wait here?"

Lainey slid a quick glance out the window, then chewed her lip while she smoothed the hem of her oversize sweater across her lap. "I'm not really dressed to go visiting."

"You look lovely," he said, and meant it. To Clay, Lainey would have been beautiful in a grain sack. Not even burlap could disguise the rolling contours of a supple body that was mature and womanly, a startling contrast to the enormous eyes and delicate facial features that from a distance appeared almost childlike. A closer look, however, revealed the wisdom gleaned by having survived the hardship and stark reality of life. That paradox and complexity was more alluring than anything Clay had ever encountered. She was without doubt the most desirable woman he'd ever met.

At the moment, however, her discomfort was evident. Propping an elbow on the steering wheel, Clay noted an unusual pallor to her fair complexion and wondered why she'd agreed to accompany him. "Lainey?"

She was engrossed in plucking fuzz balls from her sweater. "Hmm?"

"Did I do or say something that made you feel pressured into coming with me?"

Her hand hovered in midair before settling awkwardly in her lap. "Of course not. I volunteered, remember?"

Clay remembered. When he'd mentioned his plan to talk with Emma Gebloski, Lainey had surprised him by asking if she could go with him. He'd agreed without blinking and had been secretly pleased by her interest. It had been, he'd thought, a clue that she was finally willing to consider the possibility that all the factors contributing to her father's death may not have been previously explored. Now he wondered. "Why did you want to come?"

She shrugged, looked out the windshield and absently lifted her shoulder-length hair off her nape. "I'm not sure. Maybe I thought that if I recognized Ms. Gebloski, it might help me remember something about what happened that night."

That was a startling bit of news. "Don't you remember anything at all?"

"A few details. Not many." When she untangled her fingers from her hair, the glossy mane cascaded to her shoulders. She crossed her arms. "I remember a policeman coming into my bedroom. He helped me put on my robe and slippers. I was holding my kitten while the policeman carried me downstairs. Uncle Russ was there. I remember crying."

Clay cupped her small hand between his palms. "Why were you crying?" he asked softly.

Still gazing out the window, she flinched slightly. "Because Uncle Russ took my kitten away. He said Aunt Hallie was allergic."

"Did you understand what had happened to your father?"

"No, I don't think so," she whispered. "I just remember Uncle Russ saying that I was going to sleep at his house for a while."

Clay lifted her hand to his lips and gently kissed each slender finger. Finally he found the courage to ask, "How long did you stay with your uncle before your mother came for you?"

A tear slid down her cheek. She didn't answer.

Something cracked inside his chest. "Your mother never came for you, did she?" Without expecting a response, Clay rubbed Lainey's fingers against his cheek and fought the rage swelling up inside him. At that moment he despised Lainey's absent mother almost as much as he despised his own father. Clay didn't know what kind of sadistic woman could have so callously abandoned a traumatized child, but he was determined to find out. One way or another, MaryBeth Sheridan would answer for what she'd done to her daughter. Clay would see to that personally.

Until then, he couldn't bear to cause Lainey another moment of pain. He caressed her soft hand, pressed his lips to her palm and reluctantly released her.

When he fired up the ignition, Lainey looked up in surprise. "Where are we going?"

"Back to Scarlet."

"But why? I thought you wanted to speak with Ms. Gebloski."

"Another time. Right now, I think you need to go home." He shoved the transmission into drive and would have pulled away from the curb except for Lainey's restraining touch.

"I'm fine, really." For emphasis, she gently squeezed his wrist. "And if you don't mind, I'd really like to go inside with you."

After a conflicted moment Clay honored her wishes and turned off the engine. He exited the vehicle, helped Lainey out of the car, then took her arm and guided her along the cracked walkway that wound up the sloped lawn. As they mounted the porch steps, he felt her stiffen slightly. When they reached the front door, she was white as death. He slid an arm around her shoulders. "Are you sure you want to do this?"

Her response was to take a shuddering breath and press the doorbell. A melodic chime echoed inside the house. In a moment the front door cracked open and two saggy blue eyes peeked through the screen.

"I'm Clayton Cooper, Ms. Gebloski. We spoke on the telephone this morning."

The eyes turned toward Lainey, blinked twice, then glanced warily toward the street. Finally the door opened to reveal a middle-aged woman with a headful of gray-streaked, honey-brown curls. After scanning the street once more, she unlatched the screen door, then stepped back and nervously twisted the skirt of her ruffled apron. "I suppose y'all better come in."

"Thank you." Clay held the screen door open while Lainey stepped into the tidy parlor. He followed, closing both doors behind him. "I appreciate you allowing us to come by."

"Like I already told you, I've got nothing to say that hasn't already been said." With her hands still tangled in her apron, Emma tilted her round face and scrutinized Clay closely. "You don't look nothing like your daddy. Not that I knew him, mind you, but I seen him around from time to time."

Since no response was required, Clay managed a politely proper smile. "Do you remember Lainey Sheridan?"

"Lainey?" The woman's eyes widened in shock. "Land sakes, child. Is it really you?" Before Lainey could answer, Emma disentangled her hands and threw her arms around the startled young woman. "Lord have mercy," she wailed, hugging Lainey fiercely. "Look how you've growed." Finally relinquishing her grip, Emma stepped back and wiped her moist eyes. "Do you still remember how to roll popcorn balls?"

"Popcorn balls?" Lainey's confused smile suddenly widened into one of genuine delight. "You used to give popcorn balls as Halloween treats. I helped you make them."

Emma's curly head bobbed happily. "And you ate all of 'em what weren't perfectly round. Never did figure out if you were a clumsy child or a clever one 'cause danged if you didn't roll some of the strangest-looking corn balls I ever did see."

Tears sprang to Lainey's eyes. "Oh, Emma," she whispered. "How could I have ever forgotten you?"

Lainey collapsed into the woman's waiting arms. For the next ten minutes Clay shifted uncomfortably while the women alternately hugged, laughed, cried and chattered about the old neighborhood—the crotchety old man who threw dirt clods at anyone who ventured into his tulip garden, the pastor's wife who got tipsy at Fourth of July barbecues and the busybody who made rounds with the postman to sneak peeks at her neighbors' mail.

Finally Clay cleared his throat and the women looked at him as though he'd just materialized. Emma flushed. "Gracious, where are my manners? Please, sit and get comfortable. Can I get y'all something to drink... coffee, soda?"

After declining the refreshment offer, Clay settled on the homey stuffed sofa and cautiously broached the main purpose of the visit. "I understand that you were the one who reported hearing a shot the night Gerald Sheridan was, uh..." He angled a guarded glance at Lainey, who'd pursed her lips and was staring at her knees. Clay sighed, wondering how he could ask questions about that night without mentioning a word associated with death. He absently straightened a filet crochet piece protecting the sofa arm. "Could you tell us everything that you saw and heard?"

Emma nervously perched on a chair across from the sofa. "It's been a long time. My memory's not what it used to be."

"It would mean a lot to us if you'd try."

The woman rubbed her palms on her aproned lap and angled an uneasy glance toward Lainey. "I heard a popping noise, kinda like a firecracker."

"What did you hear before that?"

"I don't remember."

Clay tapped a frustrated finger on his kneecap. She remembered, all right, but the poor woman was obviously scared to death. "Did you hear voices?"

She shrugged. "Could've been something on television."

"But you didn't think so at the time, did you?"

Staring at her lap, Emma twisted a portion of the apron's ruffled hem into a spear. "Being divorced and living alone, a body tends to get kinda antsy. You know how women are, always reading awful fears into the teeniest things."

"I don't believe that."

The woman peeked up without raising her head. The corner of her mouth twitched slightly. "Me, neither. Fact is, if I'd ever met a man who had one lick of a woman's common sense, I'd still be married."

Clay smiled. "If the women I've known are representative of the gender as a whole, I tend to agree with you."

Relaxing slightly, Emma released her mangled apron and slid Lainey a questioning glance. "Are you all right with this, sugar?"

Lainey nodded. "I— That is, we would appreciate anything you can tell us."

Emma puffed her baggy cheeks and exhaled slowly. "I don't want to talk about this to no one else, hear?"

As Clay studied the older woman's fearful expression, he felt Lainey's gaze boring into his temple. "I can't make that promise, Emma. If you talk to us, you may eventually be asked to repeat your statements under oath."

She cringed. "And if'n I don't talk to you?"

"Then the official record will remain as it is now, that you called police to report hearing a gunshot—nothing more." Clay hesitated before adding, "But I think you want to be truthful with us because you believe that Lainey has a right to know what happened to her father."

At that point Lainey reached across the oblong coffee table and touched the woman's thick wrist. "Please. If you know anything that could help us sort out what went on that night, it's really important."

Emma clutched Lainey's hand between her own work-worn palms. "I'm so sorry, child," she whispered. "All these years I've been feeling so guilty because I wasn't there when you and your ma needed friends most. I'm ashamed to admit I was afraid."

"Afraid of what?" Lainey asked.

When Emma looked away, Clay played a hunch. "You were afraid of Aldrich Clark, weren't you?"

She nodded listlessly. "Next day he came to my place. Started out real sweet, talking about what I'd told the police officers after... after it happened. Pretty soon he was saying that I hadn't really seen what I seen or heard what I heard. He got mean then. Told me that everyone knew divorced women weren't nothing but lying trash, and swore if I didn't keep my mouth shut, I'd lose my job, my friends, everything."

"You worked at ChemCorp, didn't you?" Clay asked.

"For fifteen years," she whispered, wiping her face. "My plant supervisor told me that if I quit and left town, they'd give me a real good recommendation, severance pay, and a bonus to boot. Otherwise they'd fire me and I'd get nothing." She raised pleading eyes to Lainey. "With no husband bringing in money, I have to take care of my own self. It's hard to get work when you're old and don't have but a high school education. I needed that recommendation. I *needed* it."

"No one blames you." Lainey gave the woman's hand a reassuring squeeze. "They gave you no choice. It was the only thing you could do."

Clay leaned forward. "What did you see that night, Emma?"

She chewed her lip for a moment, then took a deep breath. "I was upstairs getting ready for bed. When I went to close my window, I saw a car pull up across the street."

That was interesting, since Ben Cooper had always driven a pickup truck. "What kind of car?"

"A big one. Dark paint." She shrugged apologetically. "I don't know much 'bout cars."

Clay smiled thinly. "That's all right. Go on."

"Well, three men got out. Two stayed in the front yard, but one went up to the porch and knocked. The porch light went on and Gerald, he answered the door. Him and the man on the porch, they started talking mad to each other."

"Did you hear what they said?"

"No. They weren't yelling loud enough to catch words, but none of 'em sounded too happy."

"What happened then?"

"The man on the porch grabbed Gerald's arm and kinda pulled him down the steps."

"So Gerald was on the front lawn with all three of the men who'd gotten out of the car?"

Emma nodded. "I couldn't see much after that, on account of that big ol' maple tree growing upside the pavement. But there was scuffling going on, and I heard groaning. That's when I ran downstairs to the phone. I was fixing to dial when I heard a shot, then . . . then . . ." She wiped her mouth with the back of her hand. Her voice broke. "A woman screamed. It was the awfulest thing I ever heard in my life."

Clay exhaled all at once. "Now think carefully, Emma. Did you recognize any of the men who got out of that car?"

She shook her head. "I didn't catch more'n a glimpse."

"What about the man on the porch when the light went on?"

"He was taller than Gerald." Emma eyed Clay. "'Bout your size, I'd say. What with that tree being in the way, I just caught a look now and again."

Leaning back, Clay propped his elbow on the sofa arm and recalled his first night back in Scarlet when he'd stood in front of Emma's old house trying to imagine what she might have seen from the upstairs window. The nearest streetlamp, as Clay recalled, had been at least a hundred feet from the Sheridan home. Most of the light cast by the lamp would have been obstructed by the gigantic maple that now obscured any view into the Sheridan yard. Two decades ago the tree would have been small enough that Gerald's porch could have been at least partially visible, especially from the upstairs window.

A distressed gasp jarred Clay from his thoughts. He turned. Emma was kneeling beside the sofa patting Lainey's limp hand. "Lordy, child, you're white as a pink-eyed mouse."

As Lainey swayed forward, Clay caught her trembling shoulders. Her lips were chalky, her ashen cheeks damp with perspiration. "What is it, Lainey?"

"Take me home," she whispered weakly. "Please . . . just take me home." When she looked up, her eyes were glazed with pain. And with terror.

Sandborne Hunicutt glanced at his watch, then stared out the diner window watching traffic on the bustling interstate. A marked police car moved down the off ramp, turned right and pulled into the parking lot. "He just drove in," Sandborne announced, stepping anxiously from the secluded booth at the back of the dowdy restaurant.

Across the table, a calm voice emanated from behind an open newspaper. "Bring him here."

With a nervous snort, Sandborne held a handkerchief to his nose while he scurried through the noisy diner. He arrived at the front door just as it opened. "You're late," he snapped.

"Some fool done hit a cow and tried to flag me down." Aldrich Clark tucked his hat under his arm and smoothed a hand over his bald scalp. "Is he here?"

"Of course, he's here," Sandborne replied crossly. "We've been waiting almost ten minutes." With that, he tucked the handkerchief back into his pocket, grabbed the chief's fat arm and ushered him around to the back of the drab little eatery.

Clark slid awkwardly into the booth. Sandborne sat tentatively beside him. Across the table, the newspaper rattled. An icy voice from behind the extended pages made both men flinch. "I trust you haven't been irreparably inconvenienced."

"No, sir." Clark laid his cap on the table. "I came lickety-split soon as I got Sandy's call."

Reeves folded the newspaper and laid it beside his empty coffee cup. Glancing irritably over his shoulder, he snapped his fingers. A waitress hurried over with a refill. He waved her away before she could attend to the table's other occupants. Reeves sipped his fresh coffee, seemingly lost in thought and oblivious to his partners' discomfort.

Clark absently twirled a cheap plastic salt shaker. Sandborne's head felt as if it were about to explode. Nerves, he decided, and cursed his rotten luck at having inherited sinuses that plugged up every time he started to sweat. As he reached for the nose spray, Reeves pinned him with a look that made him squirm. Sandborne dropped the bottle back into his pocket, pulled out the handkerchief and mopped his wet face.

Reeves settled the cheap stoneware cup into its saucer with the same care one used with fine china. Propping his forearms against the table's chromium edge, he clasped his hands with presidential flare. "Gentlemen, we have a problem."

To Sandborne's disgust, Clark nodded his fat head until his jowls vibrated, which was all one could expect from such a boot-licking, butt-kissing pig. But despite being a repulsive swine, Sandborne allowed that the police chief had been useful on occasion. A man who could gut a chicken with one hand and eat a sandwich with the other was obviously not bothered by handling particularly disagreeable chores. Murder, for instance.

Reeves's frosty voice broke the thought. "Are we boring you, Sandy?"

"No, sir. I was just thinking about how to resolve our, uh, problem." He wished to hell he didn't sound like he had a clothespin on his nose.

Reeves leaned forward with saccharine interest. "Oh? Then perhaps you'd be so good as to share your solution with the rest of us."

"Of course." Sandborne managed to suppress a satisfying snort. "The way I see it, McFerson is just playing games to get attention. I mean, *Banner* sales are going through the roof, and I heard tell that Broddie's looking for UPI to pick up the story."

Reeves smiled pleasantly. "What story is that?"

"Well, uh...'scuse me." Unable to deny himself another moment, Sandborne blew his nose and was instantly relieved. The moist fabric muffled the rest of his speech. "I figure that if McFerson knew anything, it would already be in print. The old coot is guessing, that's all, hoping to stir up enough interest to make a name for himself."

"I see." Reeves nodded gravely. "So your hypothesis, if I understand this correctly, is that despite the fact that McFerson quite obviously has obtained potentially damaging information about our past manufacturing problems, we should simply ignore him by crossing our fingers and hoping he'll go away." Still smiling, the tall man leaned forward until his face was inches from his terrified successor's. "Is that what you had in mind, Sandy?"

"I, uh..." Sandborne frantically dabbed his sore nose. "Maybe we could talk to him."

Reeves's smile widened. "That's an excellent idea."

Sandborne blinked. "It is?"

"Of course. We'll simply reason with the man." Reeves tugged each crisp linen cuff before adding, "After all, that same method has already proven quite effective, has it not?"

Clark chuckled. "Yessir, it sure has. Why, we'll just 'reason' with old Broddie McFerson like y'all reasoned with Gerald Sheridan, and I guaran-damn-tee we ain't gonna have no more problems."

Sandborne was horrified. Dear Lord, not again. He still had nightmares about the last time. His stomach lurched. Hiding behind the linen hanky, Sandborne mentally shook himself. No matter how distasteful the prospect, deep down he knew that they had no other choice. Reeves was right. Reeves was always right.

For twenty years Sandborne had slaved like an invisible lackey, propelled by promises that someday the ChemCorp reins would be his. That day had finally come. Now that he had the respect and prestige he deserved, no one was going to take it away. He'd worked too hard, too long. There was nothing he wouldn't do to keep what was rightfully his.

"Are we all in agreement, Sandy?"

Any trace of doubt was erased when he looked into Reeves's shrewd eyes. Sandborne straightened until his shoulder blades painfully pressed into the stiff vinyl booth. "Yes," he said forcefully. "We're in agreement."

"Good." Lifting his coffee cup, Reeves acknowledged his successor with a wry salute. "After McFerson has been silenced, Cooper must naturally be attended to in the same fashion."

"Natur'ly." Clark rubbed his hands together. "I'm really gonna enjoy that."

Suppressing another wave of nausea, Sandborne angled a disgusted glance at Clark and automatically moved as far away as the narrow booth bench would allow. "Cooper's already gone," Sandborne said. "Since he obviously left town without the information he was seeking, it seems pointless to pursue him."

Reeves pursed his lips, issued an inflated sigh and replied with the exaggerated patience frequently used with animals and small children. "Cooper has simply gone underground. Even if he's not staying in Scarlet, he's most certainly close by, and we must consider that if this book of his is published, there will be renewed interest in the old Sheridan case."

The possibility reclogged Sandborne's sinuses. "I thought we'd taken care of all that. The lawsuit is going to tie up Cooper's manuscript for years and cost a fortune for legal defense. As soon as Lainey Sheridan files for injunction, Cooper's publishers will drop him like a hot rock."

Reeves frowned. "Unfortunately, the young lady has decided against pursuing legal action."

"What?" Sandborne reached for a napkin, knocked over an empty coffee cup and somehow managed to fumble the chipped vessel back into its saucer.

This was dreadful news, the absolute worst. Even if Cooper couldn't complete the project, a draft of the manuscript was probably already in some editor's hands. Unless publication could be legally thwarted, the book could still be marketed in one form or another.

With his terrified brain whizzing, Sandborne struggled to supply another option. "Perhaps the company itself might have legal recourse."

"Perhaps," Reeves replied thoughtfully. "But if Miss Sheridan were to experience a change of heart and support Cooper's venture, company opposition could result in raising suspicions rather than alleviating them."

Clark scratched his bald scalp. "That don't seem likely. Russ and Hallie'll keep the girl in line."

"Since the Clemmonses have evidently lost control of their niece, I'm afraid the unhappy duty of enlightening Miss Sheridan about her unruly behavior has also fallen on us." Raising his hand, Reeves made a subtle gesture.

The waitress appeared out of nowhere, laid the check at the edge of the table, then melted discreetly into the background. As Reeves buttoned his suit coat, he added, "In other words, gentlemen, Miss Sheridan must also be reasoned with."

After that chilling pronouncement, Reeves pushed the check in front of Hunicutt, then stood, spun on his polished heel and left.

Chapter 10

It was a silent drive back to the lakeside cabin where Lainey's car was parked. She had spent the time staring out the passenger window, answering Clay's concerned questions with succinct, noncommittal replies. After being assured that she was not ill, he'd respected her need for private thought. Although Lainey wasn't used to such sensitivity, she was nonetheless grateful for it.

As he pulled into the clearing, she angled a covert glance to her left. It was a mistake. Just the sight of him made her tingle. His patrician profile was so strong, so confident, yet there was a hint of vulnerability in those startlingly full lips . . . lips that had caressed her own with both exquisite tenderness and stunning passion. Even the memory of his kiss left her breathless.

She turned away, absently laying a palm over her racing heart. The car slowed to a stop. The engine whirred briefly, then fell silent.

"We're here, Lainey."

She nodded without comment, lifted her purse from the floorboard and pushed open the door. By the time she stepped out, Clay had exited the vehicle and moved quickly to her side.

He solicitously took her arm. "Come inside. I'll make coffee."

The offer was tempting. Not so much the coffee as the thought of spending a few more minutes with Clay. His presence calmed her, made her feel safe. Once she left this protected place—left him—she'd be alone with her demons again.

When he slid a comforting arm around her waist, Lainey melted against his blessed warmth and didn't resist as he led her into the cabin. He smoothed the wrinkled sheet covering the sofa and patted the cushions. "Put your feet up. Relax."

Accepting the invitation, Lainey settled comfortably, kicked off her shoes and allowed him to lift her feet onto the sofa.

He hovered anxiously. "Comfy?"

"Yes, thank you."

Feeling thoroughly pampered, she snuggled against the soft cushions and sighed. "I'm not used to being coddled. It's nice."

"You deserve to be coddled." Facing her, Clay sat on the edge of the sofa with his hip pressed against her thigh. "You deserve to be waited on and cared for and showered with every luxury life has to offer."

She smiled. "Hmm. That sounds lovely."

"Does it?" The husky whisper sent shivers down her spine. Wrapping strong fingers around the taut muscles at the juncture of her neck and shoulders, he began a slow, rhythmic massage. "Let me wait on you, Lainey. Let me shower you with luxuries."

Beneath his kneading fingers, her tension melted like ice in summer. She closed her eyes, indulging the warm sensations, the gentle motion of his soothing hands. "I can't think of anything more luxurious than this," she murmured.

"The world is filled with wondrous things," he said softly. "Furs and fancy clothes, diamonds and gold, mansions with dozens of bustling servants ready to fulfill your every wish. What would make you happy, Lainey? If you could choose anything, what would you want most?"

"Anything?" she repeated, drowsily going along with the whimsical request.

"Anything at all."

"Well, there is one thing... Oo-ooh, that feels wonderful." She rolled her head, moaning in pleasure as the expert massage appeased the knotted muscles at the base of her skull.

"What is it?" Clay whispered, so close she felt his warm breath on her cheek.

"It's very extravagant," she teased, certain that they were simply playing some kind of happy wishing game. "How rich are you?"

His smile was a little sad. "Would you be disappointed if I told you that I wasn't rich at all?"

"Dreadfully disappointed." Stretching lazily, she opened her eyes and winked. "Isn't it just like a man to make promises he can't keep."

"I always keep my promises."

"Really? So, what if I told you that I've always wanted a sixty-foot yacht?"

"I don't think a sixty-foot yacht would fit in Tupaloosa Creek."

"Don't be silly. I'd dock it at the marina."

"Scarlet doesn't have a marina."

"Palm Beach does."

"Ah. And would this be a private marina adjacent to your beachfront estate?"

"Of course."

His forehead puckered into an exaggerated frown. "That would certainly max out my MasterCard."

"Lucky for you that asking what I would like is not the same as promising to provide it."

He regarded her thoughtfully. "Is that what you really want, Lainey, a Palm Beach estate and a sixty-foot yacht?"

"Are you serious?" When a quick scan of his somber expression indicated that he was indeed serious, she hastened to reassure him. "Oh, for heaven's sake. I get seasick in a rowboat and need sunscreen to walk across the street. I was just joking. I thought you were, too."

"I was and I wasn't." He touched her cheek, a caress so infinitely tender that she wondered if she'd imagined it. After a moment he sighed. "When I was a kid, my mother gave me a diary of my own. She told me it would be my special friend, that I could tell it things I could never share with anyone else. I used to play this 'what if' game..." With a sheepish smile, he avoided her gaze by studying her shoulder and nervously fidgeting with the seam of her sweater. "That sounds pretty silly, doesn't it?"

"It doesn't sound silly at all." She laid a hand over his jittery fingers. "I was an only child, too, remember? I understand what it's like when the only escape from loneliness is your own imagination."

The gratitude in his gaze brought a lump to her throat. "I used to list the things I would buy if I had all the money in the world."

"What kind of things?"

"Impossible things," he replied softly. "Shoes that didn't pinch, pants without someone else's patches sewn on the knees, a bicycle that worked. Sometimes I'd even be generous and wish my mother a new dress or a frivolous nightie with lace on the collar. She loved pretty things."

As he spoke, his eyes softened with a faraway light that touched Lainey's heart. In her mind she could picture that stoic little boy hunched over his list of austere wishes. "Do you ever look back over those pages and check off the wishes that came true?"

The tiny lines bracketing his mouth instantly tightened. "I threw the book away."

"But...why?"

"Because I saw my mother's journal become public entertainment. Her private thoughts and intimate feelings were not only exposed, they were ridiculed. She was mocked, humiliated, emotionally shattered." With conscious effort, Clay displayed what Lainey assumed was supposed to be a smile but bore greater resemblance to an agonized grimace. "I learned rather quickly not to write anything down that I didn't want to read in the morning paper."

There was a paradox to Clay's words that Lainey couldn't reconcile. "Then how can you possibly justify violating her privacy by wanting to publish her personal journal?"

He seemed offended by the question and stung that she would ask it. "That journal will never be published. Do you think I want to write a tabloid exposé of my own mother?"

"Of course not," she whispered, well aware that Clay had planned a book that would pay homage to Catherine's courage and eloquence. "For some reason, I just assumed you were planning to include her diary."

"Parts of it, of course, passages that reveal her inner beauty and intellectual brilliance. But I'd never betray her trust by including intimate details and expressions of her heart that were never meant to be shared."

"I'm sure you wouldn't," she murmured, chagrined by having doubted him. "I didn't mean to imply otherwise."

He stared at her for a moment, then sighed. "And I didn't mean to snap your head off. Apparently I'm more sensitive about the subject than I realized."

After a silent moment Lainey asked a question that had been bothering her since she'd read the journal. "You mentioned Catherine's intellectual brilliance—and I agree that the person who wrote those words was extraordinarily gifted—but I couldn't help wonder why she, well, stayed with your father for so many years." When he glanced away and appeared pained, Lainey hastened to clarify her meaning. "The journal never described any outrageous cruelties, of course, but there was always an underlying aura of..." She struggled to express herself without alienating Clay completely. "Not fear exactly, but certainly a sense of apprehension."

Clay absently massaged his chin, staring at the hardwood floor as though fascinated by the scarred planking under his feet. Finally he spoke in a voice both thoughtful and incredibly sad. "I'm not sure I can answer your question because I've asked it so many times myself. I guess my mother must have been in denial. She equated meanness with male temperament and refused to recognize the clues that her husband was a criminal."

"What clues?"

He shrugged. "Cash wads appearing out of the blue, weapons stashed in odd places throughout the house, that kind of thing."

"Perhaps she loved him," Lainey suggested, although she didn't really believe that. In the journal's early entries Catherine had expressed an abiding loyalty to her husband but never any deep emotional feelings.

Evidently Clay agreed. "I don't believe she loved him, although in the beginning she may have confused gratitude and dependence with love."

"That's very sad," Lainey murmured. "But as you pointed out, Catherine was an intelligent woman. Over the years, she must surely have come to understand the shaky foundation on which her marriage was based."

"My mother *was* intelligent, yes, but she was also emotionally repressed. She'd been raised in an atmosphere of discipline so strict it bordered on abuse. To her, a certain amount of violence was normal in any family." Clay rolled his head, wincing as though the movement caused pain. He rubbed the back of his neck and sighed. "By the time my parents married, my mother's self-esteem had been seriously eroded. She believed herself to be ignorant and unattractive. Since her childhood was so unhappy, she always felt indebted to my father for having rescued her."

"This must be difficult for you to talk about," Lainey whispered.

"At one time it would have been. I've come to terms with my heritage, but at the moment I'm in the mood for something more pleasant." Still seated on the outer edge of the cushion, Clay propped his elbow on the sofa back to form a human bridge over Lainey's partially prone body. "So let's go back to the game."

"The game?" Frowning, Lainey readjusted her mind to what they'd be discussing before the subject of Cooper history came up. "Oh! The wish game."

"Right. You said there was one thing you really wanted."

She folded her arms. "Promise you won't laugh?"

"That depends on how funny it is. If your deepest wish is to own a hamster wheel the size of Boston, a small chuckle might slip out."

"How small?"

"Minuscule," he assured her. "Barely a snort."

Partially placated, she cleared her throat. "I've always wanted a really good mixer, the kind that comes with dough hooks and whisk beaters and a detachable meat grinder—Why are you looking at me like that?" she demanded, embarrassed by his incredulous expression.

"I, uh..." He coughed away a minute but noticeable lip twitch. "With all the frills and fancies life has to offer, all you can come up with is a kitchen appliance?"

"It's a very valuable kitchen appliance," she insisted defensively. "And expensive. Very expensive."

"So are diamonds. This is a wish game, Lainey. You're not supposed to be practical. Think of something else."

She gave him a narrowed stare. "All right. A Cuisinart." Ignoring his dumfounded stare, she defiantly lifted her chin. "And not the teeny little economy model, either. I want the big one with all the attachments."

His jaw drooped. "Good grief, are you planning to spend your life in a kitchen?"

"Would that be so awful?" She hated the temperamental squeak in her voice, but Clay was acting as if a kitchen were nothing more than a dowdy prison for the intellectually disadvantaged. Since Lainey was happiest with a loaf of homemade bread in the oven, Clay's attitude—coupled with what he'd just confided about his mother's lack of education—made her feel like a second-class citizen.

He absently scratched an arched brow. "Well, no, it wouldn't be awful, but there aren't many people who can brag about owning their own newspaper. I figured the least you'd wish for would be a high-speed press or one of those multicolor overprint doomawhatchies."

She didn't bother to hide her annoyance. "Printing presses give me a headache, the smell of black ink makes me sick and if I could spend the rest of my life without touching another computer keyboard, I would die with a smile on my face."

"You're kidding." He studied her irked expression. "Good grief, you're serious. You hate the newspaper, don't you?"

"Hate is a pretty strong word," she mumbled, realizing that she'd probably sounded like a whining, ungrateful brat. "The truth is that the *Banner* will always be a part of my father. He loved it, so I guess I love it, too."

"But you don't want to work there."

She fidgeted with a loose thread on her knitted cuff. "That's not a big secret. Everyone in the newsroom knows that I'm not really qualified for my job. Some people resent that, and I can't say that I blame them. I, like your mother, don't have a college degree."

"You say that like you expect me to faint in horror. Do I really seem that pompous to you?"

"Of course not." She cleared her throat. "I suppose hearing that Catherine felt inadequate because she lacked an education must have struck a nerve."

"Granted, my mother was pulled out of school in the eighth grade, but she was a voracious reader and as far as I'm concerned, she damn well educated herself." He skewed a sideways glance. "A degree is helpful but hardly an accurate measure of a person's worth. I'm sorry if I've given you the impression that I believed otherwise."

"You didn't." She smiled and shrugged. "It's just a touchy subject, so now it's my turn to apologize for being cross."

"I guess we're just a couple of grumps." Clay returned her smile. "But for the record, my interest was in you, Lainey, in filling in the blanks of your life."

"Why?"

"Because I care." The corners of his eyes were wonderfully crinkled. "And because you already know my entire life's story, so I figure it's time for you to return the favor."

She emitted a dry laugh. "My life's an open and very boring book. What do you want to know?"

"Would another college question set you off?"

Her smile froze a moment then melted under the warmth of his twinkling eyes. "Ask away."

With his elbow still propped on the sofa back, he bent his arm and rested his cheek against his folded hand. "The newspaper has made a fairly good profit over the years. Surely your father's share would have been enough to provide for your education."

She fiddled with the hem of her sweater. "I wasn't entitled to any of the *Banner*'s profits until last year."

He frowned. "So where has the money been going all this time?"

"My mother was Daddy's prime beneficiary," Lainey explained. "He made every effort to take care of both Mother and I equally. He established a college trust for me and postponed inheritance of the newspaper so I'd have time to finish school."

"If money wasn't a problem, why didn't you go to college?"

"I did. And I liked it, too. I just couldn't..." Embarrassed, she looked away. "I couldn't stay."

"Why not?" When she didn't answer, Clay laid a compassionate hand on her shoulder. "It's nothing to be ashamed of, Lainey."

The perplexing statement caught her by surprise. "What are you talking about?"

"We've already ascertained that college isn't for everyone. You have other talents, I'm sure."

Astonished and humiliated, her voice rose with an embarrassing squeak. "Are you implying that I flunked out?" Without allowing him to reply, she shook an indignant finger in his face. "What gall! For your information, I earned straight A's for my entire first semester—except for that B-plus in trigonometry because I had the flu during finals. In fact, if I hadn't been forced to drop out, I could have—no, I *would* have—graduated in the top five percent of my class, and I deeply resent any insinuation to the contrary." She refilled her lungs, as irritated by her own overreaction as by Clay's mistaken assumption.

"Congratulations," he replied quietly. "I apologize for having jumped to an erroneous conclusion."

Deflated, she brushed her spotless sweater, folded her arms and hoped the entire subject would die naturally. It didn't.

Clay studied her thoughtfully. "Then, why did you quit?"

She shrugged. "Things happened."

"What things?"

Fluffing her bangs with her fingers, she bought a moment to compose herself. Finally she decided that there was no shame in simply admitting the truth. "Aunt Hallie hurt herself doing laundry and needed more surgery to repair the damage. Afterward, she simply couldn't manage alone."

Clay's arm dangled against the sofa back as he lifted his head. "You gave up an education to take care of your aunt? Why on earth didn't they just hire a housekeeper?"

"They couldn't afford that. The medical bills were enormous." Lainey shook her head. "You don't understand. My aunt and uncle were never wealthy people. When they took me in, the last thing they needed was another mouth to feed. They could have turned their backs on me, but they didn't. They worked hard to give me everything I needed, even if it meant they had to do without. I owed them so much."

"Did you owe them your future?"

Lainey took a sharp breath, then reminded herself that Clay had no way of knowing she had no future. At least, none that excited her. Her fate had been sealed long before the Clemmonses had entered her young life. But her secret torment was private, something that Clay Cooper must never know.

Her troubled contemplation was broken as Clay leaned forward until his face was inches from her own. His eyes glowed like moonstones. "You cashed in your trust fund to pay your aunt's medical bills, didn't you?"

There seemed no reason to deny it. "Yes."

His gaze delved deep inside her, so deep she could actually feel its heat burrowing into her very core. "Lainey, Lainey," he murmured, his hip pressing insistently against her thigh. "What am I going to do with you?"

She would have made a shocking suggestion, except the image made her blush. Instead she squirmed silently, acutely aware that her shoulders were pressed deeply against the sofa arm and her legs were conveniently extended across the plush seat cushions. With just a subtle downward scoot, she'd be positioned for the ultimate joining, a delicious blending of reality with the erotic visions racing through her mind. And she wanted that desperately.

Eyes smoldering with promise, he moved his hand from her shoulder and gently cupped the side of her throat. His thumb caressed her jaw with exquisite tenderness. "Has anyone told you how beautiful you are?"

She licked her lips. The seduction was beginning. This was the point at which she usually slid away with a flip remark or a deflating snicker. But she couldn't move—and didn't want to, fearing the slightest motion would break the spell and this mesmerizing moment would disappear forever.

Clay's fingers slid around her nape, tangling in her thick hair as his palm cupped the back of her skull. A strange throbbing circled her belly, spiraling outward like warm ripples on a silky pond.

His head bent closer. Their cheeks brushed. She closed her eyes, waiting, and felt a tickle at her temple. "You smell so good," he murmured against her ear. "Honeysuckles on a spring night."

"I-it's my shampoo." Now there was a provocative reply. "You smell good, too."

He nuzzled her earlobe. "Forest Spice."

"E-excuse—" she shivered "—me?"

"My after-shave. Forest Spice."

"Ah...it's nice. Smells piney." Another chill slid down her spine. "And spicy," she murmured stupidly. "Piney and spicy."

His lips teased the corner of her mouth. "I'm glad you like it."

Oh, yes, she liked it just fine. The masculine fragrance mingled with the aroma of sweet musk wafting from his neatly scissored hair was probably the most sensual scent she'd ever encountered. She was overwhelmed with sensations, inside, outside, mind and body. Every glide of his gentle fingers made her skin quiver—and yet she was excruciatingly aware that he'd yet to touch her below the shoulders. The fantasy of imagining his warm palms cupping her waiting breasts was so delicious that her nipples actually began to ache. Moaning in frustration, she yearned for the courage to take the initiative and move his searching hand under her sweater.

Alas, the brazen act was beyond her muster of courage, so she simply rolled her head back, allowing his lips access to the throbbing pulse point at the base of her throat. He instantly accepted the invitation, his lips blazing a moist trail down to the lowest point of the V-neck, then slowly moving upward with titillating flicks of his tongue. It was the most erotic experience of her life. She could barely breathe.

By the time his mouth covered hers, she was shaking all over. He kissed her deeply, with a passion so intense that the world could have exploded around them and she'd have never noticed. There was nothing else on earth but this man, this moment, this absolute bliss.

She responded without thought, without shame, winding her arms around him as though her life depended upon the strength of her grip. Sensations overwhelmed her, a coursing heat that seared her to the bone and made her crazy inside.

And then it was over.

The kiss was broken. Clay brushed his lips across her cheek, caressed her hair, then reached back to loosen her convulsive arms from around his neck. One tug and they slid away like limp noodles and flopped onto her lap. She was weak. She was dizzy. She was bewildered. "Now what's wrong?"

Smiling affectionately, he combed her mussed bangs with his fingers. "I promised you coffee, remember?"

Coffee? He'd snatched away paradise because he'd promised her *coffee?* Lainey rubbed her eyes, certain she'd misheard. The sofa cushion expanded gently and when she looked up, Clay was in the kitchen area pumping water into a blue steel pot.

He set the pot on the stove and lit the gas burner. "It'll only take a few minutes to perk," he said cheerfully, dumping in a handful of coffee grounds.

Lainey wished she had something to throw. Pivoting until her feet touched the floor, she fumbled for her shoes. "I should be going."

"Wait a while. You still look a bit shaken."

She slid him a dry look and stuffed one foot into a squashed sneaker. "I'm fine."

His lean legs moved him quickly across the room. "Lainey, I'm sorry. I know it was all my fault, but I never meant to upset you."

The shoelace froze in her fingers. "I'm not upset," she lied, assuming that he was referring to the romantic moment they'd just shared.

"Of course you're upset." He bent in front of the coffee table and picked up her left sneaker. "You almost fainted."

She snatched her shoe away. "You have a pretty high opinion of yourself, don't you?" The fact that she had indeed nearly fainted was beside the point. A gentleman would never be so crass as to have mentioned it.

Looking totally confused, Clay sat on the low table with his knees absurdly bent and poking out at odd angles. Finally, comprehension clouded his eyes along with a reflection of misery. "You're right. It was arrogant and self-important for me to coax you into something you weren't ready to face simply so I could prove I was right. I don't blame you for being angry with me."

As she tied the final lace, Lainey began to realize that she and Clay might not be on the same wavelength. "Exactly what is it that you don't think I was ready to face?"

He hesitated. "It's fairly obvious that taking you to see Emma Gebloski was a mistake."

The reminder made the blood drain from her face. Emma. The memories. The dream.

Clay reached out to steady her. "Lainey? What is it?"

She couldn't answer. The mention of Emma's name brought back the terror she'd felt as the woman had related hearing angry male voices. When Emma had spoken of a woman's scream, a bolt of sheer panic had jolted Lainey to her toes. She'd felt faint, nauseated. The image of polka-dotted clown legs had raced through her mind, and she'd been sickened to realize that the nightmare must have something to do with her father's death.

As she saw alarm building in Clay's eyes, she wanted desperately to share what she feared. He was the champion of her dream, her protector...but something warned her to keep silent. If she told him about the frightening images in her mind, he might believe her to be hysterical, or worse, emotionally frail. Lainey wouldn't be able to bear that.

Clay took her hands. "Lainey, look at me."

Reluctantly she did as he asked.

"There's only one person who can answer all the questions and put this matter to rest once and for all. We both know who that is, don't we?"

"I've told you that I won't discuss this." Lainey pulled her hands away and stood. "I'm leaving now."

"Lainey, wait!" Lurching forward, he grasped her arm and nearly fell off the table in the process. Without releasing her, he struggled to his feet. "Look, I know MaryBeth hurt you deeply. I don't blame you for not wanting to see her, and you don't have to. Just tell me where she is."

Eyes darting, Lainey clawed at his restraining fingers. "I have to go. Turn me loose!"

"Your mother was there, Lainey, right upstairs. If Emma Gebloski heard voices clear across the street, then your mother must have heard them, too. She might even have recognized—"

"Stop it!" Taking advantage of Clay's momentary confusion, Lainey ripped away and stumbled toward the door. Grabbing the knob, she whirled and held up her palm. "Don't...just don't."

Clay froze in midstep.

Stark panic swelled up inside. She yanked open the door and dashed to her car, knowing that Clay Cooper would never give up his search for her mother. One way or another, he was determined to learn the truth.

And that was most terrifying of all.

Clay parked down the street and walked the darkened sidewalk toward the Clemmonses' house. He glanced around, satisfied that the quiet residential area was deserted. He'd expected as much. At this time of the evening, most folks were tucked inside their snug little houses enjoying an evening meal.

When he reached the edge of the Clemmonses' property, he saw the house was alight. There was activity in the kitchen, as he'd expected, but the woman standing in front of the sink wasn't Lainey. His heart sank.

Ever since Lainey had rushed from the cabin two hours ago, Clay had been kicking himself for not having followed her. He'd actually jumped into his van and turned on the ignition before rethinking the impulsive act. Obviously he'd done or said something that had upset her deeply. Although he'd desperately wanted to apologize, to right whatever wrong had been committed, he'd realized that a vehicular pursuit wasn't likely to further his cause.

So he'd allowed time for her to return home—the longest twenty minutes of his life—then telephoned the Clemmonses' house and asked for Lainey without identifying himself. Her uncle had gruffly stated that she wasn't there and hung up. Two subsequent calls had netted the same result.

Clay had even called McFerson, who'd claimed that he hadn't seen Lainey all day. Strangely enough, the old man hadn't seemed particularly worried. He'd made a blithe comment about it being Saturday and had told Clay to sit tight, adding that she'd probably show up by morning. *By morning,* for heaven's sake! This from a man who went berserk if Lainey was ten minutes late getting to work. It didn't make sense. McFerson loved Lainey like a daughter, yet he'd acted as if it were no big deal that her whereabouts were unknown.

To Clay, it was one hell of a big deal.

So while the town's rich and powerful were huddled somewhere trying to figure out how to get their hands on him, Clay was slinking through the Clemmonses' yard like a common thief. Go figure.

The Clemmonses' garage was set back from the house. Clay circled the bleak frame structure and found no windows. Since the garage door was locked, there was no way to tell if Lainey's car was inside.

He moved quietly to the back porch, which was nothing more than three steps and a four-foot concrete slab, and peeked through the door window. Hallie was still standing at the sink, rinsing dishes. No one else was in the room. Clay hesitated, then tapped on the glass.

Hallie frowned, wiped her wet hands on a tea towel, then unhooked her canes from the counter edge and awkwardly crossed the room to open the door.

"Good evening, Mrs. Clemmons," Clay said pleasantly. "I'm here to see Lainey."

"She's not home. It's Saturday." The woman eyed him skeptically. "Who're you?"

Again the reminder that it was Saturday. Clay's heart sank even lower. "Is she out on a date?"

Hallie snorted. "Lainey don't have 'dates.'" She bent forward and stared up into Clay's face. "You're that Cooper boy."

Ignoring the flat statement, Clay gazed over the woman's head and noticed several empty bags from the local Burger Barn. A peculiar sense of foreboding settled over him. If Lainey had been home, the Clemmonses certainly wouldn't be supping on greasy take-out. Apparently the lazy slobs allowed their niece at least one night a week away from her housekeeping duties, although Clay wasn't in the mood to view their motives charitably. Besides, he was convinced by Hallie's shrewd expression the woman knew exactly where Lainey was.

He cleared his throat and forced a pleasant smile. "Do you know where I might find her?"

"Seems to me that's none of your business." Hallie shifted her weight to the right cane and glanced tensely over her shoulder, as though expecting someone. She turned back to Clay, lowering her voice. "You got some nerve, coming here, what with half the town fixing to knot you a new tie."

Clay balled his fists at his side and fought to maintain an even expression. "It's important that I speak with Lainey tonight."

A crafty gleam lit the woman's tiny eyes. "Tell me where you're staying. I'll have her call when she gets home."

Right, Clay thought dryly. And there really is a tooth fairy. He knew perfectly well that advertising his own whereabouts would be an invitation to share Sunday brunch with Lloyd Reeves's henchmen. Since he couldn't tell Hallie where he was staying, all he could do was hope the woman might actually pass on a message. It was a stupid notion, but it was all Clay had. And he was desperate.

After a brief search of his pockets, he found a stick of gum and scrawled his untraceable cellular phone number on the back of the wrapper. "She can reach me here anytime," Clay said, holding out the scrap.

Shifted her weight, the woman let the unused cane dangle from her hand as she took the paper. The water pipes suddenly vibrated as though a toilet had been flushed. Hallie pivoted, looking anxiously back toward the living room. "Best be on your way," she muttered. "My husband finds you here, he's not likely to be as tolerant as me."

Clay hesitated. "You'll give Lainey the message?"

"I said I would," she growled, then slammed the door in his face. After twisting the lock, Hallie peered out the window until Clay Cooper had disappeared behind the latticework trellis.

Hearing footsteps in the hallway, Hallie thumped across the kitchen as fast as her canes could carry her and was correctly positioned by the sink when Russ entered the kitchen adjusting his belt and carrying a copy of *Sports Illustrated* under his arm. "I thought I heard voices." He tossed the magazine on the table. "Was someone here?"

"No one was here," Hallie replied, still staring out the kitchen window. "Must've been the wind."

Grunting an acknowledgment, Russ pulled a beer out of the refrigerator and ambled into the living room. In a moment, the television was blaring.

Hallie opened her hand and looked at the telephone number Cooper had written down. With a triumphant smile, she slipped the scrap into her pocket and continued rinsing dishes.

Chapter 11

It was after dark by the time Lainey arrived at the rambling, nondescript structure outside Greenville. Grabbing her purse and the purchase she'd made less than an hour ago, she hurried though the unmarked entrance into a plain, sparsely furnished lobby.

The perky young woman behind a circular counter greeted her. "Good evening, Miss Sheridan. Running a little late?"

Lainey tucked the department store bag under her arm and managed a tight smile. "It's been one of those days."

The receptionist nodded. "Know what you mean. Sometimes there just aren't enough hours—" A ringing phone captured the woman's attention, much to Lainey's relief.

As the receptionist tucked the receiver under her chin, Lainey mouthed "See you later" and pushed open the swinging double doors leading to a long, sterile hallway. She walked briskly, soundlessly, turning right, left, then right again, the same route she'd taken every Saturday afternoon for more years than she cared to remember. She stopped in front of the same doorway, taking a deep breath before entering the dimly lit room.

Light flickered from a television bolted to one of the unadorned walls. A white towel was draped over the steel back of an armless chair that had been shoved into the corner beside a barred window. There was a plastic water pitcher and a glass on a gray metal nightstand, which also held a curved desk lamp providing illumination for the cramped room. The only other furniture was a narrow bed, adjusted to raise the occupant's upper body into a sitting position.

Lainey's attention was focused on that occupant, a middle-aged skeleton of a woman, physically and emotionally deteriorated from decades of confinement. Lainey crossed the room, dropped her purse and parcel on the chair, then went to the bed and took the woman's emaciated hand. "Hello, Mother," she whispered. "I'm sorry I'm late."

The woman stared vapidly out the window. "I declare, did you ever see such a fine day? The sky is so blue in summer."

Swallowing, Lainey followed her mother's gaze and saw only the blackness of a cold autumn night. "Yes, it's a lovely day." She sat on the edge of the mattress and smoothed a stringy blond strand from the gaunt face. "How are you feeling?"

MaryBeth sighed longingly. "The clouds are so white and fluffy. Like a sky full of kittens."

"Yes," Lainey agreed softly. "Just like kittens."

Lainey sat silently for several moments, fighting the familiar sting of tears. She felt so alone, so desperately alone. Of those few people who understood her mother's plight—Aunt Hallie, Uncle Russ, Broddie, and of course, Lloyd Reeves—none had offered Lainey the comfort she so desperately needed. Broddie had tried, bless him, but like the Clemmonses, he'd become so distressed by the mere mention of MaryBeth's illness that Lainey found it easier to avoid the subject completely.

Besides, in Scarlet the walls really did have ears. If anyone else in that tattling town ever learned MaryBeth's secret, Lainey would die of shame. From church pews to street corners, canasta games to quilting bees, the entire population would be whispering, watching, waiting for the second generation of madness. Lainey would be pitied, reviled and ridiculed, an outcast among the only people she'd ever known.

She stood suddenly and went to the chair. "I brought you a present, Mother." Reaching into the bag, she pulled out a soft lap robe. "Isn't it a lovely shade of aqua? It matches your eyes, don't you think?" She expected no response and got none. "Would you like to try it on?"

"The sun is so bright." MaryBeth placidly allowed her daughter to extract each thin arm from the worn cotton duster she wore. "I love the sun."

"Of course you do. Lean forward...there." Lainey finished removing the faded print garment, tossed it aside and wrapped the new robe around the woman's thin shoulders. "Put your arms in...that's good." Lainey fastened the front buttons and tied a neat bow beneath the Peter Pan collar. "Now, how does that feel?"

"A lady must never take sun without a parasol. Freckles mar the complexion." MaryBeth finally looked at Lainey as though seeing her for the first time. "I don't believe we've been properly introduced."

The repetitive statement never ceased to hurt. "My name is Lainey."

"So pleased to meet you." With a gracious smile, MaryBeth gestured regally toward a naked wall. "Shall we have tea on the veranda?"

"Another time."

"Perhaps you'll have supper with my husband and I," MaryBeth said, a dreamy expression giving life to her dreary eyes. "Every night he takes me to the finest restaurants. Afterward we go dancing or to the theater...I do adore the theater."

"That sounds lovely."

Suddenly MaryBeth's gaze went vacant. Her lips slackened, her chin drooped and she quietly slipped into the familiar comatose state where she spent most of her waking hours.

Lainey caressed her mother's hair for a moment, then reached into the nightstand drawer for the brush and barrettes she'd bought for her. "How would you like your hair today, Mother? Shall we twist it at the nape?" Without awaiting the answer that would never come, Lainey gently guided the nylon bristles through the long strands of dull, limp hair.

As always, Lainey chatted as she worked, relaying tidbits of news from Scarlet in the vain hope that some name would jog a memory, a cohesive thought. The doctors had repeatedly told her that would never happen. She refused to believe them. After all, those same doctors couldn't state with any degree of certainty what had originally compelled MaryBeth to withdraw into a world of her own making. They had theories, of course, some kind of inane conjuncture about suppressed childhood trauma or subliminal deniability, whatever that meant. Eventually Lainey had come to her own conclusion, one that would haunt and alter the entire course of her adult life: that if the curse was genetic, her own future could be reflected in her mother's empty eyes.

That was the terror Lainey lived with, the horrifying fear that someday she, too, might suddenly go mad, emotionally scarring her children and driving her husband into the arms of another. Because she could never allow that to happen, she'd long ago decided that she would never marry, never have a family of her own.

The decision had been wrenched from anguish, but Lainey had learned to accept it. Or at least she'd thought she had. Now that Clay Cooper had returned to her life, this decision threatened to rip her heart out.

Clay held the cellular phone with his chin and poured another cup of coffee, his third in the past hour. "You found nothing, not even a traffic ticket?"

"MaryBeth Sheridan never had a driver's license, at least, not under that name" came the crackling reply. "So far her social security number is a big zipperoo. No payroll, bank or credit records for the past twenty years. She's crafty, that one."

"Damn." Clay shifted the telephone to his left hand and carried his coffee to the table. The investigator on the other end of the line was one of the best in the business. Clay had found his information to be accurate, well documented and an invaluable research tool for several past projects. "What about income tax?"

"Haven't checked government records yet. I'll start Monday, but it'll be slow going."

"Why?"

"Because each government data base is like an island without a phone. Communication by boat only. Boats are slow, see? And sometimes the wind carries 'em off course. But no worries, mate. I've made the trip before." A crunch echoed into the line, as though he'd taken a bite of an apple or something equally crisp. When he spoke again, his voice was muffled. "Since it doesn't look like—" he paused to swallow "—Ms. Sheridan has ever held a job, not much chance of finding tax records, but I'll check, anyway." Another chomp was followed by noisy chewing sounds. "'Ere's al'ays 'elfare—"

"Excuse me?"

"Sorry, mate." Gulp. "In my line of work, you have to take your nourishment on the run. I was saying, there's always welfare records...financial aid, disability, social security, that kind of thing. Maybe our lady has been living off the state."

"Which state?"

"Well, you see, that's the thing." Crunch. "Coul' be any o'em."

Setting his cup on the table, Clay rubbed his forehead as the extent of the search finally sank in. "This will take weeks."

"Ummmph."

"What if she's using another name?" Clay asked when the chewing sounds had stopped.

There was a pause. "Could be a problem."

"You mean, we might never find her?"

"Distinct possibility, that. But let's not panic before the 'roos stampede... Oops. Got another call. Later, mate." The line clicked and went dead.

Sighing, Clay flipped off the phone and dropped it on a stack of file folders. He sat at the table, rocked the chair back until it was balancing on two legs and stared into space. That had not been the news he'd wanted to hear. After talking to Emma Gebloski, Clay was more convinced than ever that MaryBeth Sheridan was the key to what had happened the night her husband died. Emma had heard a woman's scream. That woman could only have been MaryBeth.

MaryBeth Sheridan had seen something, dammit, something that police and prosecutors had swept under the rug. And who had the power and money to have mobilized such a conspiracy and silence tongues in a town where loose lips were a badge of honor? There was only one person in Scarlet with that kind of authority—Lloyd Reeves.

Rocking forward until all four chair legs hugged the floor, Clay took a sip of coffee. Emma had described a large dark car. Reeves had always driven black Continentals, probably because the big Lincolns resembled limousines and represented an irresistible status symbol. There had been three men in the car. Reeves and who else?

Frustrated, Clay balanced the mug on his knee. He was grasping at straws. At any given time in the past two decades, there'd probably been hundreds of big dark cars within cruising distance of Scarlet. But a woman's scream...that *had* to have been MaryBeth Sheridan.

Clay closed his eyes and constructed a scenario in his mind. According to both the original and doctored versions of the police report, MaryBeth had been upstairs asleep. She'd been awakened by a shot and come downstairs to find her husband's dead body on the lawn. What if she had been awakened before the shot by, say, loud voices? What if she'd looked out the upstairs window and seen her husband's attackers? What if—?

Clay's blood suddenly ran cold. If MaryBeth had indeed witnessed her husband's murder, her abrupt disappearance might not have been voluntary. After all, a dead woman can't testify.

That would certainly explain Marybeth's absence from the trial, her abandonment of her child and why a top-notch investigator hadn't turned a clue as to her whereabouts for the past twenty years. It would also destroy Clay's best hope of uncovering the truth of what had happened that night.

With a groan of despair, he stood and paced the small room. The answer to one set of questions simply opened up an entire set of new ones. If MaryBeth was dead, did Lainey know? Did McFerson? Both of them had been evasive to the point of paranoia each time the woman's name was mentioned.

But Lainey had been so young then, it was more logical that she, too, had been deceived and devastated by what she must surely have perceived as deliberate abandonment. That would explain the horrible sadness that crept into Lainey's eyes whenever her mother was mentioned.

Clay concluded that if MaryBeth had indeed been killed, Lainey didn't know it. But, McFerson . . . that was another story. Pulling information about MaryBeth Sheridan from that tight-lipped newsman was like yanking elephant teeth with tweezers. The thought occurred to Clay that if McFerson knew what had happened to MaryBeth Sheridan, he might also have been involved. And if the woman was dead, that meant that McFerson—

Clay's teeth vibrated at the thought. Rationally, the frightening theory made perfect sense, but his gut didn't buy it. There was something missing, a vital clue that hadn't been uncovered yet. So Clay was back where he'd started with nothing to go on except supposition and suspicion.

Well, not exactly where he'd started. His participation in this project had never been that of a neutral observer—it was difficult to remain impartial where one's family was concerned—but he'd come to Scarlet with a blank sheet and a determination to expose the bitter truth regardless of consequence. Now he wasn't sure he could do that, not if it caused more pain for Lainey. She meant too much to him. He cared so deeply that even the silent acknowledgment of such resonant feelings was unsettling.

He glanced at his watch. Ten-thirty. Damn. He should have known Hallie wouldn't give Lainey the message. Or maybe she had. Maybe Lainey hadn't called because she didn't want to talk to Clay. Worse, maybe she hadn't even gotten home yet. Maybe she'd had an accident. The possibility made his heart pound with fear.

Wiping both hands over his damp face, he stood there trembling, wondering how he could live if anything had happened to Lainey. He'd never be able to bear the guilt, the unending sorrow of losing her. Although Clay knew that Lainey Sheridan had become the most important person in his world, it never occurred to him that he might be falling in love with her.

It was past midnight. Lainey sat in the cushioned window seat gazing out her bedroom window. By the time she'd returned from the hospital, her aunt and uncle had been asleep. She'd crept upstairs, bone tired, and quietly dressed for bed. That had been two hours ago. Now every muscle in her body ached, but she was afraid to close her eyes, afraid the dream would return. There was a message in that dream, something more frightening than the nightmare itself. What was her mind trying to tell her?

The silent question was met by a stabbing pain in her temple. *Don't think about it,* she told herself. *If you don't think about it, the pain will go away.* Holding her pounding skull between her palms, she concentrated on mundane matters—the pot roast for tomorrow's supper, the floor that had to be scoured, the huge pile of linens waiting to be washed. After a moment the throbbing eased.

Sighing, Lainey returned her gaze to the window. The word "coward" popped into her mind. What would happen, she wondered, if she ignored the ache and forced her reluctant mind to reveal its painful secret? Perhaps there was no secret at all; perhaps there was nothing except fear, the terror of things hidden in blackness. After all, a dark room is filled with frightening shapes, eerie imaginings. One only has to turn on a lamp and the room becomes a warm, inviting retreat.

Light dispels shadows—in a room, in a mind.

As Lainey contemplated the obscure theory, she absently glanced toward the ash tree in the front yard that had always reminded her of the huge maple at her parents' home. Moonlight was filtering through the swaying ash leaves, casting dappled shadows on the ground. The effect was familiar, oddly perturbing. Lainey remembered that the moon had been particularly bright the night her father had died. Her head started to ache.

Squinting through the pain, she stared out at silver dollars of moonlight dancing on the lawn. An image formed in her mind. She recalled that the policeman had carried her outside, and assumed that must have been when she'd noticed the bright moon. Lainey also remembered seeing neighbors clustered on the sidewalk; police cars lined the curb with flashing red lights that made everyone look strangely devilish.

As the long-ago scene focused in her memory, the pain in her head grew more intense.

...She was at the circus. Polka-dotted clown legs surrounded a sleeping figure. She hugged her kitten and started to cry. The ballooned pants suddenly transformed into trousers spattered with blood. And the sleeping figure had her father's face...

Lainey gasped. "No," she whispered to the night. The whisper turned into a moan, the moan into a scream. Pressing a knuckle to her lips, she stood and stumbled back from the window, crying out again and again as the memories flooded her terrified mind.

"Lainey!"

Someone opened her bedroom door.

"Good Lord, girl! What'n hell is wrong with you?" Was that her uncle's voice?

Strong male fingers bit into her upper arms, holding her upright. "Are you sick? Answer me!"

Aunt Hallie appeared in the doorway. "What is it? What's wrong with her?"

Russ growled over his shoulder. "Damned if I know. She won't talk."

Gesturing feebly, Lainey fought to find her voice. "I...remember." She limply pushed against her uncle's chest. When he released her, she grabbed the footboard to steady herself and spoke again, more clearly this time. "I *remember.*"

Hallie limped into the room. "Remember what, child?"

"It wasn't a dream," Lainey murmured. "The polka-dot clowns... the sleeping man... it was real."

In a halting voice she related details of the nightmare that had haunted her for years. When Russ and Hallie exchanged a telling look, Lainey was frantic to make them understand the significance of what she'd remembered.

"Don't you understand? I was in the yard when the men came for my father." She clutched her uncle's sleeve. "I saw it! I saw what happened—"

Russ whirled on her, shaking his finger in her face. "You saw nothing, hear? Nothing!"

Lainey blinked in confusion. "But I did. I'd sneaked outside to get my kitten and saw men in the front yard. Daddy was talking to them—"

"Who were they?" Russ demanded furiously. "Did you see faces?"

"Ah..." She closed her eyes and massaged her aching temples. "Their faces were shadowed." Dappled shadows, from moonlight filtering through the giant maple tree. "One had his back to me. One was on the porch with Daddy. The other...the other..." God, her head hurt. "I can't see them," she said finally. "I just can't see them."

"You can't see them because they were never there. *It didn't happen.*" Russ grabbed Lainey's shoulders and roughly shook her. "It was a dream, that's all, a damned stupid dream. Don't you go telling anybody about such foolishness, hear me? Not a living soul."

Stunned, Lainey looked toward her aunt. "But why?"

Hallie's face was ashen. "You know why, child."

An icy terror gripped her spine. "My... mother?"

Hallie nodded grimly. "MaryBeth was always imagining things, foolish things like this dream of yours. You start spouting such stuff and nonsense, no telling what people will think."

"I'll tell you what they'll think," Russ interjected. "Like mother, like daughter, that's what."

Though the dire statement played on her worst fears, Lainey was nonetheless aware that neither her aunt nor uncle were making sense. "But nobody even knows about Mother."

Hallie slid an anxious glance toward her husband. "Broddie knows... and Lloyd Reeves."

Lainey dismissed that as irrelevant. "If they were going to blab it around, they would have done it years ago. Besides, Broddie would never do anything to hurt me, and Mr. Reeves certainly doesn't want to advertise that a blood cousin has, uh, that kind of problem."

A heavy silence fell over the room. After several long moments, Russ gave Lainey a glacial stare. "Lloyd and Broddie kept quiet for your sake. If it happens again, won't much matter who knows."

"If *what* happens again?" The room began to spin as her uncle's meaning became clear. If Lainey suffered her mother's fate, there'd be no reason to keep MaryBeth's secret. Lainey clutched the spindle at the foot of her bed and stiffened her shoulders. "I'm not crazy. I know what I saw."

"That's what your ma used to say." Russ regarded her sadly, then left the room, shaking his head. After casting an imploring glance at her niece, Hallie followed.

When Lainey's legs stopped shaking, she crossed the room and closed her bedroom door. The cruel reminder that she could spend the last part of her own life locked in a dreary institution had done its job; she began to doubt herself.

Perhaps her aunt and uncle were right. For years Lainey had been under siege. The dream had been her enemy. Perhaps that enemy had finally won. Perhaps her benumbed brain had already traded reality for the nonsensical ramblings of a deteriorating mind. Perhaps she was already insane.

And perhaps Broddie really did see leprechauns at the bottom of a whiskey bottle.

With a disgusted sigh, Lainey rubbed her eyes and realized that tonight hadn't been the first time Russ and Hallie had pulled out the do-what-we-say-or-end-up-like-your-mother routine. They had, in fact, used that intimidation tactic frequently over the years, turning her legitimate concern into an obsessive, consuming terror.

In the past she'd assumed that they were genuinely grieved about her future and, despite heavy-handed methods, had her best interest at heart. Now she wasn't inclined to be so magnanimous. There was something in their eyes tonight, a veiled threat that had been more frightening than words. When Russ had asked if she'd seen faces, his eyes hadn't reflected skepticism. They'd reflected terror.

Although Lainey briefly wondered if the Clemmonses knew more about her father's death than they'd been willing to admit, she quickly dismissed the notion. Reading sinister intent into every little thing really *would* be crazy. Besides, she had enough trouble accepting the facts that she now knew to be true, facts that were as terrifying as the nightmare had been.

Because Lainey *had* been outside the night the men drove up. And she'd watched her father die.

"Did I wake you?" Lainey asked as Clay opened the cabin door.

An odd relief softened his handsome features. "No. I've been up for a couple of hours."

She fidgeted with her purse strap. "It's Sunday. I thought you might want to sleep in."

"I haven't slept much lately." Standing back to let her enter, he mussed his hair with his fingers. "I've been worried about you. Didn't you get my message?"

"Message?"

He sighed. "I should have known she wouldn't tell you."

"Who?" Lainey dropped her purse on the sofa and shimmied out of her wool church coat. "Tell me what?"

"Your aunt." He took her jacket and draped it neatly over a chair. "I stopped by last night. You weren't home, so I gave your aunt my cell-phone number and asked her to have you call me."

"I got home late. Aunt Hallie was already in bed—" She blinked as the impact of what he'd done hit home. "You went to the house?" When he nodded, Lainey stared dumbly for a moment, unable to believe that he'd taken such a risk. "Good grief, what if you'd been seen? Someone could have followed you back here and . . . and . . ."

"And what?" His rakish grin melted her heart. "What would they do, stone me with pinecones? Throw me in the lake? Let the air out of my tires?"

"Why are you being so flippant? They could do a lot worse and you know it."

"It's been a long time since anyone worried about me. I like it." Still smiling, he crossed the room and reached for the coffeepot. "One sugar, no cream, right?"

"Um? Oh. Right." Lainey wondered why she'd never noticed what a sexy walk he had, how his tight hips rotated with every forceful step. Clay usually wore tailored slacks, pleated, loose, very fashionable. This morning, however, he was wearing jeans tight enough to be dangerous and a cotton knit body shirt that looked as if it had been painted on. The effect was unsettling. She hadn't realized that his normal business attire of crisp dress shirts and tasteful ties concealed a body to die for, with sculpted pecs and sinewy biceps that any athlete would have been proud to display. And displayed they were, an enticing exhibition of flexing masculinity that made her pulse race and her heart pound.

Holding two cups of coffee, Clay turned and Lainey quickly looked away, hoping he hadn't noticed that she'd been brazenly gaping his body. She absently thumbed a few loose papers spread over the table and was excruciatingly aware that he'd moved to within touching distance.

He held out a steaming mug. "Here you go."

"Hmm?" She glanced up casually, as though she'd just noticed he was standing there. "Oh. Thanks."

"So you got home late?"

She offered a noncommittal shrug and sipped her coffee, hoping he wouldn't quiz her on where she'd been.

He regarded her for a long moment. "I guess it's none of my business where you were."

"I guess it isn't." She avoided his gaze, angry with herself for having issued such a sharp retort when his only crime was being concerned. "I had some shopping to do," she added, hoping the half-truth would ease the sting of rudeness. "What did you want to talk about last night?"

He sighed. "I wanted to apologize for upsetting you."

For a moment she wasn't certain what he meant. Then she remembered how she'd fled in anger after being pressed by questions about her mother. "There's no need to apologize. I shouldn't have stomped off like that. It was inconsiderate of me."

"It was my fault. Sometimes I get pushy..." He studied the floor, as though contemplating something profound. Finally he spoke quietly, choosing his words with great care. "I should have been more sensitive to your feelings. I promise not to mention, uh, that subject again."

Both understood that he was referring to the subject of MaryBeth Sheridan.

Although relieved that Clay had apparently given up the search for her mother, Lainey couldn't shake off a disquieting guilt at having deliberately withheld the truth. But she had no choice. Long before Lainey had been old enough to understand what insanity meant, the family had taken extraordinary steps to safeguard her mother's shameful secret, even going so far as having MaryBeth admitted to the hospital under a false name.

Over the years Lainey had been privy to all manner of covert activities, including furtive financial arrangements so that her mother's share of *Banner* proceeds was laundered like drug money, then shipped to the overseas account used to pay MaryBeth's hospital bills. The lies and deception were all for Lainey's sake, or so she'd been repeatedly told.

As a child, she'd been subjected to Aunt Hallie's grim warnings of the terrible things that would happen if anyone found out about her mother. At ten, Lainey insisted on seeing MaryBeth for the first time. Hallie and Russ had been dead set against the idea. There had been a terrible row.

Finally Broddie had convinced the Clemmonses that she had a right to know her mother, regardless of the circumstance. For the next six years Broddie had spent most of his Saturdays chauffeuring Lainey to Greenville. After that, she'd been old enough to drive herself and rarely missed a week.

Sometimes the visits were disheartening—sometimes frightening. That didn't matter. Lainey loved her mother. Nothing would ever change that.

"Are you all right?" Clay asked suddenly.

Blinking, Lainey glanced around and realized that she'd been lost in thought. "I'm fine."

"You seemed to be a million miles away. What were you thinking about?"

"I was hoping you wouldn't go into town again." More lies. She took a sip of cool coffee to compose herself, then added, "It's too dangerous. There are people out there who would do anything to stop you from finding the truth about my father's murder."

Clay set his cup down. "What people?"

Shadowed people. Faceless men. She turned away. "I don't know."

He came up behind her, so close his body heat made her tremble. "Does this mean that you now believe there's an unrevealed truth to be found?"

She clutched the mug with both hands to quell her trembling fingers. "Yes."

A soothing warmth calmed her as he stroked her shoulders. "What changed your mind?" When she didn't respond, he turned her gently around and tipped her chin up. His eyes searched hers. "You've been crying. Why? What is it, Lainey? Please, tell me what's wrong?"

With fresh tears seeping over her lashes, she met his gaze and for once told him the truth. "Emma was right. Three men came to our house that night."

Clay's fingers tightened around her upper arms. "How do you know?"

"Because I was there," she whispered. "Oh God, Clay. I saw who killed my father."

Chapter 12

Clay looked like he'd been struck. "What . . . are you saying?

A nebulous flood of words rushed out. "I've been having this dream about polka-dot clowns, only it wasn't a dream at all . . . and last night I remembered the trousers and the blood and the shadows and . . . and . . ."

"Shh." Clay embraced her gently. "Slow down. We've got all the time in the world."

She took a shuddering breath, then nuzzled against his warm chest. "I must sound like a basket case."

"You sound upset and apparently for good reason." He guided her to the sofa. "Sit down, take a deep breath . . . that's good." He settled beside her and took her hand. "Now let's start from the beginning. On the night your father died, what's the very first thing you remember?"

Closing her eyes, Lainey forced her mind back in time and heard a voice that sounded much like her own. "Daddy gave me a cookie. It was bedtime, but I wasn't sleepy, so Daddy let me have a snack."

"Then what happened?" Clay asked gently.

Lainey remembered taking her father's hand as he'd led her into the warm kitchen. It smelled of lemon and fresh bread.

She'd climbed into a chair so big her feet couldn't touch the floor and giggled happily as Daddy took a fat oatmeal cookie from the bumblebee jar.

He put the cookie on a china plate and poured a tall glass of milk. "Here you go, Peaches. Can't have that little tummy growling all night, can we?"

"Uh-uh." Using both hands, she picked up the cookie, nibbled the edge, then held it out. "Want a bite?"

Daddy smiled and sat across the table from her. "No, that's all for you."

A ball of black fur suddenly sprang into Lainey's lap. "Bad kitty," she scolded, struggling to hold her treat away from the curious animal. Thwarted, the kitten jumped to the table and tried to push its head into the milk glass. "Daddy!" Lainey wailed.

Daddy slid a gentle hand under the kitten and lifted it up so they were face to furry face. "Where are your manners, Fuzz? You're supposed to ask permission before helping yourself."

Fuzz meowed. Lainey giggled.

"That's better," he said, winking at his tickled daughter. "And because you've been such a polite kitty, you can have your very own saucer of milk on the back porch."

Lainey crunched her cookie while Daddy fixed Fuzz a midnight snack and carried the kitten outside. "Can Fuzz sleep with me tonight?" she asked as soon as he'd returned to the kitchen.

"You know how your mommy feels about that."

"I'll close my door so he can't get out and scare Mommy like he did the last time. He'll be real quiet."

Bending close, Daddy brushed crumbs from Lainey's little mouth, then kissed her cheek and lifted her up into his strong arms. "Not tonight, Peaches. Mommy's not feeling well."

Lainey's lip quivered. "Is she bad sick?"

"Just a little headache." He reassured her with a hug. "Let's go kiss Mommy good-night, okay?"

"Okay." She wound her arms around Daddy's neck as he carried her upstairs and tapped on Mommy's door. A tired voice said to come in. They did.

Mommy was in bed reading a magazine. She smiled when she saw them. "Is that a new nightie?"

"Uh-huh. Daddy bought it for me." Lainey proudly smoothed the pleated lace bodice. "It's your favorite color."

Mommy absently touched her own satin gown, which was the same brilliant aqua as her daughter's. "Why, so it is. I declare, you look just like a little angel," she murmured, turning her cheek for her daughter's kiss. "Good night, dear."

"G'night, Mommy." Lainey wanted to hug her so bad it hurt, but she knew Mommy didn't like hugs, probably because she was so fragile. Lainey wasn't sure what "fragile" meant but figured it must have had something to do with being sad all the time.

Daddy quietly closed Mommy's door, carried Lainey into her own room and tucked her into a squishy soft bed. "Sleep tight, Precious."

"Daddy..."

He paused in the doorway.

"I think I'm still hungry."

He smiled tolerantly. "Are you really hungry?"

"Maybe."

She sighed, not understanding the emptiness inside her yet knowing that food wouldn't make it go away. "I guess I can wait till breakfast."

Daddy blew her a kiss. Lainey caught it. Daddy closed the door. Lainey put Daddy's kiss under the pillow and scrunched beneath the covers. She couldn't sleep. The moon was too bright. Slipping out of bed, she went to the window and looked down into the yard. A shadow scurried across the lawn, disappearing into the bushes by the front porch.

"Fuzz," she whispered. "Here, Fuzz." As long as the kitten came into her room all by himself, Lainey figured she wasn't really disobeying. Of course, her room *was* on the second floor and Fuzz *was* still a baby. She finally decided that since it wasn't his fault he was so little, it shouldn't count if she gave him just a tiny bit of help.

Sneaking into the dim hallway, Lainey tiptoed downstairs. Daddy was in the living room watching television. She moved ever so quietly into the kitchen and slowly opened the back door. The night air was colder than she'd expected. She shivered and would have retreated, except she wanted her kitten so bad. Fuzz liked to be hugged. He never turned his head when Lainey kissed him. Whenever she snuggled with Fuzz, she felt all toasty inside and the emptiness went away.

So she carefully shut the kitchen door and went out into the yard.

Clay's voice floated into the memory. "What did you do then, Lainey?"

She licked her lips. "I went to the bushes by the front porch. But I couldn't see Fuzz because he was black and it was nighttime."

"Was the porch light on?"

"No."

"Did you find your kitten?"

"Yes," she said dully. "I crawled into the bushes on my hands and knees, whispering his name. He came to me." When Clay gently brushed his thumb across her cheek, she realized that she was crying. Her throat felt full, swollen. It was difficult to talk. "There . . . were headlights."

"A car pulled in front of your house?"

"Yes."

"What did the car look like?"

"I couldn't see it. The bushes were in the way and the maple tree blocked any view of the curb." Turning her head, Lainey discreetly sniffed and wiped her face with the back of her hand. She fumbled in her purse, which was on the floor beside the sofa, and pulled out a small pack of tissues. "The headlights went off. I heard car doors slam—"

"How many doors?"

"I don't remember." She blotted her eyes. "I heard voices, though. Men's voices." With quiet cry of despair, she shook her head, unable to go on.

Clay reached out and gently cupped the back of her neck. "Take your time," he murmured, guiding her head to his shoulder.

She rolled her face into his warmth, absorbing his strength, his compassion. Clay embraced her gently, firmly, holding her close to his heart. It had been so long since she'd felt this safe. He was brushing the hair from her face with soothing whispers that made her feel as though nothing in the world would ever hurt her again.

"Let's stop for a while," he said finally.

Lainey swallowed hard. "No."

"This is too difficult for you."

With some effort, she peeled herself from his chest and fought for composure. "I'll be all right. We both need for me to do this."

He touched her face, urging her to look at him as he searched her eyes and apparently found the inner strength he sought. "All right. You were in the bushes and you heard men's voices."

A chill shook her to the bone. She hugged herself, rubbing her arms to warm them. "The men came around the tree into the yard. They frightened me."

"Why?"

"Because they were speckled." Frustrated, she rubbed her eyes and tried to clarify the memory. "Moonlight was filtered by the maple tree," she said finally. "When the men came into our yard, they looked all blotchy, like some kind of alien light creatures were crawling all over them."

"Did you see their faces?"

"Yes." She shrugged apologetically. "But all I remember are distorted shadows and eerie patches of light." Lainey looked up apprehensively, expecting Clay to be disappointed by the fact that she hadn't recognized the men. All she saw was an encouraging smile.

He squeezed her hand. "What did the men do?"

Closing her eyes, she bit her lip and concentrated on the dark image in her mind. "One went to the front porch and rang the doorbell. The porch light went on. Daddy opened the door."

As Lainey spoke, she tightened her lids to keep the tears from squeezing through as she remembered her father's voice, low and angry. He'd come out, closing the door behind him. The man on the porch had been angry, too. Their voices rose into shouts. She couldn't remember what was said, but she remembered feeling that her daddy was being threatened. There were bad words, cuss words that Lainey couldn't repeat. The man on the porch hit her father, hit him so hard that he stumbled and fell down the steps onto the front lawn. The other two men grabbed him....

"They held my father while the third man beat him," Lainey whispered. There'd been a swish of blue satin when she'd turned away and cowered in the bushes. "One of the voices became so shrill and piercing...I couldn't stand it. I buried my face in my kitten's fur and pulled my nightie up over my head, thinking if I couldn't see what was happening, then it wouldn't be real." Something soft and absorbent touched Lainey's cheek. She realized that Clay was using a fresh tissue to dry her face. "I wanted to cover my ears, too, but I didn't have enough hands."

"What did you hear?"

"That shrill voice. The sound of blows, like a pillow being punched. Then—" she winced "—a sharp noise. The air smelled funny. I thought one of the men had thrown a firecracker, so I looked up—" Her voice cracked like a shattered mirror. A metallic taste flooded her mouth. She felt faint, nauseated.

Clay massaged the back of her neck and waited silently.

Finally she shuddered so hard her teeth rattled. "Daddy was on the ground," she whispered. "The men were standing around him with their trousers spotted with blood. Someone was screaming and screaming and—"

"Shh." Clay gathered her into his arms, rocking her gently. "It's all right, honey. Everything's going to be all right."

"T-they killed him, Clay." Speaking brokenly between sobs, Lainey tangled her fingers in his stretchy T-shirt and let all the pain, all the suppressed anguish, rush out. "They m-murdered my father and—" she shuddered violently "—and I just r-ran away."

Clay's lips brushed her damp forehead. "You were just a little girl, honey. There was nothing you could do."

"But I *ran.*" She feebly swatted his chest with her fist. "I crawled out of the bushes and ran back into the kitchen and I—I ran upstairs to my room and pulled the covers over my head—"

Clay gently captured her flailing hand, holding it against his heart while violent sobs racked her slender body. He ached for her, for the years of torment she'd endured, suppressing memories too gruesome to accept. So much pain, so much anguish. Dear God, how could something so horrible have happened to someone so dear, so very precious?

As he stroked her gently, massaging her quaking shoulders, brushing away the damp strands of hair clinging to her wet face, something deep inside Clay cracked. Nothing mattered anymore—not vengeance, not justice, nothing except this woman, this cherished soul who had suffered so much.

Yet he felt so damnably helpless, as helpless as that little girl who'd watched her father die and could do nothing to stop it.

So he gave what he had—his body, his soul, his heart—and held her until the racking sobs had subsided.

"Are you feeling better?"

"Yes, thank you." Lainey took the mug of fresh coffee Clay offered with a grateful, slightly tenuous smile. She balanced the mug on one knee and self-consciously touched her puffy eyes. "I must look a sight."

Clay sat beside her on the sofa. "Just awful," he teased. "Like a hung-over raccoon."

"Oh, Lord. My mascara." Ducking her head, she reached into her purse and pulled out a small mirror.

Clay covered the mirror with his hand. "Trust me. You don't want to know."

She slid him an apprehensive glance. "That bad?"

"Worse." He smoothed her bangs away from her forehead and gently kissed the soft curve between her brows. "But don't worry about the mascara. It slid off your chin half an hour ago."

She laughed softly. "Is that supposed to make me feel better?"

"Does it?"

"Yes."

"Then that's what it was supposed to do."

Still smiling, she pulled one knee onto the sofa, modestly smoothing her skirt over her bare thigh as she twisted sideways to face him. She took a sip of coffee, then peered over the rim of the mug. "You really are quite extraordinary."

The statement took him by surprise, as did the admiration he saw in her shining eyes. He felt worthy of neither and spoke more gruffly than he'd intended. "I'm nothing special."

She tilted her head quizzically. "Modest, too. I like that in a man."

Avoiding her gaze, he stared across the cabin as though studying the breakfast dishes piled beside the sink. "I'm not being modest, Lainey. I'm being realistic. I know who I am and I know where I came from."

"What is that supposed to mean?" As she bent to set her mug on the coffee table, the scooped neckline of her cream-colored blouse drooped just enough to allow an enticing glimpse of cleavage. "That a poor boy from the wrong side of the tracks can't really rise above the mediocrity of his youth? Your success has already proven the fallacy of that theory."

"Success is a rather superficial measure of worth, don't you think?" With some effort, he forced his gaze away from the tantalizing view until she straightened and leaned one shoulder against the sofa cushions.

Seeming oblivious to the effect she was having on him, Lainey regarded him with concern. "Is that really how you measure yourself, Clay?"

"No, and neither should you." He raked his fingers through his hair. "That's the point, Lainey. I could earn a million dollars and have my name peppered all over the best-seller lists, but it wouldn't change who I am."

She regarded him cautiously. "And who are you?"

"I'm Ben Cooper's son," he snapped, regretting his harsh tone yet unable to control the seething anger bubbling up from inside. "All my life I've been told and I've been shown that violence is normal, that's it's okay to hit and to hurt and to kill if that's what it takes. That kind of environment creates monsters, people without conscience or compassion. That kind of environment created *me.*"

"You can't honestly believe that." Lainey pressed a trembling hand to her throat. "You're not a monster. I've never known a more compassionate man, a man of greater honor."

"How do you know what kind of man I am? You don't know what's buried inside me, what I might someday become." Unable to bear the shock in her eyes, Clay stood quickly, crossed the room and stared sightlessly out the window. Folding his arms, he shook his head, struggling to explain something he feared but didn't fully understand. "I'm part of him," he said finally. "His blood runs in my veins. That... scares me."

Clay leaned against the windowsill and listened to the silence. He had finally done it, pushed Lainey away with a brutal reminder of who he was and where he'd come from. Or was it himself he was reminding? It didn't matter. Returning to Scarlet had brought back all the old feelings—the pain of rejection, the humiliation of being feared and reviled—emotions buried but not forgotten.

An unexpected touch startled him, a sweet hand resting on his taut forearm. He looked down, mesmerized by the possessive curve of her slender fingers, the sensual contrast between softness and strength. Her hand was delicate, porcelain pale, with curved nails tinted with subtle pearlescense. So gentle, so infinitely kind, her silky fingertips grazed the corded muscles from shoulder to elbow, elbow to wrist. That the airy touch made him tremble seemed as ludicrous as a fluttering butterfly dislodging a granite perch; yet he *was* trembling. Her fragrance enveloped him. Her nearness caused an odd tightness in his chest.

Her soft whisper sent warm ripples down his spine. "You've been through so much. I didn't realize."

Was that pity in her voice? His heart sank. He forced a stiff smile. "Didn't realize that I was an incorrigible whiner?"

As she studied his strained expression, Clay hoped she'd go along with his feeble attempt to lighten the mood. She didn't. "You're a lot of things, Clay Cooper, but a whiner isn't one of them."

"How about a self-indulgent sniveler?"

She finally smiled and affectionately rubbed his arm, generating so much heat he thought his skin might steam. "How about a courageous man who beat the odds by rising above the poverty and violence of his childhood?"

Embarrassed by the unexpected praise, Clay winced. "That sounds like a plot summary."

"You're right. Maybe your next project should be an autobiography." Her smile faded. "I'm serious, Clay. You should be proud of yourself and what you've accomplished."

"I suppose that I am, in a way. It's just that—" He clamped his lips together and shook his head.

She encouraged him softly. "What is it, Clay? Why don't you feel that you deserve joy in your life?"

Stunned that she'd verbalized so simply what had always been a vague, melancholy shadow, Clay couldn't respond. He searched her perceptive eyes, wondering how a woman so young could be so wise until he remembered what she'd endured, the hardships that had molded her life. And he was ashamed of the bitterness in his heart, the anger that he'd been too puerile to release. "I keep wondering how many lives could have been better if I'd only done something to change things."

"What could you have done?"

"That's the problem. I don't know."

She considered that. "I have to admit that after reading Catherine's journal, I realized that her life—and yours—had been more difficult than I could ever have imagined. She wrote that your father was an unhappy and volatile man, yet she seemed to pity him more often than she feared him. And I never felt that she'd doubted his love. In fact, I recall several passages where she described him quite kindly."

"That's the insidious thing," Clay said. "All people are a mixture of good and evil, kindness and cruelty. Only the proportions are different. Circumstance tips the balance between what we are and what we show the world. It's easy to be generous when there's enough to go around. Hardship is the mirror of the soul."

Tipping her head, she regarded him curiously. "That's very profound," she murmured. "Unfortunately, I don't have a clue what it means."

Clay chuckled softly. "Haven't you heard? Writers are a pompous lot. We enjoy being obtuse."

"Ah. Well, you're quite good at it."

"I've had a plenty of practice." Because he couldn't help himself, he brushed his thumb over her satiny cheek. Her eyes widened, but she didn't flinch or pull away. He traced a gentle line along her throat, then allowed his hand to settle at the curve of her shoulder, extending his thumb just far enough to touch smooth skin beyond the fabric's edge. "What I meant was that there was a time when my father tried to be the man society expected. When life soured, the metamorphosis began. He became hard and brutal, a man without conscience. Even so, he had several faces—the one he showed to my mother, the one he showed to me and the one he showed to rest of the world."

"He could have made different choices."

"Perhaps."

"*You* have made different choices."

"The circumstances have been different for me. Deep down, I know that if my family were starving, I could steal. If they were in danger, I could kill. So how am I any better than he was?"

"Did your father steal because his family was starving?"

A tiny glimmer of comprehension glowed in the back of his mind. The fact was that Ben Cooper had been a thief because stealing was easier than working and because of insatiable greed. And there was another, more chilling reason. "I think that he got some kind of perverse thrill from feeling more powerful than his victim."

Her dark eyes searched his with a compassion that warmed his marrow. She laid a sweet hand against his chest and whispered, "In here, in the most deepest corner of your heart, do you hide a secret wish to hurt and humiliate and overpower?" She responded to his horrified expression with a knowing smile. "No, of course you don't, because you are a good and decent man. You are not now, and you never have been—never could be—like your father."

There was admiration in her eyes, an unconditional acceptance so intense that he was touched to the core. "You almost make me believe that."

"Believe it, Clay, believe it because it's true."

He covered her slender hand with his palm, pressing her even closer to his heart. Perhaps it was the respect shining in her eyes that affected him so deeply. Perhaps it was the fullness swelling in his chest, a unique sense of being special, at least to her. Whatever the reasons, she was at that moment the most beautiful woman he'd ever seen. There was an aura about her, a shimmering spirit of goodness and purity that took his breath away. She was so close that her light enveloped him, too, surrounding him, penetrating the deepest caverns of his soul until he actually believed that he was what she saw, a man of tender strength and infinite love.

Lifting her hand, he brushed his lips across her fingertips then turned her wrist and kissed her smooth palm. "Do you believe in destiny?" he whispered against her fragrant skin.

She trembled. "Yes."

"I never have." His lips slid to the translucent pulse point at her wrist. "Until now."

"And what do—" she gasped as his sensual exploration moved up her forearm "—you believe now?"

"I believe that the first time we saw each other, there was some kind of...I don't know...a connection, I guess." Suddenly embarrassed, he studied the tiny lines crisscrossing her palm. "I guess that sounds pretty hokey."

"Not to me. I felt it, too, you know."

Angling a quick glance at her face, he was relieved to find no trace of amusement in her solemn expression. "Did you?"

"Yes," she murmured. "I know we were both children, but to me, you seemed so big and so strong. Whenever I felt weak and lonely, I'd pretend that you were with me, as a friend and a protector. It made me feel safe."

"I'm glad."

She regarded him wistfully. "On some level I must have known that you were the only one who could stop the nightmare."

"I didn't stop it, Lainey. You did. You had the courage to accept what the dream was telling you . . . and to remember."

"I don't feel very courageous." She gazed down at her wrist, which was still nested in his palm. "But I don't need courage when I'm with you. You have enough for both of us."

"No." Because he couldn't help himself, he kissed a tiny crease above her brow. "Perhaps we feel strong because we're together."

"I like that idea," she whispered so softly he could barely hear. "Would . . . you do something for me?"

"Anything."

"Would you hold me?"

The breath caught in his throat. If he held her, if he took her in his arms, he wasn't certain he'd ever be able to let her go.

Misreading his hesitation, her eyes clouded with embarrassment, then were concealed by a curtain of black lashes as she lowered her gaze. "I'm sorry. That was...brazen of me."

"No," he whispered. "It was honest." He tipped up her chin. "Haven't you heard? Men love bold women."

She managed a smile. "Do they?"

"Oh, yes." He embraced her then, silently, warmly, and she melted into his arms like sweet chocolate. With a contented sigh, she hooked her arms around his back and nuzzled against his chest. One hand cradled her head while Clay laid his cheek against her soft hair, deeply inhaling the subtle fragrance of honeysuckle clinging to the shiny strands.

He rolled his fingertips across the malleable muscle between her shoulder blades, marveling at the contrast of rigid bone and buttery soft flesh hidden beneath the silky fabric. How like the woman herself, a steely core inside a deceptive veneer of delicacy. Simply holding her in his arms, embracing the enigma of her soft strength, made him feel mystically empowered. Complete. Content. Exquisitely alive.

Rubbing her cheek against his chest, she made a purring sound deep in her throat. "That day in the *Banner* newsroom, the first time I saw you all grown-up, I wondered what it would be like to be this close to you."

Clay smiled, recalling his own thoughts at that moment. "And I wondered if I'd ever be able to breathe again."

She twisted her head just enough to look up quizzically. "Were you ill?"

He laughed. If infatuation was an illness, then he'd been sick as a dog. "You were so beautiful you took my breath away."

Her lashes gave a demure flutter. "Flatterer."

"Truth is not flattery, Lainey. Don't you know how very beautiful you are?"

"I've never felt beautiful," she replied honestly. "Not many people are entranced by muddy brown eyes and hair that resembles a muskrat pelt. Besides, I'm too thin and my feet are too big. Aunt Hallie says I look like a broomstick on skis."

Clay's jaw clenched in anger, assuming that Hallie had been deliberately demeaning to serve her own selfish needs. After all, if Lainey realized how attractive she was to men, she might wind up married and the Clemmonses, God forbid, might actually have to take care of themselves. "Your aunt is wrong, Lainey. You're perfect, absolutely perfect."

She blinked. "I am?"

"Have you ever seen a broomstick shaped like this?" Clay slid his hands slowly down her rib cage until his fingers touched, then traced the narrow band of her skirt. "Your waist is so small I could span it with my hands. And the curve of your hips—" ignoring her tiny gasp, his knuckles brushed the sensual swell of warm flesh "—is enough to make a man dizzy."

As he spoke, he was entranced by the nervous dart of her tongue. The movement focused attention on her lips, which were tinted an inviting hue of palest pink. Her upper lip was slim, sharply arched like a traditional cupid's bow. But it was the lower lip that was most fascinating, overly full, exceptionally plush yet without the objectionable pout that made fashion models look like disagreeable morons.

As he scrutinized her features, she ducked her head shyly, pressing her curled hands against his chest. "You always know the right thing to say."

"It's the truth," he whispered. "At this very minute, I want to kiss you so badly it hurts."

That delicious pink tip slipped out to moisten her lips. "Then why don't you?"

He stiffened slightly, then flexed his fingers and raised his hands to frame her face. "Do you want me to?"

Her answer was to lift her mouth, lips parted in silent invitation. It was an invitation he was too weak to resist. He bent his head slowly, eyes focused on the gleaming prize. His trembling fingertips cradled her face as he tasted her gently at first, then took her mouth with a sudden fierceness that both shocked and shook him.

She responded eagerly, moaning when the kiss deepened and returning his bold entrance with a tentative caress so erotic his legs threatened to give way. Her fingers tangled in his shirt, twisting the stretchy fabric with talonlike intensity. Their mouths grappled, desperate for ever-increasing intimacy. Breath came in tortured gasps, his breath and hers, a shared sweetness from one to the other that left both shaken and wanting more.

Clay withdrew slightly, so their lips were almost but not quite touching and moved his hands down to cup her firm bottom. The heavy flesh quivered at his touch. Lashes fluttering, Lainey emitted a tiny cry, an erotic half moan that slid down his spine like white lightning. He wanted her. Dear God, he wanted her more than he wanted another day of life.

So he asked without words. When the answer he sought was reflected in her smoldering eyes, Clay lifted Lainey into his arms and carried her into the bedroom.

Broddie gulped the last drop of cold coffee and balanced the cup on the stack of soiled dishes clogging the kitchen sink. He gave the dirty mess a guilty look. In the eight years since his wife's death, the kitchen hadn't seen a clean day. He briefly wondered if Maddie was up there clucking and shaking her finger. Probably. Poor woman never did know when to give up on a lost cause. God, he missed her. The last years of her life had been nothing but grief—grief he had caused, along with the damnable whiskey that had left him less than a man.

Somber and sober, Broddie pulled a partially filled bottle from the bare cupboard. For years this had been his solace, a place to hide from his own failure. No more. No bloody more.

He uncapped the bottle and poured the contents over the dirty dishes. Grinning, he dropped the empty container into the trash, brushed his hands together and sauntered into the living room, whistling softly. He hoped his beloved Maddie had been watching the proud moment. It was for her he was doing this, and for Gerald. Broddie owed them for all the wasted years. He only hoped it wasn't too late to be making amends.

At the dining room table, he shuffled through a disheveled mass of papers and plucked out the one he sought. He shivered in excitement, rereading the fading form that held the key to what had happened to Batch #74-38692. "This is it, Gerald, m'lad. You never knew how close you were."

Grabbing his jacket from a carved wall peg, Broddie tucked the lab report in his shirt pocket and sauntered out the front door. He could hardly wait to show Clay what he'd found.

The day was a chiller, so Broddie paused to don his jacket before climbing into his blocky old sedan. He settled behind the wheel as the comfortable seat molded around his familiar form. After patting his shirt pocket to reassure himself that the vital form was still there, he flipped the ignition and smiled as the sturdy engine roared to life.

"Good ol' girl." He affectionately patted the aging Buick's dashboard. Folks at the newsroom were always chirping at Broddie to get rid of Big Bertha, but he wouldn't hear of it. Bertha had style and substance. Those flimsy, newfangled cars made a man feel like he was squeezed inside a roller skate.

After steering the big Buick away from the curb, Broddie drove through Scarlet's small business district, sparing ChemCorp a quick glance before turning up the winding road that led into the mountains. He briefly wondered if he should have let Clay know he was coming, then discarded the thought. Nothing the lad was doing could be half as important as what Broddie had in his pocket.

Feeling oddly buoyant, he whistled a happy folk tune from his childhood. Outside, rolling farmland evolved into a mountainous forest. When the road veered sharply, Broddie touched the brake. Nothing happened. Cursing under his breath, he twisted the steering wheel and frantically pumped the brake pedal. Halfway through the curve, his foot suddenly hit the floor. Tires squealed. The car fishtailed wildly. Broddie jerked the wheel. The car spun around and careened toward a steep ravine.

Covering his face, Broddie screamed his wife's name and plummeted into the abyss.

Chapter 13

With her heart pounding, Lainey locked her arms around Clay's neck and buried her face in the curve of his corded throat. He kicked the bedroom door open. She uttered a hushed gasp, tightened her grip and started to tremble.

This was what she'd wanted, what she'd craved since that day in the newsroom. Clay Cooper was her destiny, the man of her heart. Like their star-crossed parents, they could never have a future together, but they had this moment, a moment Lainey could cherish forever.

Yet she was afraid. Well, not afraid exactly, but definitely apprehensive. She wasn't very experienced at this sort of thing, after all. What if he was disappointed? What if she did something foolish, like giggle at an inopportune moment, or worse, burst into tears? She'd be mortified.

Lainey realized that they'd stopped moving and that Clay was lowering her legs to the floor. Squeezing her eyes shut, she silently begged her knees to remain rigid. Miraculously, they did. She swayed slightly but thankfully Clay's strong arms held her upright. A subtle shiver started at her nape and quivered a leisurely path to her toes. She wondered if he'd noticed.

His lips brushed her earlobe. "Are you cold?"

Her heart sank. He must think her painfully inept. "A little," she lied, not wanting him to know that she was ready to hyperventilate.

Clay kissed Lainey's forehead, then released her and squatted to ignite a small propane heater in the corner. Since he'd been holding her up, his sudden withdrawal was a jolt. She wobbled backward until her calves touched cotton batting, then she steadied herself on a loop of rolled steel at the foot of the cot. By the time Clay had straightened, she was stiff as a pole, clutching the stupid metal tube as though her life depended on it.

"That should take the chill off," he told her.

She stared dumbly at the orange glow spreading across the heater's woven wire face and issued a response that displayed her incredible intellectual prowess. "Uh-huh."

He nodded without comment. Shifting uncomfortably, he tucked the thumb of one hand through his belt loop and absently scratched the back of his neck with the other. He glanced uneasily around the sparse room. "Not exactly the Hilton, is it?"

"It's, uh..." She winced as the heated air dislodged a dust bunny. "Quaint."

Clay morosely watched the fat fuzzball rolling lazily across the floor. "At least the linens are clean."

"Very clean," she assured him quickly. "And white. Very white."

"They were stored in plastic."

"Yes, I remember."

"Of course. I forgot that you unpacked them." He looked pained.

"They were very clean," she repeated lamely, wondering if it were possible to actually die of embarrassment. This wasn't happening the way she had planned. Her glorious daydreams of this moment hadn't included a discussion of laundry and dust balls punctuated by awkward silence. She'd imagined a movie-type seduction, swept away by the throes of passion, and conversation had been limited to provocative moans and whimpers.

Because she didn't know what else to do, she slid a covert peek at Clay, hoping he'd give her a hint as to what was expected of her. To Lainey's surprise, he was studying the toe of his sneaker and appeared every bit as apprehensive as she was. His thick ebony hair was ruffled like an unmade bed, with untidy strands flopped endearingly across his forehead. Holding one hand on his trim hip and the other behind his neck,. he looked every bit of a man in turmoil—lips pursed, forehead creased, teeth clicking.

She cleared her throat.

He glanced up expectantly.

"I—I'm warmer now," she said.

He smiled stiffly. There was terror in his eyes. "Good."

Licking her lips, she took a deep breath and fanned her face with her hand. "Gosh. It's really getting hot, isn't it?"

His smile faded. "I'll turn off the heater."

"No! I mean, it's probably just this heavy blouse." She feebly touched the flimsy satin bodice and swallowed hard. "Maybe I should, you know, loosen it."

A luminous warmth softened his tense gaze. "May I help you?"

She exhaled all at once as her arms dropped limply to her side. "Yes, please."

He approached her hesitantly, stopping when their toes touched and their bodies were close enough to exchange heat. His fingertips grazed the back of her hands, then moved up to caress her wrists. She closed her eyes, overwhelmed by the sensuality of his delicate touch. The sweet exploration continued as his tender hands slowly moved to her elbows, her upper arms, then slid smoothly down to begin the seductive process all over again.

"Like silk," he murmured. "Your skin is so soft."

"It's my bath oil."

He dipped his head and brushed his lips at the curve of her throat. "Smells good."

"Thank you." She shivered, arching her neck to allow him greater access. "You smell good, too."

"I know. Piney and spicy."

She could literally feel his smile against her throat and was embarrassed by the reminder of a previous verbal blunder. Sighing, she decided that since the man was obviously aware that she didn't know what she was doing, she might as well confess. "I'm afraid that I'm not very experienced at this sort of thing."

"I didn't think you were." He lifted his head and regarded her kindly. "Since we're being honest, perhaps you'd forgive a blunt question."

She eyed him anxiously. "How blunt?"

"Are you a...I mean..." He coughed nervously and stared over her head. "Have you ever done this before?"

Her eyes widened. "I'm twenty-six years old, Clay."

"Well, of course, you are." He puffed his cheeks and blew out a breath. "I didn't mean to insult you."

"I'm not insulted." She shook her head miserably, realizing that her only love affair had taken place so long ago that it practically didn't count. "The truth is that there was a man—a boy, actually—when I was in college."

"There was only one?"

Now she was insulted. "What were you expecting, a computerized data base sorted by physical attributes?"

"I only meant—"

"I know what you meant. I'm not a naive schoolgirl. This is the place where we're supposed to exchange partner information, right? Well, excuse me if I've breached some unspoken etiquette, but I didn't bring references." She folded her arms and glared at him. "Did you?"

His astonished expression melted into one of amusement. "I'm afraid I don't have references, either. There, uh, wouldn't be a lot of them."

She poked a dust wad with her toe. "How many is 'a lot'?"

"Let's just say I could count them on my fingers."

"One hand or two."

"Two." He shrugged sheepishly. "Okay, okay. One hand and a thumb."

Trying not to smile, she peeked up. "Long-term or one-night stands?"

"Oh, for crying out loud—"

Her grin broke free. "Just kidding."

Clay shook his head and laughed. "You really are a brat."

"So I've been told."

An odd glow lit his pale eyes. "I love brats," he murmured, tracing her scooped neckline with the back of his knuckle. "They're my favorite kind of people."

A nervous tremor swept down her spine. "Why's that?"

His finger hooked over the first button. "Because they're not coy or deceptive." A quick twist and the first inch of fabric parted. "Brats are guileless—" twist "—candid—" twist "—and say what they mean." With a final twist, the entire front of her blouse fell apart to expose her lace bra and a sliver of skin extending to her waist.

When he hesitated, Lainey tentatively touched his T-shirt just above the point where the garment was tucked into his jeans. Gathering her courage, she tugged the shirt free and awkwardly pushed it up to his rib cage. Thankfully he took over at that point, crossing his arms and pulling the shirt over his head to expose a chest so beautiful, so perfectly formed, that it took her breath away. The sculpted muscles were defined by a light smattering of black hair. A thicker nest in the center of his chest narrowed into a dark route downward, encircling his navel before disappearing beneath the denim barrier slung low on his lean hips.

Because she couldn't help herself, she explored the hard flesh with her fingertips, marveling at the hidden strength, the leashed energy throbbing beneath his smooth skin. Clay took a sharp breath but made no effort to dissuade her as she buried one finger in the center tuft, then slowly grazed a path down to the end of the silken trail. She eyed the brass button, which seemed as formidable as a padlocked gate. She traced the embossed sphere with the tip of her nail. A furtive glance confirmed that once the button barrier was breached, the distended fly would probably unzip itself.

Holding her breath, she delicately pinched the denim flap, easing the button through the wrapped opening. The flap popped open. As predicted, so did the zipper, although she was startled by the size of the cotton-clad bulge protruding through the gap. The thing pulsated with raw power, as though preparing to leap out and grab her. Which was, of course, the eventual plan.

Still, she was so taken aback that it took a moment to realize Clay had been speaking to her. With some effort, she pulled her gaze upward. "Excuse me?"

His eyes twinkled with undisguised amusement as he slid his hand around her waist and tapped the plastic button fastening the band of her prim pleated skirt. "I asked if it was my turn."

Realizing that her intense scrutiny of his assets had been duly noted, a stinging flush crept up her throat. She managed to answer his question with a quick nod. There was a tiny tickle at the small of her back. The brown wool slid into a crumpled heap at her feet. She nervously rubbed her palms together, then picked up the skirt, folded it neatly and draped it over the footboard.

Clay grinned. "Ever the tidy little homemaker."

"It's an expensive skirt," she said defensively.

"That's not the point. This is how one discards clothes in the heat of passion." To demonstrate, he shoved his jeans down his lean thighs, then unceremoniously kicked the limp garment across the floor. It plopped against the wall and settled into a rumpled blue heap. "See? Now you try it."

Lainey could only gape at the cheerful man who seemed blissfully unconcerned that he was wearing nothing but his underwear. "I don't want to throw my clothes at a wall."

"It'll help get you in the mood."

She fidgeted with the loose opening of her blouse. "Do I look like I need help getting in the mood?"

The teasing glint faded from his eyes. He brushed a tender fingertip across her cheek. "I wasn't making fun of you. I just tend to get a little silly when I'm nervous."

She smiled gratefully, knowing he understood her own anxiety and was trying to ease it. "Have I told you recently what a wonderful man you are?"

"Tell me again." As he spoke, he casually moved his hands to the opening of her silk blouse.

Lainey shivered as his thumbs grazed beneath the fabric. "You're wonderful," she whispered.

Smiling, he slid his hands upward over her collarbone. A gentle push and the satin blouse flowed over her shoulders. As it floated toward the floor, he caught the garment and laid it neatly atop the folded wool skirt.

When he straightened and looked at her, his eyes seemed lit from within. He touched the top of her shoulder, tracing the lace bra strap with his fingertip. "You're so beautiful," he said huskily. "I knew you would be but..."

The words evaporated as she tentatively mirrored his exploration of her onto his body, delicately running her fingers over the hard contours of his chest. The muscles quivered beneath her touch, empowering her to attempt an even bolder examination. She brushed her knuckles around his ribs, following the soft black belly hairs to the elastic edge of his briefs.

As her fingers lingered there, she felt a subtle touch between her shoulder blades. The lace cups of her bra drooped, then the straps slid to her elbows. She lowered her arms. The bra fell to the floor. Suddenly embarrassed, she stared at the lace puddle, acutely aware of Clay's hushed gasp and the fact that he seemed to be holding his breath. She didn't know what to do now.

Clay did. He gently stroked her sides, moving from waist to ribs and back again. When she made a soft purring sound and was pliable as putty, his caress became more intimate, moving closer and closer to her breasts until each soft mound was neatly cupped in one of his warm palms. Eyes closed, her head lolled back in absolute ecstasy. Her own hands were pressed against his chest, fingers curling and uncurling in rhythm with the funny little humming sounds that seemed to be emanating from deep in her throat.

When he deliberately used the heel of his hands to brush the sensitive nipples, her lips fell apart in a soundless cry of surprise. Each movement, each thrilling caress, sent a new wave of pure sensation coursing through her veins. Without conscious permission, her spine arched, allowing him greater access as she clutched his biceps to prevent her boneless body from collapsing completely.

Grasping her waist, Clay bent his head to take advantage of the silent invitation. He smothered her exposed throat with moist kisses before blazing a fiery trail downward. When his lips rested between her breasts, Lainey squirmed restlessly. As his mouth sought and found an erect nipple, she cried out and dug her fingernails into his upper arms. A frantic heat was building in her belly, spiraling out in wave after scalding wave.

Instinctively pressing her hips against his, she felt her body's reactive motion with a vague sense of shock. Through thin fabric barriers, Clay's distended manhood crowded her belly with a series of tiny spasms that penetrated her flesh and ignited a fiery blaze deep inside her.

The intimacy was so intense, so moving, it was as if they were physically joined. He was cherishing her with his mouth, caressing her with his body, building a frenetic fire inside her feminine core, a passionate inferno swirling beyond the depth of her experience, beyond the limits of her imagination.

His lips moved from her breast, and her disappointed whimper turned into a moan of sheer delight as his warm mouth slid downward. He knelt, sweeping away her flimsy panties as he kissed the soft swell of her belly. Of their own volition, her fingers seemed to tangle themselves in his thick hair while his moist mouth set a thousand raging bonfires, fires spread beyond the scope of his touch to ignite the very core of her being.

Desire made her dizzy. She was frantic with need, with wanting all of him. Barely aware that he'd managed to disentangle her clutching fingers, she was bewildered when he suddenly stood, crushed her in a steely embrace and took her lips with a fervency that left her gasping.

He tightened his grip with one arm, allowing his free hand to roam her body with increasing boldness. Each stroke left its own tingling wake until every inch of skin quivered with electric sensation.

Moving lower, his seeking hands brushed the silky barrier at the apex of her thighs, then beyond. The impact of the intimate touch jolted her right off her feet. She cried out and by the time she realized that Clay had actually lifted her, he was laying her gently on the cot.

He kissed her cheek, whispered, "Wait for me," then quickly crossed the room and started digging through his suitcase.

Dazed, Lainey propped herself up on one elbow. "W-what's wrong?"

"Nothing, honey. I'll be right there." He burrowed through the folded fabric and finally pulled out a leather case the size of a small purse. He unzipped the case, muttering, "I know they're in here.... I saw them a few months ago...ah!" Triumphantly palming whatever he'd found, he stood and took his tiny prize to the window.

Lainey's heart gave a resounding thud as she recognized the flat foil packet. She nearly moaned aloud, realizing that in her fervor, she hadn't even given a thought to protection. Thank goodness, Clay was better at this than she was, although she couldn't for the life of her figure out why it was necessary to inspect the unopened package so carefully. A distressing thought struck her. "Has it been damaged?"

"Hmm?" He glanced up and offered a reassuring smile. "No. I'm just checking the expiration date."

She nearly choked. "You mean condoms are perishable?"

When he ducked his head, she could have sworn he was blushing. "Well, not exactly, but after a few years they lose elasticity or something."

"A few *years?*" Fortunately she was too stunned to burst out laughing. "Just how long has it been since you've had to, uh, check expiration dates?"

Avoiding her gaze, he evasively mumbled, "A while."

When he flipped the package over and inspected the other side, Lainey's heart sank. "Is it still good?"

A slow flush crept up his throat. "I hope so."

"No date, huh?"

"Nope. Maybe this one has a lifetime guarantee." Clay padded back to the cot and slid the package neatly under the pillow, apparently so it would be unobtrusively available when the big moment arrived.

When he lay down beside her, she noted the red stain lingering on his neck and realized that he really had been embarrassed. The endearing vulnerability made her heart swell. She tenderly caressed his cheek, wanting to tell him how very dear he was and how much she cared. But she couldn't utter the words and so expressed her feelings with a deep, slow kiss, to which he responded with rewarding ardor.

In moments they were both afire, bodies slick, hands seeking, surrounded by soft sounds of pleasure and the erotic scent of mutual passion. The cot squeaked with frantic movement. Lainey was crazed with need, oblivious to everything but this man, this beautiful man who had haunted her nights for so long. He was here. He was real. And for these precious moments, he was hers.

She couldn't get enough of him. Her mouth moved frantically from his face to his gorgeous chest, tasting and touching and teasing until he could stand no more.

Groaning, he rolled over and reached under the pillow. While his hands were occupied, Lainey nuzzled his earlobe and impatiently nipped at his shoulder. When he'd completed his task, she purred deep in her throat and tugged at his shoulders.

"Easy, honey," he murmured against her ear. "I'm ready to pop as it is."

Instead of calming her, the idea that he might "pop" without her made her even more frantic. When he moved over her, she wound her legs around him and lifted her hips, oblivious to how shocking the brazen act might seem to Clay. Oddly enough, he didn't seem to notice that she'd suddenly turned into a hussy, probably because he was busily examining her earlobe with his tongue.

Suddenly he lifted his head, framed her face with his hands and searched her eyes. She clutched his wrists, blinking back tears of joy as his body pressed intimately against hers. Then gently, deliberately, he moved into her and began the slow, rhythmic dance of love. Sighing, Lainey hugged him to her heart. She was complete.

Nested in the crook of Clay's arm, Lainey watched a shaft of sunlight crawl slowly along the wall. They had been lying silently for more than an hour, savoring what had been shared while trying to postpone as long as possible the inevitable onset of reality.

Although her body was relaxed, humming with the afterglow of love, her mind was in turmoil. She'd wanted one moment to cherish; now she was torn, realizing that she'd fallen in love with Clay. One moment could never be enough. She wanted a lifetime.

But she couldn't have that. Her uncertain future was clouded by doubt and the fear that she, like her mother, could someday end up locked in a sterile room with empty eyes and drool on her chin. The concept made her shudder.

Beside her, Clay stirred. "Honey? Are you all right?"

She lifted the arm draped around her waist and kissed the back of his hand. "I'm wonderful."

When she released his hand, he raised up on one elbow and gently stroked her mussed hair. "Are you sure? You've been awfully quiet."

"I'm sure," she said softly, willing herself not to cry. She didn't want to spoil these precious moments with fear or self-pity. There'd be time for that later, after Clay had returned to Atlanta.

Clay watched Lainey's melancholy expression with increasing anxiety. He recognized the secret worry in her eyes and believed that he understood it. Now that the memories about her father's killers had surfaced, she was obviously concerned for her safety.

So was Clay. In fact, he was scared to death. The men who'd murdered Gerald Sheridan were ruthless. They wouldn't think twice about eliminating anyone who became a threat. The fact that she couldn't remember their faces may not be enough of a deterrent. After all, last week she hadn't even remembered being there. It was impossible to guess what memories might surge forth next week or the week after.

Clay doubted that Gerald's killers would wait around to find out. Once they discovered that Lainey had been watching from the bushes, her life wouldn't be worth a plug nickel. That scared the liver out of him. If anything happened to Lainey, he wouldn't be able to live with himself. She meant more to him than anyone on this earth and there was nothing he wouldn't do to protect her. Nothing.

Automatically pulling her closer, Clay laid his cheek against the top of her head. "What's the deadline for tomorrow's edition of the *Banner?*"

She twisted to look up. "That depends on whether it's front page or filler. Why?"

He separated a strand from her glossy brown hair and curled it around his finger. "I want you to write a front-page article."

"About what?"

"About the book project."

Pushing herself up, she pulled up her knees, pivoted on the narrow mattress, modestly holding the sheet over her bare breasts. "Are you going to leak information about the men who killed my father?"

"Good Lord, no! And neither are you, Lainey." To emphasize his point, he grasped her shoulders. "Promise me that you won't tell anyone what you've remembered."

"But I don't understand wh—"

"Promise!"

She winced. "You're hurting me."

As Clay's hands sprang from her shoulders, he was appalled at the pale pink imprints his fingers had left on her delicate flesh. "Oh, God, honey... I'm so sorry." His voice broke as he embraced her, hugging her to his chest and rocking her gently. "Forgive me."

"It's all right," she murmured against his throat. "It was an accident."

But Clay was inconsolable, unable to endure knowing that he'd caused her pain. He didn't deserve her forgiveness. He didn't deserve—

"Hey!" Lainey took hold of his face, forcing him to look at her. "No, you are *not* like your father."

His jaw drooped. "How did you know what I was—"

She interrupted with an impatient gesture. "I always know what you're thinking. Your eyes are like glass. Now get rid of those negative thoughts right this minute. That's an order."

Astonished, he could only blink and nod dumbly.

"Good." She reached out to smooth a tousled lock of his hair. "Now as far as that promise goes, I'm afraid it's too late."

Fear gripped him like an icy hand. "What do you mean?"

"I've already told my aunt and uncle."

Groaning, Clay rubbed one eyelid and tried to control burgeoning panic.

"What difference does it make?" she asked. "I mean, everything is going to come out as soon as the book is published."

"No, it's not. There isn't going to be any book." Sighing, Clay let his head roll back against the steel headboard. "Tomorrow's *Banner* will announce that there will be no book because I've come to the conclusion that my father was justly convicted."

Lainey vibrated as though struck. "But that's a lie."

"Maybe." Leaning forward, Clay took her hands. "Listen to me, honey. Even if what you remember is true—"

"Of course it's true!"

"Don't you see that it doesn't matter?"

She stared in disbelief. "Doesn't matter? You've spent half your life trying to prove your father was unjustly convicted for murder. Now that we have proof, how can you possibly say it doesn't matter?"

"Because we don't have any proof. You say there were three men, but you can't remember their faces. My father could have been one of those men."

"He wasn't!"

"How do you know?"

"I—I...just know." She miserably plucked at the bedclothes. "Besides, your father drove a truck. I saw a car, a big, dark-colored car."

"Which could have belonged to one of the other two men." He held up a hand to silence her protest. "Any prosecutor worth his salt would point out that a man bent on revenge might well have taken a couple of goons to make certain the odds were in his favor."

"But would this vengeful killer remove the murder weapon from an anonymous mystery car and lay it in plain view on the front seat of his own pickup? I don't think so."

Clay shrugged. "It doesn't matter what we think. All that matters is what can be proved, which at this point is absolutely nothing."

Lainey ducked her head, silently staring at the sheet corner she'd twisted into a wrinkled roll. When she looked up, her eyes were bright with unshed tears. "But wouldn't my testimony and Emma's show that pertinent evidence was omitted, deliberately or otherwise, from the original case?"

He couldn't deny that. "Yes."

"Then someone should answer for that."

"Lainey, listen to me. Once word gets out that you saw your father's killers, do you honestly think those three men—regardless of where they are now—will stand quietly by to find out whether or not you can identify them?"

The comprehension dawning in her dark eyes was quickly followed by fear. "Then Emma could be in danger, too?"

"These men are murderers. Anyone who threatens them could be in danger."

Her eyes widened. "You threaten them, Clay."

"Not any more." Frustrated, he raked his hair. It galled him to be so close, so damnably close, only to be driven away by fear. But nothing was worth jeopardizing Lainey's safety and his mother would have been the first to agree. Forcing what he hoped was a reassuring smile, he affectionately touched the tip of her nose. "Everything will be fine, honey. We'll explain things to Broddie and he'll take it from there."

After brushing her brow with his lips, he swung his legs over the edge of the bed and plucked his rumpled briefs off the floor. He'd donned the undergarment and gathered the rest of his clothes when he noticed that Lainey was still as he'd left her, cocooned in bedclothes, staring sadly into space. Her poignant expression broke his heart.

He swallowed hard, scooped her dainty undergarments from the floor and laid them in front of her. "We'd better put on some clothes before heading to town or Scarlet tongues will be wagging until Christmas."

She fingered the lace bra. "What if I remember their faces?"

Clay's jaw twitched. "You won't."

"But what if I do?"

"Then pretend you didn't. Don't tell anyone, Lainey. No one at all."

"Not even you?"

"Not even me." Unable to endure her soulful gaze, Clay turned away.

They dressed silently, then climbed into Clay's van and drove through the woods toward town. During the trip, Clay was lost in thought, realizing that if Lainey ever remembered those faces, she'd be in mortal danger. By revealing that explosive information, she'd be instantly vulnerable to a careless whisper, a prying ear. Yet as he thought of the two people she'd already told, he had the sickening feeling that his warning had come too late.

Suddenly Lainey clutched his arm. "Clay, look!"

His gaze swung in the direction of her frantic gesture. Touching the brake, he slowed as they approached a group of vehicles and heavy equipment gathered along the road. Along with a police car and two public works trucks, a massive crane was hauling something up the steep slope.

When a crumpled blue wreck emerged from the ravine, Lainey emitted a sharp cry. Clay's stomach turned. That twisted mass of steel was all that remained of Broddie McFerson's beloved Buick. And, quite possibly, all that remained of the man himself.

Chapter 14

Settling into his padded leather, Lloyd glanced at his watch, then gazed out the window, waiting patiently. At the appointed time, his private telephone rang. He hesitated—an important man never answers on the first ring—then lifted the receiver.

A raspy voice greeted him. "It's done."

"Good." Lloyd absently straightened his cuff. "Where are you calling from?"

"Pay phone down by the slough."

"Were there any problems?"

A nervous cough filtered through the line. "McFerson's a tough old bird. Banged up but still breathing."

Lloyd's smile faded. He sighed, wishing that his brilliant plan had been executed with sufficient skill to have assured a more permanent solution.

The caller, evidently alerted by the lengthening silence, added, "Mebbe I should, y'know, finish things."

Lloyd rubbed his chin thoughtfully. Broddie McFerson was stubborn, not stupid. "That shouldn't be necessary, Aldrich. I assume the meddlesome old fool has learned a valuable lesson, one he won't wish to repeat. What happened to McFerson's car?"

"Had it towed to the impound lot."

Lloyd frowned, knowing that city mechanics would have access to the vehicle. "Do you think that was wise?"

"Ain't no one gonna find nothing." Clark's voice lowered to a conspiratorial whisper. "Hell, that little nick in the brake line coulda been done by damn near anything."

Tapping his desk, Lloyd considered that and decided that for once his idiot brother-in-law was probably right. Since the car had careened over an embankment, the undercarriage had undoubtedly suffered serious damage. No one would be able to state with any degree of certainty exactly what had caused the minor blemish or when it had occurred.

"Got some good news," Clark said suddenly, his voice bubbling with pride. "I found Cooper. Him and the Sheridan gal came driving down the highway while we was dragging McFerson's old pile of bolts outta the ravine."

Lloyd straightened, cautiously optimistic about the unanticipated stroke of luck. "Where is he?"

"Now? Prob'ly took the gal to the hospital. She was a mite upset."

Lloyd blew out a slow breath. This was the chance he'd been hoping for. He could have someone stake out the hospital, ready to follow when Cooper emerged. That could be risky, though. The surveillance car could be spotted and outmaneuvered, as McFerson had done last week after the motel fiasco.

"Where exactly was Cooper when you first saw him?" Lloyd asked.

"This side of the Greenville turnoff, coming toward town."

That meant that Cooper's hideout was probably somewhere between Scarlet and Greenville. Unless, of course, he'd taken the old fork leading into the mountains, which offered any number of secluded locations for one wishing to maintain a low profile. Lloyd pursed his lips thoughtfully. Unfortunately the woods were pocketed with dirt roads, most of which were unmapped and led nowhere. Except, of course, for the road to that little catfish lake at the head of Tupaloosa Creek.

Lloyd swiveled his chair, bent across his polished desk and checked his leather-bound appointment book. "Arrange a meeting tonight at the Clemmonses' place," he said brusquely. "Eleven o'clock."

"But I been up since dawn," Clark sniveled. "What're we gonna do in the middle of the damned night?"

Leaning contentedly back, Lloyd tucked a hand behind his head and stretched out his lean legs. "We're going fishing, my boy. And this time, I intend to hook the big one."

Rushing down the sterile hospital hallway, Lainey dodged a white-coated technician and an unoccupied gurney, lost in the glossy linoleum maze. She jolted to a stop where two corridors joined, fighting tears as her frantic gaze darted left, then right.

A comforting grasp encircled her elbow. "This way," Clay said, guiding her forward.

She offered no resistance, grateful that Clay had maintained at least a modicum of composure. If not for his soothing strength, Lainey would have dissolved into sobbing hysteria, useless to Broddie, useless to herself. Instead she'd managed to control her burgeoning panic. Temporarily.

But when Clay opened the door to Broddie's room, Lainey uttered a gasp of horror at the sight of her dearest friend lying helpless and wan, his frail body impaled by a terrifying assortment of wires and tubes. An arm encased in plaster jutted awkwardly from a partial body cast encircling his bony chest; one immobilized leg was suspended from metal rods that rose like satellite antennae from a bed pocketed with all manner of buttons, levers and other space-age gadgetry.

Beside the bed, a man wearing a sloppy green scrub suit was studying a metal clipboard. He glanced up and acknowledged them with a nod. "Are you Miss Sheridan?"

Since Broddie had always referred to Lainey as his adopted next of kin, the benign question made her knees weak. Closing her eyes, she sagged against Clay and was barely able to whisper an affirmative reply.

"Good. He's been asking for you." The clipboard snapped shut. "Maybe you can convince this pigheaded fool to sign the surgical consent form."

That stunning pronouncement was followed by indecipherable muttering, weak but wonderfully familiar. When Lainey looked up, the bedclothes were vibrating and Broddie was trying unsuccessfully to peer around his hoisted leg. "Lainey, lass?"

"I—I'm here." She nearly fainted from joy and relief, but her wobbly legs managed to carry her across the room. When she was alongside the bed, she bit her lower lip to keep from crying.

A thick gauze pad was taped to Broddie's forehead and an ugly purple bruise stained one side of his swollen face. His bright blue eyes, however, were clear, lucid and flashing with indignation as the doctor bent to inspect an IV needle taped to the back of his unswathed hand. "Would a wee bit of privacy be too much to ask?"

With a pained sigh, the doctor straightened and spoke to Lainey. "Apparently Mr. McFerson is so frightened of surgery that he'd risk permanent damage rather than allow repair of his torn knee ligaments."

Bristling at the suggestion of cowardice, Broddie fixed the young physician with a furious stare. "Listen to me, you cocky whippersnapper, you and your bloodthirsty cohorts can do all the cutting you want when my business is finished—my *private* business, if you please. Now if you'd be so good as to torment someone else for a while, I'll be getting on with my affairs."

The frustrated physician shoved the chart under his arm and spared Lainey a sympathetic glance before stalking out of the room.

When the door clicked shut, Lainey gently touched the cloud of white hair. "The doctors are only trying to help you. Why are you being so difficult?"

Broddie's somber gaze swung from Lainey to Clay. "I couldn't be letting them knock me out until I told you."

"Told us what?" Clay asked.

"Quality control. In 1974, ChemCorp didn't have in-house testing facilities, so batch samples went to outside labs for analysis. Thing is, it took two or three weeks to get results."

Although that meant nothing to Lainey, the information seemed inordinately intriguing to Clay. "Meanwhile the finished product took up expensive warehouse space waiting for an okay to ship."

"Right you are, laddie. And would you be caring to guess how the blokes in charge planned to save a few pennies?"

Clay rubbed his eyelids. "I don't have to guess. We already have copies of shipping documents proving the batch was bagged and shipped within forty-eight hours of manufacture. Apparently someone didn't think it necessary to wait for quality control sign-off."

"Aye. By the time the lab reports were done, bags of contaminated fertilizer had most likely been distributed halfway around the States."

Lainey's puzzled gaze swung from Broddie to Clay and back again. "Contaminated with what?"

The old man's response was succinct and terrifying. "Arsenic."

Clay moaned and shook his head. "Snail bait."

Broddie nodded somberly. "Right you are, lad. In the early days, the same mixing vats were used for everything from herbicides to fertilizer to rat poison."

"Wait a minute." Frustrated and confused, Lainey held her hands in a time-out gesture until she had both men's attention. "I don't understand what snail bait has to do with contaminated fertilizer."

"The questionable batch was produced in Production Area Three," Clay explained. "According to the logs, that area had just been used to manufacture granulated snail bait."

Although Lainey was no chemist, she knew that arsenic was a primary ingredient for many snail control products. "So you're saying that somehow the vat wasn't cleaned properly between batches?"

With a shrug, Clay cast a perplexed glance at Broddie.

A troubled expression clouded the old man's face. "That's the thing. Such carelessness might have left a trace, but not the high percentage showed by the lab report."

Clay frowned. "I don't remember seeing a lab report."

"You haven't seen it because the bloody thing is still in my shirt pocket." With a limp gesture, Broddie pointed toward a narrow door at the far side of the room. "In the closet, lad."

Following instructions, Clay found a plastic bag stuffed with Broddie's possessions. He pulled out a torn plaid shirt and extracted a folded paper from the breast pocket. Broddie chortled happily, "That's it! Thanks be to the blessed saints. I've been fretting that it might have been lost in all the hoopla."

Lainey watched nervously as Clay inspected the fragile sheet. "What does it say?"

"It confirms what Broddie just told us, that the sample was loaded with arsenic and unsuitable for the purpose for which it was intended." Clay carefully refolded and pocketed the report. "If that fertilizer was actually used, it could have caused a hell of a big problem."

"It couldn't have been used," Lainey blurted, horrified by even the thought that a deadly poison could have been inadvertently spread over thousands of acres to contaminate crops, water supplies, livestock and, God forbid, humans. "Once ChemCorp learned of the problem, surely they would have issued a recall."

"Maybe," Clay replied, although his expression clearly conveyed doubt. "In minute proportions, arsenic is a natural element, found almost everywhere on earth. Once diluted by rains, the evidence would have dissipated considerably. After a few seasons, there probably wouldn't have been more than a trace left."

"Is it possible that the contamination might not have done any serious damage?" Lainey asked.

"I honestly don't know," Clay replied.

It was all too much for Lainey to grasp. She pulled up a nearby chair and sat beside the bed, trying to comprehend the far-reaching implications if Clay's speculative theory was proven to be true. "What you're saying is that there was some kind of conspiracy to cover up the accident even though people's lives would be jeopardized." When Clay moved beside her, she reached up and took his hand. "I can't believe that. I simply can't accept that people I grew up with would have so little regard for human life."

Clay touched her cheek, his eyes reflecting empathy and something deeper. He said nothing. He didn't have to. His expression was a chilling reminder that her father had been investigating the same incident when he'd been killed.

Lainey had always believed—hoped—that had been a coincidence. Now the mounting evidence indicated that someone from the company, perhaps even someone she knew, had been involved in her father's murder.

Cradling Broddie's head, Lainey held a water glass to his cracked lips. After a few tentative sips, he turned away. She set the glass on his nightstand and used a tissue to dab a drip off his chin. "Can I get you anything else?"

"No, lass. Having your sweet self at my side is all the medicine I'm needing." Broddie sighed as she lowered his head back to the pillow. "Poor Bertha. Saved my life, she did."

Lainey shivered. The massive old Buick, having been built like a tank, had absorbed most of the impact. A smaller vehicle would have collapsed like an accordion. Broddie would have been crushed to death.

Since the thought made her ill, Lainey abruptly switched subjects. "When Clay comes back with the doctor, I want you to sign those consent forms without any more shenanigans, okay?"

With a startled snort, Broddie blinked pitifully. "Such a bossy lass you are."

She smiled. "The doctor said that if you didn't have surgery tomorrow morning, your leg might not heal properly. I'm worried about you. So is Clay."

"Ah, Clay is it?" Broddie's bright eyes narrowed shrewdly. "Is that a bit of cupid's arrow I see sticking out of your heart?"

A slow heat crawled up her throat. "Don't be silly."

"Now, I've known you since you were knee-high to a leprechaun and never have I seen such light in those bonnie brown eyes." He smiled kindly. "You could do worse, lass. A fine man, that one. He'll be a good husband."

The warmth instantly receded as her skin turned cold as ice. Emotion tightened her voice. "That won't happen."

"How can you be saying that? A blind man could see how much he cares."

Lowering her gaze, she smoothed the bedclothes and tried not to cry. "Clay and I have no future together, and you know why."

A reflective sadness dulled Broddie's gaze. "What happened to your mother is a terrible thing, Lainey, but you've got to go on with your life."

"How can I?" she blurted, wiping the angry tears suddenly spurting from her eyes. "I won't subject Clay or any man to the horror of waking up beside a human vegetable. And, dear God, what if there were children? Do you think I'd allow my own children to suffer the humiliation, not to mention the guilt and pain of believing that they must have been very, very bad to have driven their mommy insane? I would never do that! Never!"

"Sweet Mother of God," Broddie whispered. "All these years, is that what you've been thinking, that 'twas you who caused your mother's breakdown?"

"Yes. No." Unable to look at him, Lainey sat in the chair and covered her face with her hands. "My mother was born with a...weakness. Having a child just made things worse for her."

"Oh, lass. You're wrong, so very wrong. What happened to your mother, God bless her, had nothing to do with you. 'Twas the shock of Gerald's death pushed her over the edge."

Lowering her hands, she took a shuddering breath and stared at the floor. "Sooner or later, it would have happened, anyway. Aunt Hallie said that Mother had always been different, unable to cope, and was already at the edge before Daddy died."

After a silent moment Broddie confirmed that with words that seemed to have been chosen with great care. "True enough, your mother was emotionally fragile, but she wasn't born that way." He hesitated then issued a heartfelt sigh. "If only I'd understood what you were feeling, I would have been telling you this long ago."

Lainey looked up and was alarmed to see that the old man's color had faded to a sickly pallor. "Telling me what?"

Looking miserable, Broddie closed his eyes and sunk back until the pillow seemed to swallow his swollen head. He spoke tentatively, in a quavering voice. "A terrible thing happened when your mother was a child. There was a stranger who offered her candy. She took it and went with him." The old man didn't speak for several moments. Finally he opened his red eyes and fixed Lainey with a gaze so poignant that her heart nearly stopped. "They found little MaryBeth a few hours later, down by the slough. The whole thing was hushed up, of course, but the poor lass was never the same."

Curling her hands under her chin, Lainey tried to comprehend the horror Broddie was describing. "Are you saying that my mother was . . . was . . . molested?"

"Aye." Broddie licked his lips. "Gerald knew, of course. That's why he was so patient, always hoping that his love would ease her out of that terrified shell. Your mother did try, God help her, but then you were born and things were worse than ever."

Guilty tears pricked her eyes. "I was a difficult birth," she whispered.

Broddie scoffed at the notion. "Stuff and nonsense. Why, MaryBeth hadn't been in labor long enough to work up a sweat before you popped out like a greased melon seed."

The brusque contradiction of what Lainey had been told came as a jolt. "But Aunt Hallie said—"

"I don't give a fiddle what your aunt said," he growled. "Hallie wasn't even there. But your daddy was." The old man's lips curved at the memory. "And a prouder man never walked the face of the earth. Shot four rolls of film, he did, and you not even six hours old."

Ordinarily Lainey would have been eager to hear stories about her father's love, but at the moment she was completely overwhelmed. All her life she'd been led to believe that her mother had been born with an evil curse that could be passed down through generations. "Are you telling me that my mother's mental problems are not genetic?"

"I can't speak about that, child. I'm not a scientist." Broddie's good shoulder rotated in a halfhearted shrug. "All I can tell you is what I believe, which is that poor MaryBeth suffered enough heartache to break the strongest mind."

Lainey's head was spinning. "But if she wasn't traumatized by childbirth, then why did she resent me?"

"She didn't resent you, lass. MaryBeth loved you deeply, but watching you grow brought back all the fear and the shame that she'd never been able to face."

A glimmer of comprehension flickered deep in her mind. "Oh, Lord," Lainey murmured. "When she looked at me, she saw herself as a child, didn't she? I was a reminder of what had happened to her."

If Broddie's interpretation was correct—and Lainey desperately wanted to believe that it was—then MaryBeth would have seen in her daughter a mirror of the past, a constant reminder of her own haunted childhood. It made sense. Dear God, it made sense.

Tears flowed freely now, but they were tears of joy. For the first time in her life, Lainey allowed herself hope for the future. She finally had a chance to find happiness and love. After so many desperate years, it was a chance she simply had to take.

* * *

Clay held the door as Lainey entered the dark cabin. "Wait here," he said. "I'll fire up the oil lamp."

Light from the full moon spilled into the room, illuminating his movements. In a moment a golden glow from the lamp joined the silvery moonlight. He straightened, smiled at her, then went to the kitchen and pumped water into a saucepan to make the tea he'd promised.

Lainey didn't really want any tea, but she didn't want to go home, either. With a quick phone call from the hospital, she'd informed the Clemmonses of the accident and that she'd be home late. After confirming that Broddie's surgery was scheduled for early tomorrow morning, Clay had driven her back to the cabin, ostensibly to pick up her car. Now she fidgeted nervously, wondering what he'd think if she asked to spend the night.

She slid a furtive glance toward the kitchen, where he was poking a match into the antiquated gas burner. A tiny flame flared, flickered and disappeared.

Lainey kicked off her shoes.

Clay muttered under his breath, rifled through a small box on the counter and plucked out another match.

Lainey quietly crossed the room and came up behind him.

Clay lit the match, twisted the stove knob and carefully held it to the hissing jet. A ring of blue flames encircled the burner.

Lainey laid her cheek against his back, then slid her arms around his waist.

Clay lifted one of her hands to his lips, then turned in her embrace and cupped her face with his hands. "Hi, beautiful," he murmured, then brushed her lips with a sweet kiss.

"Hi, yourself," she whispered as a courageous warmth radiated the length of her trembling body. Taking a deep breath, she turned off the flaming burner.

Clay arched a brow. "You don't want tea, right?"

"Right." Reaching back, she unbuttoned her waistband and stepped out of her skirt. Gathering her courage, she carefully avoided his startled gaze and carefully picked the pleated wool off the floor. After a nervous pause, she hauled back and flung her skirt against the nearest wall.

In the shocked silence that followed, Lainey felt supremely stupid. What must Clay think of her? She managed a thin smile. "You're right. It really does help get one, uh, in the mood."

Clay's eyes started to glow softly and a slow smile spread across his handsome face. "I told you so."

Crossing his arms, he pulled off his T-shirt and hurled it at the same spot. By the time the garment had settled on top of the crumpled wool skirt, Lainey was shrugging off her blouse. With a major league windup, she aimed and threw. It hit with a satisfying splat and slid into a satin puddle atop the growing pile. A wad of heavy denim followed, thudding against the wall hard enough to vibrate the thin cedar paneling.

Breathing hard and clad only in their underwear, they stood there like a couple of grinning fools.

Clay appreciatively eyed her scanty attire. "Ladies first," he said, gesturing toward the rumpled clothes heap.

"No, you first."

"On the count of three, then."

Lainey reached back and took hold of her bra clasp. "One..."

Clay hooked his thumbs over the elastic waistband of his briefs. "Two..."

"Three!"

The simultaneous chant was followed by a flurry of activity and flying fabric. Laughing madly, they dashed into the bedroom, dived onto the nearest cot and rolled into a giggling tangle of groping hands and clenched legs. Lips touched, lingering until the taste of passion erupted into a burning inferno and their laughter had melted into lusty moans.

Clay's hands were everywhere, stroking her breasts, caressing the soft curve of her hips, igniting a blaze of erotic desire so intense she feared she might die of the heat. His mouth created its own magic, steaming a moist trail down to her waiting breasts. He kissed each one gently. When he took one swollen tip into his mouth and rolled the erect nipple between his lips, Lainey whimpered for more. She'd never experienced such agony of joy. Her body tingled, her skin sizzled, her belly throbbed with intimate need.

Writhing against him, she hooked an ankle possessively over his muscular calf and shamelessly explored his body. His skin was warm, slick, pulsating like a living thing. Emboldened by his soft groans of pleasure, her fingertips followed the silky path down his hard belly and beyond, to the woolly portal of his masculinity. Then her hand crept lower, brushing the moist tip. He shuddered violently and returned the favor, stroking her with a caress so intimate she cried out in ecstasy.

With a groan that seemed to have been torn from his very soul, Clay reached under the pillow, rolled over and knelt between her thighs. Eyes glowing, he fumbled with the packet.

Fascinated, Lainey watched the sensual sheathing with unbearable anticipation. Beyond doubt, the provocative movements were the most erotic she'd ever seen and by the time he'd completed the task, she was ready to leap out of her skin. She clutched his shoulders, lifting her hips as he moved toward the completion that she so desperately craved. Then, in a spiraling rapture of body and soul, they merged into the ecstasy of love.

Hours later Lainey was sated and content, lulled by the rhythmic beat of Clay's heart and the comforting cadence of his breath. Nuzzling her cheek even closer to his warm chest, she reveled in the tickle of soft hairs brushing her skin. The living room oil lamp cast a golden glow through the open doorway, illuminating her lover's repose. With his sharp features softened by sleep, he was even more beautiful, more appealing. A slumbering man, she discovered, was enticingly vulnerable and she was captivated by the touching display of trust.

Dear God, how she loved him. In all her life she'd never experienced such a sweet, wrenching ache of emotion. She was so full inside, her heart so swollen with love that it threatened to burst through her ribs. And Clay loved her, too, she knew it in her bones. No man could express such tenderness, such poignant passion except through the power of his love.

She was suddenly struck by an overwhelming urge to look at him, to examine the extraordinary landscape of flesh and muscle until she'd memorized every crease, every sculpted curve of his body. Taking care not to awaken him, she slowly raised herself up on one elbow. Reveling in his magnificence, her greedy gaze caressed his sleeping form. She was part of him now, as he was part of her.

A surge of powerful emotion swelled up inside her with a frightening intensity that was both awesome and humbling. It was hard to believe that this remarkable man could love her; but undeniably, he did. He hadn't said so—yet—but a woman knows these things. Lainey felt blessed, exhilarated and deliriously happy.

Smiling to herself, she let her mind wander. She pictured herself puttering in her own immaculate kitchen, baking fresh bread, making homemade baby food. Their life together would be perfect, absolutely perfect. Clay would have his own office, a place where he could work in peace and churn out dozens of bestsellers. She'd keep the children quiet and on Saturdays...

Lainey's smile faded. On Saturdays she'd be at the nursing home with her mother.

A cold finger of fear slid down her spine as she remembered that Clay didn't know about MaryBeth. She'd have to tell him because... because she had to, that's all.

Lainey licked her lips, silently imagining herself leading Clay into her demented mother's room. If they were lucky, MaryBeth might actually realize someone was there; or perhaps she'd simply stare vacuously into space, an empty vessel oblivious to any existence beyond her own silent torment. And if it was one of the really bad days, MaryBeth might scream and tear at her skin as though trying to rip away the madness.

Squeezing her eyes shut, Lainey covered her ears to block out the memory of her mother's bloodcurdling shrieks, her moaning wails of despair.

How could Clay—or anyone else—accept MaryBeth's condition without recoiling? Afterward, would he secretly consider Lainey to be pitiable and wonder if she, too, carried some hideous hidden flaw?

She cringed at the thought. Even if Broddie's contention was true and the seeds of MaryBeth's mental problem had been sown by childhood trauma, there would always be a shadow of doubt, a cloud of suspicion. A lump of pure terror wedged in her throat. She loved Clay too much to deceive him; yet if she told the truth, she risked losing him forever.

Conflicted and sick at heart, Lainey slipped out of bed, tiptoed into the living room and quietly dressed. Maybe there was some other way, an option she hadn't discovered. Maybe not. In either case, she needed time to think, to sort things out in her mind.

With a final longing glance around the tiny cabin, she picked up her purse and walked into the night.

Chapter 15

Lainey drove down the Clemmonses' driveway, past the kitchen door and parked in front of the garage, which was situated fifty feet behind the rear of the house. As she exited the vehicle, she wondered why the house lights were on. Russ and Hallie were usually in bed by ten, so she'd figured they would have retired an hour ago. Lainey hoped they weren't waiting up for her. When she'd called to tell them she'd be late, they'd presumed that she'd be at the hospital all evening. Lainey hadn't bothered to correct that erroneous notion. Now she nervously wondered if they'd discovered her deception. If so, she'd have to lie about where she'd been. And with whom.

The back porch light went on. Lainey sighed. Mentally fortifying herself for the imminent inquisition, she pulled her purse from the front seat and closed the car door just as Uncle Russ emerged onto the porch.

He peered around a latticework trellis and looked anxiously toward the front yard. "Best get inside, girl. Hallie needs you."

Lainey's heart flipped. "Has she had another one of her spells?"

"Hmm?" Russ tore his gaze from the dark street in front of the house. "Spells? Yeah, that's it. Hurry on, now."

Still standing on the porch, he pushed open the kitchen door and motioned her inside. Just as Lainey crossed the driveway, headlights strobed the house. Russ swore under his breath as the car pulled up at the curb.

Lainey frowned. "Visitors at this hour?"

Reaching inside the open door, Russ flipped off the porch light. "Get inside," he ordered. "Stay there." Without waiting for a response, Russ quickly descended the porch steps and hurried to greet the car's occupants.

Since her uncle had evidently been expecting the car and its occupants, his apprehensive behavior piqued Lainey's curiosity. Instead of going inside as Russ had instructed, she quietly wandered up the driveway. A car door slammed; then another and another. Three slams, three men in the front yard. Uncle Russ was the fourth.

Lainey froze, feeling a odd sense of déjà vu. A shadow lay on the drive like a black corpse; it was her own shadow, cast by the moon hovering behind her left shoulder. The spray of silvery light filtered through the latticed redwood, forming a dappled pattern over the cropped lawn. *Like moonlight through leaves,* she thought fuzzily. *Dappled shadows. Three slams, three men in the front yard. Her father had been the fourth.*

Suddenly she wasn't standing in her uncle's driveway. She was crouched in the bushes beside her parents' home. She saw her father in the front yard, confronted by three men.

One of the men was holding a handkerchief to his face. The largest of the group—the one who'd pinned her father's arms behind his back—was distinguished by a glint of reddish hair. Another man—a tall one—was methodically fitting his hands into a pair of leather gloves. Then the tall man smiled and buried a black fist into her father's stomach.

As cobwebs cleared from her memory, Lainey remembered details—black leather gloves, an embroidered monogram on the handkerchief. She remembered the men's clothing and voices and words. And she remembered their faces.

* * *

A stealthy coldness seeped into Clay's bones. He turned groggily, pulling up the covers as he reached out for Lainey's comforting warmth. His fingers brushed empty air. Rising up on one elbow, he scanned the darkened room. A frisson of fear skittered down his spine.

Whipping off the bedclothes, Clay swung his feet to the floor and gazed anxiously out the open doorway. "Lainey?" He cocked his head, listening. Silence answered.

With a sinking sensation, Clay padded into the main room. He found what he'd both feared and expected. The room was empty. Lainey was gone.

After lighting the oil lamp, Clay wandered aimlessly around the cabin as Lainey's laughter echoed in his mind. A few hours ago the walls had resonated with happiness and love. Now a murky hush had settled over the night, a foreboding silence broken only by the mournful cry of a distant owl and the muted moan of the wind.

His gaze was drawn to the clothing heaped at the base of the wall where they'd been flung with such joyous abandon. He picked up his cotton briefs, his jeans and gray T-shirt. The silky blouse was missing, as was Lainey's brown wool skirt and filmy undergarments. All of her possessions had been scrupulously removed. It was as if she'd never been there at all, as if their lovemaking had been nothing more than a glorious dream. Then he caught her scent, a trace of sweet honeysuckle lingering in the cool air, and he knew it had been real.

And it had been sublime. They had cherished each other with a physical and emotional coupling so intense that Clay's mind resonated with her passionate whimpers and his lips still savored her honeyed sweetness. The memory warmed him. He closed his eyes, drawing emotional sustenance from the sublime image. His heart swelled with feelings that were frightening in their intensity. He loved her. Dear God, he loved her more than life itself, and yet she had left him.

A black void opened to swallow the happy memories. He looked at the clock. It was nearly eleven. He brooded about whether to call or simply jump in the van and go after her.

In the end, he decided to do neither. If she'd wanted to be with him, she wouldn't have left. Obviously she needed time alone. He would respect that, although his mind crawled with horrible options he didn't even want to consider. Worst was the fear that she didn't share his feelings. For Clay, tonight had been a spiritual awakening of mind and heart and of soul.

Clay was in love; perhaps Lainey wasn't.

Certainly she'd never said that she loved him—at least not with words. He'd felt the love radiating from her every touch, her every breath. Yet she'd walked away without so much as a fond farewell. And he couldn't shake the chilling sensation that she might never be back.

Having been alerted by Lainey's hushed gasp, Russ whirled and swore angrily. His big legs carried him quickly across the yard. "I told you to get into the house," he growled, grabbing her wrist and trying to haul her back up the driveway.

She yanked out of his grasp. "You," she whispered. "It was you."

Russ's bewildered expression melted into one of stark terror. After a quick glance confirmed that the tall man was walking toward them, he seized Lainey's arms and shook her soundly. "Don't say another word," he rasped harshly, then called over his shoulder, "Y'all wait for me in the car."

Lloyd Reeves emerged from the shadows. "Is there a problem?"

"No problem. The gal's just asking about her aunt's medicine, that's all."

Lainey stood frozen, her numb gaze shifting from the blocky figure still at the curb to Sandborne Hunicutt, who'd come up behind Reeves and was screwing the top on a plastic atomizer.

"Are we going to stand out here in the cold all night?" Hunicutt whined. "My sinuses are killing me."

Ignoring his sniveling companion, Reeves focused his shrewd eyes on Lainey. "You seem upset, my dear. Is there something I can do to help?"

She stared at Reeves's gloved hands, remembering the cruel blows they had delivered to her helpless father. Fury boiled up inside her, an overwhelming rage surmounting any sense of danger. She glowered at Reeves without thought of retribution. "You bastard."

Reeves stiffened.

Russ sucked in a quick breath and released one of Lainey's arms long enough to deliver a stinging blow to her cheek. Before her ears stopped ringing, her uncle was shaking her furiously. "Go into the house!" he shouted, dragging her up the driveway.

Planting her feet, Lainey struggled violently, arms flailing, fists ineffectually pounding her uncle's thick chest. "You killed my father! You're all murderers . . . *murderers!*"

Suddenly she was free. Panting, she backed away and saw that the fourth man had left the car and was ambling toward them. When he moved into the light, her heart leapt in relief. Aldrich Clark was wearing plaid flannel and a hunting cap, but uniformed or not, he was still the police chief and her only hope of rescue. Lainey dashed forward and threw herself at the startled man.

"What'n tarnation . . ." Clark stared down at the woman clinging to his chest as if she were a ghostly apparition.

Lainey wiggled a frantic finger at the three men clumped in the driveway. "Arrest them! They killed my father!"

Clark's jowls sagged. Hunicutt gagged and fumbled for a hanky. Reeves stared icily.

Russ covered his eyes, groaned and shook his head.

Lainey's fingers tangled in the flannel shirt stretched across the chief's fat belly. "They did it! I saw them!" Nearly hysterical, she yanked at the fleecy fabric in a frenzied attempt to make him understand. "Please . . . you have to arrest them. *They're murderers!*"

Clark peeled away her clutching fingers, but instead of moving toward the three men, he clamped a meaty hand around Lainey's wrist, uttered a graphic oath, and spoke to Reeves. "What're we gonna do now?"

Rushing forward, Russ positioned himself between Lainey and her captor. He took hold of the chief's arm. "Turn her loose," he said calmly. "I'll take care of her. The girl doesn't know what's she's saying."

Reeves made a production of smoothing the black leather between each finger. "She sounds rather sure of herself to me."

"Lainey's just like her ma," Russ insisted, his voice cracking. "Not right in the head. No one's gonna listen to her—y'all know that."

Seeing the fear in her uncle's eyes affected Lainey like a bucket of ice water. She also saw corruption on Clark's contorted face and evil in his eyes. At that moment she realized what she had done. Although the police chief hadn't been at her parents' house the night her father had died, he'd obviously been involved in the sinister conspiracy.

Lainey gasped as Clark tightened his bruising grip on her wrist. His flabby mouth twisted as he yanked her forward, dragging her up the driveway and forcing her into the house.

The other men followed. After they were all inside the kitchen, Hallie appeared in the doorway, leaning on her canes. "Land sakes, turn that girl loose!"

Wringing his handkerchief into a soggy spear, Hunicutt rushed over to Hallie. "She knows," he whispered significantly, then cringed at the woman's hostile glare.

Hallie turned to her husband. "What the devil is this little weasel blabbering about now?" Without awaiting an answer, she swished one of her canes at the police chief. "Turn her loose or I'll crack that fat skull of yours."

Sidestepping the feeble thrust, Clark jerked Lainey's wrist and snarled as Hallie raised the cane again. "Back off, woman, or I'll wrap that thing around your skinny neck."

In less than a heartbeat, Russ was at his wife's side easing the wooden staff downward. "Cool down," he murmured to his furious wife. "You're just making things worse."

Hallie anxiously searched her husband's somber face. "What're these fools doing in my kitchen?"

"We have—" he coughed nervously "—a problem."

The woman slid a narrowed glance at her niece. "A problem with Lainey?"

Russ nodded miserably. "She just told God and everyone that she saw us that night at Gerald's."

As Hallie's eyes widened in horrified comprehension, Lainey's skin went cold. "You knew," she whispered as her aunt's guilty gaze slid to the floor. "All this time, you knew the truth and you let an innocent man go to prison. My God, these men killed your brother. How could you protect them?"

"Quiet, child! You don't know what you're saying." Hallie took a limping step forward.

"Don't..." Lainey swallowed a sob of despair. "You betrayed my father and you betrayed me."

"Her mind is cracking," Hallie insisted, slipping a desperate glance around the room. "It's the nightmares. She don't know what's real anymore."

Sweating bullets, Hunicutt stepped forward. "But the girl said that she saw us."

Lips quivering, Hallie turned a pleading gaze on Lloyd Reeves. "Lainey makes up stories...to get attention, you know? She's always been that way. You can't believe nothing she says."

"Perhaps." Reeves glanced nonchalantly around the tidy kitchen. "Unfortunately, she can't be allowed to continue making up such stories."

Hunicutt's Adam's apple bounced erratically. "How're we going to keep her quiet?"

Smiling coolly, Reeves slid a gloved finger beneath Lainey's chin. She glared up defiantly, turning her face when he caressed her cheek. "Such a pretty girl," he murmured. "Such a terrible waste."

Russ stiffened. Hallie whimpered. They both knew that Lainey had to die.

Having given up any thought of sleep, Clay set a pan of water to heat and rifled through his meager stock of herb teas. He decided on chamomile. It smelled awful, but he'd read somewhere that it had some kind of tranquilizing ingredient. Actually, Clay would have preferred a stiff belt of hundred proof, but since there wasn't a drop of liquor in the cabin, he hoped the foul tea would have a similar mind-numbing effect.

He dropped the bag into an empty cup and stared at the bubbles forming inside the saucepan. A wisp of steam curled up. As he waited for the water to boil, he idly wondered about the adage about watched pots. Maybe he should turn his back.

Shaking his head, he glumly clicked his teeth, tapped his fingers on the counter and decided that love really did make people nuts. Here he was fretting about the physics of boiling water when all he really wanted to do was drive into Scarlet, burst into the Clemmonses' house and retrieve the woman he loved as Richard Gere had done in *An Officer and a Gentleman.*

Clay had originally considered that scene to be ridiculously corny; now it seemed incredibly romantic.

He was mentally musing the depth to which emotional entanglements seemed to alter one's perspective when his cellular phone rang. His heart leapt. He spun around, knocking the ceramic cup off the counter as he stumbled toward the heaped table. A loose pile of papers vibrated with the next jarring ring.

Clay dug through the clutter, found the phone and flipped the switch. "Lainey? Where are you—"

A vaguely familiar voice rasped, "Mr. Cooper?"

Deeply disappointed, Clay suddenly recalled telling the hospital staff to call if McFerson's condition worsened. He tightened his grip on the tiny phone and answered roughly. "This is Clay Cooper. Who's calling?"

"Come quickly" came the strained reply.

"Has something happened to Mac?"

"No, no. It's Lainey."

"Lainey?" he repeated stupidly. "What about Lainey?"

The grating voice sounded even more distraught. "Please hurry. You have to stop them."

"Stop who? I don't understand." Completely baffled, Clay massaged his forehead and tried to recall where he'd heard the voice before. "Who is this?"

"T-there isn't much time. They have her—they know what she saw."

That got Clay's attention. "Who are you talking about?" he asked warily. "And exactly what is it that these people believe Lainey has seen?"

After a taut silence, the voice rose in thinly veiled hysteria. "Lainey saw what they done to Gerry. You've got to come! Please—"

"Hallie? Is that you?"

"They've got Lainey," the woman wailed. "You got to help her."

Clay stiffened. "Where is she?"

"Here... at the house."

"Call the police," he snapped. "I'm on my way."

"Won't do no good," Hallie insisted.

"Why not?"

"The chief... he's one of them."

Clay swore under his breath. "Are Reeves and Hunicutt involved?" He barely heard her affirmative whisper.

"Do you have any weapons in the house?"

"Just Russ's old .38."

"Get it. Don't let them take Lainey out of the house." The command was one of pure desperation. If the men were also armed, he doubted poor Hallie would be able to hold them off, even for the twenty minutes it would take for him to get there. He grabbed his keys and dashed out the door, still holding the phone to his ear. "I'm on my way," he told the terrified woman.

"Hurry," she whispered urgently. "They're fixing to kill her."

As Reeves held the basement door open, Clark painfully twisted Lainey's arm behind her back, roughly shoving her down the creaking stairs into the chilling darkness.

From somewhere behind came her uncle's voice. "You don't have to do this," Russ was saying. "We can send her away, have her committed. No one'll ever pay a lick of mind to anything she has to say."

Reeves flipped a wall switch. A dim bulb glowed at the end of a frayed chain as he descended the stairs, followed by Russ and Hunicutt, who was sweating profusely and clawing his collar.

"I'm inclined to agree with Clemmons," Hunicutt said. "Surely a suitable, uh, incarceration would alleviate the problem."

Clark muttered a succinct oath. "I ain't willing to wait around with a thumb up my rear while she spills her guts to some Greenville shrink. Y'all know what'll happen if someone else starts snooping around."

"It pains me to admit that Aldrich is correct." Pursing his lips, Reeves regarded Lainey with an expression that under other circumstances might have passed as remorse. "I am sorry, my dear. Unfortunately, you leave us little choice."

Playing for time, Lainey stopped struggling against the police chief's brutal grip. Instead she lifted her chin and confronted Reeves, since he was obviously the murderous clique's leader. "Do you think I'm the only one who knows what you've done?"

Although Hunicutt nearly swallowed his Adam's apple, Reeves merely shrugged. "If you're referring to Cooper, I can assure you that his fate has already been assured."

The realization that Clay was in danger made her physically ill. She sagged forward, fighting a nauseous surge. "H-he doesn't know anything," she said finally. "I never told him."

"Really?" Reeves's skeptical smile didn't reach his eyes. "Then his untimely demise will be all the more tragic."

A forceful shove propelled Lainey across the cluttered room. As she stumbled over a cardboard box of Christmas decorations, the chief grabbed her elbow and redirected her onto a splintered bench.

Russ lunged forward and spun the paunchy man around. "You don't have to be so damn rough with her."

Angrily raising his fists, Clark's fat mouth contorted in anger before curving into a twisted grin. He dropped his hands to his fat belly, yanked up his droopy pants and chuckled. "Fair 'nough, Clemmons. We promise to kill her real gentle-like."

Russ went white. He looked helplessly at Lainey, raked his crinkly red-gold hair and turned away.

Reeves stared at the chief with undisguised disdain. "Apparently you require a reminder that this is an unfortunate situation which no one besides yourself finds the least bit enjoyable. Please refrain from further—" The reprimand was drowned out by a series of loud overhead thumps.

Hunicutt flinched as though shot and plastered himself against a rusty heating oil vat, eyes darting wildly. "What the hell was that?"

"Just Hallie," Russ replied dully. "Her canes make a ruckus."

Eyes narrowed suspiciously, Reeves inspected the vibrating basement ceiling. "I thought she went to bed."

"She's . . . upset." Russ cast a soulful glance at Lainey. "Maybe I should see to her."

Reeves nodded curtly. "That would be best."

Avoiding Lainey's gaze, Russ spun and headed for the stairs. On the third step he paused and his shoulders heaved under the force of a shuddering breath. For one bright moment Lainey hoped that her uncle had finally come to his senses. She reached out to him. "Please . . . it's not too late. Don't let them do this."

Russ slowly looked over his shoulder with tears sliding down his ruddy face. "I'm sorry," he whispered. Then he ascended the stairs and was gone.

Slumping in despair, Lainey tried to quell her mounting panic and force her benumbed brain into action. If she was going to survive this harrowing ordeal, she'd have to draw on her own wit. She'd have to save herself.

As her three remaining captors huddled at the foot of the stairs to discuss her fate, Lainey's desperate gaze circled the dank cellar, searching for something—anything—she could use to defend herself. There were several mounds of sealed cardboard boxes. She briefly considered pushing the stacks over but discarded the idea when she realized that in doing so she'd cut off her own access to the stairs. There was no other escape route—no windows, no storm doors—just a pitted cinder block tomb.

After a furtive glance confirmed that the men were still engrossed in hushed conversation, Lainey's gaze fell on a row of garden tools pegged on the far wall. She eyed a long-handled hoe, realizing that even if she could get her hands on the dumb thing, it wasn't likely she'd be able to fend off three men. She'd already noted that the police chief's transformation to civilian attire had not included the holstered service revolver that was normally strapped around his bloated belly.

In fact, it didn't appear that any of the men were armed. If she could get hold of that hoe or even the thick spade hanging beside it, a surprise attack might stun them long enough for her to get out of the basement.

And run smack-dab into the aunt and uncle who'd already betrayed her.

A lump wedged in her throat. Lainey had never deluded herself into believing that Russ and Hallie had feelings of deep parental-type love; but she'd always presumed that if they hadn't cared about her, they never would have taken her in and raised her as their own. Now she realized that they'd done so out of guilt, a sick atonement for having taken part in her father's murder.

Shaking off thoughts of Russ and Hallie's treachery, Lainey placed both feet flat on the floor in preparation for a desperate sprint to freedom. Scooting until her hips were balanced on the very edge of the bench, she leaned forward, ready to spring.

At that moment Hunicutt stepped away from the group. Lainey tensed as the twitchy little fellow twisted his collar and plucked his shirt buttons. "There will be an investigation. With all those homicide detectives crawling around sniffing out clues, we'll never get away with it."

Clark snorted in disgust. "First off, them 'detectives' work for me. Second, there ain't gonna be no investigation 'cause there ain't gonna be no murder."

Hunicutt brightened and wiped a quivering hand across his wet forehead.

"The chief is right," Reeves said to no one in particular. "Suicide raises fewer questions. It will quite naturally be assumed that the unfortunate young woman inherited her mother's mental instability."

A bitter taste flooded Lainey's mouth as she realized that Reeves was right. If her death appeared to be self-inflicted, there would be lots of sad murmurs and head-shaking, but the town's whispered wisdom would doubtless conclude that the poor Sheridan girl had killed herself to keep from ending up like her mother. The murderers would go free. Again.

As Hunicutt sat heavily on the first stair step, Clark waddled into the center of the room, craning his flaccid neck to inspect the ceiling beams. "Got a rope?"

Reeves slid him a contemptuous look. "That's cruel and barbaric."

Offended, Clark puffed like a flabby blowfish. "It's not like I was gonna let her flop till her eyes bugged. Once she's a hanging, just a little jerk—" cracking his tongue, he twisted his hands as though snapping a twig "—makes it quick and clean."

Hunicutt gagged and dropped his head between his knees.

With her own head spinning, Lainey fought to stay conscious. If she fainted, she'd be lost forever. She took a deep gulp of air and prayed that when she made a move, her quivering legs wouldn't give way. Forcing her head up, she speared Reeves with a defiant stare. "Why don't you just pump a few pills down my throat?"

With a pained grimace, he waved away the suggestion. "Admittedly that would be neater than the chief's crude proposal, although the process would be rather lengthy. Since we have a full schedule this evening, I'm afraid we'll have to resort to a more expedient—and ironically appropriate—method."

Reeves reached into his tailored overcoat and pulled out the snub-nosed revolver that Lainey recognized instantly as her uncle's gun. Russ must have handed the weapon to Reeves earlier while Clark had been escorting Lainey to the basement. She felt ill. In less than a heartbeat the success potential of her escape plan had plummeted from unlikely to impossible.

Hunicutt, who was still hunched on the first stair step, looked up and saw the weapon. He blanched, dropped his head back into his hands and moaned. "Ohmygod."

"Quit sniveling," Clark growled, then examined the revolver nested in Reeves's gloved palm. "Where'd you get that?"

Reeves smiled. "Let's just say it's Mr. Clemmons's donation to the cause. We wouldn't want a weapon of questionable origin evoking unnecessary inquiry."

Clark's homely face quivered into a grin. "So she's gonna whack herself with her uncle's gun, huh? Can't no one quibble with that."

"Exactly." Reeves handed the weapon to Clark. "First shot through the temple," he instructed brusquely. "After that, we'll place the gun in her hand and fire a second."

Nodding, Clark took the gun. "That'll set a hefty load of powder residue on her hand, just in case one o' my boys gets anxious enough to test on his own time."

As the chief spun the cylinder to check the load, Lainey leaned forward until her weight was on the balls of her feet. When a renewed round of thumps upstairs drew attention to the ceiling, she leapt up, lurched forward and rammed her head into Clark's belly.

Grunting, the chief stumbled backward. The gun went off, pumping a round into the cinder block wall.

As Lainey dived toward the tools, Reeves grabbed her arm and spun her around. She bounced off his chest, then brought up her knee. Reeves dropped to the floor, gasping and clutching his groin.

Hunicutt leapt to his feet. "Ohmygod, ohmygod."

Lainey wrapped her fingers around the nearest handle and ripped it away from the wall. She swung wildly. Clark ducked, cussing madly. Reeves reared up and grabbed her ankle. Lainey cried out, hopping on one foot as she tried to kick free. For a split second, the distraction took her mind off Clark. It was a fatal mistake.

Before she realized what was happening, the handle was torn from her grasping fingers. Clark flung the tool across the room and slammed Lainey onto the wooden bench. When she tried to stand, Clark's vicious backhand knocked her into the wall. By the time she'd shaken the cobwebs from her brain and pushed a disheveled mass of hair out of her face, the gun barrel was aimed directly at her nose.

Reeves was on his feet, slightly bent and in obvious pain. "A little spitfire, aren't you? Like mother, like daughter, I suppose." He nodded at Clark, who had Lainey pinned against the wall. "Get it over with."

A tingling sensation slid down Lainey's spine. *Like mother, like daughter*... The words revolved around her mind, creating images that were strangely familiar...the swirl of a satin hem, the sound of gunfire, a woman's scream. *Like mother, like daughter...*

The ceiling reverberated like thunder. Cold metal pressed against her temple. *Like mother, like daughter...*

The hammer clicked into firing position. Lainey realized that she was going to die, yet all she could think about was glimmering silk and a burst of blue fire. There was a pounding in her brain, like a thousand fists beating against her skull. She heard voices, barked orders.

Like mother, like daughter...

The final elusive memory flashed through Lainey's troubled mind. She whimpered. Then everything went black.

Chapter 16

"The paramedics are here, Mr. Cooper. You'll have to step aside."

Without taking his eyes off the woman reclining on the living room sofa, Clay shook off the trooper's restraining hand. "Lainey...honey, can you hear me?" Kneeling, he caressed his lover's pale cheek. She moaned. Her head rolled on the cushions, then her eyes fluttered open.

A massive wave of relief shook Clay to his knees. She was alive. Thank God, he hadn't been too late.

After having alerted the state police, Clay had driven frantically into town, arriving at the same time as the squad cars. When the troopers had burst through the door, a hysterical Hallie screamed that there'd been a gunshot in the basement. Armed officers had rushed downstairs with Clay right on their heels.

When he'd seen Lainey lying on the basement floor, his entire world had exploded. He'd thought she was dead. Never in his life had he experienced such grief, such utter desolation.

Oblivious to the chaos around him, he'd scooped Lainey into his arms and carried her upstairs. After his anxious examination revealed no gunshot wounds, Clay's heart had returned to a nearly normal rhythm, and Hallie's anguished wails had subsided into quiet sobs.

Now the distressed woman wept silently, not even looking up as the officers hustled her handcuffed husband and his cohorts to the squad cars outside. Because Hallie had saved her niece's life and was cooperating with the investigation, she hadn't been placed under arrest. Later on there'd be questions about what Hallie knew and exactly when she'd known it, but the investigating officer had remarked that early evidence suggested the woman had remained silent out of fear rather than criminal intent. The final decision rested with the D.A., of course, but with a good attorney and a plea bargain, it seemed doubtful Hallie would serve any jail time.

The insistent hand returned to Clay's shoulder, a kind voice resonated in his ear. "Please let the paramedics do their job."

Reluctantly Clay stood and stepped back. Two white-shirted individuals, a man and a woman, converged on the sofa. Clay hovered anxiously. "There's a lump on her forehead...she might have a concussion. Is her pulse strong? Will she be all right?"

The female paramedic, who was wrapping a blood-pressure cuff around Lainey's limp arm, spoke without looking up. "I'm sure she'll be just fine, sir."

"She has to be," he murmured. "She has to be."

Clay backed further away to allow a third paramedic access to the sofa. As he raked his hair in helpless frustration, a movement caught his eye. He turned and saw Hallie's bony frame hunched miserably on a nearby chair. When a glance at the sofa confirmed that Lainey was awake and speaking to the medics, Clay went over and knelt by Hallie's chair. "Lainey will be all right," he told the shaken woman. "You saved her life."

Raising reddened eyes, Hallie shook her head. "It's all my fault. After what happened to Gerry, I should have known..." The words dissipated as her gaze dropped. She stared numbly at her lap.

Clay took her hand and gently stroked the swollen knuckles. "You were Gerald's secret informant, weren't you?"

Her shoulders quivered. "I loved my brother. As God is my witness, I never meant him any harm."

"I know that." Clay took a deep breath. Since McFerson had supplied company records indicating Russ had been the supervisor of Production Area Three when the accident had occurred, Clay guessed that Clemmons might have confided in his wife. "Hallie, do you know how the accident happened?"

She rubbed her baggy eyelids. "Some kind of manufacturing screwup. Russ said they'd been using Vat Three to mix snail bait—you know, that granulated stuff?" She paused until Clay nodded to indicate that he understood. "Anyway, after that production order had been filled, they cleaned the equipment and got ready for the next batch."

"That was the chemical fertilizer, right?"

She nodded. "Ingredients for each product were separated and loaded into barrels so workers could measure the stuff into the mixing vats. Russ figured someone must've got the buckets mixed up, on account of powdered arsenic looks just like fertilizer bonding agent."

"When was the problem discovered?"

"When the reports came back." Hallie plucked the skirt of her faded cotton dress. "Weren't nothing supposed to ship until the lab work was done, but the company had so many back orders, they didn't want to wait."

Clay knew that Sandborne Hunicutt had been in charge of the shipping department when that crucial decision had been made, but his lowly position wouldn't have allowed him authority to breach quality control policy. It was logical to assume, therefore, that then-CEO Reeves must have given the order to ship without lab clearance.

As the theory formed in Clay's mind, Hallie continued to speak in a dull monotone. "Reeves swore everyone to secrecy, saying liability lawsuits would bankrupt the company. He said there wasn't enough poison in the stuff to really hurt anyone and, at worst, crop runoff might kill a few fish and maybe some livestock."

"Didn't he realize that any human who came in contact with contaminated soil or water could also have been at risk?"

"Reeves said if that happened, folks would most likely figure someone got careless." She shrugged listlessly. "Farmers always got a barnful of rat poison and such."

"And your husband didn't have a problem with that?"

Hallie's voice quivered. "Russ isn't a bad man, just a weak one. He was afraid of losing his job and having to start all over somewhere else. By the time things started getting out of hand, he was in too deep."

"Why did you leak the story to your brother?"

"No one else was doing anything to stop it. I figured Gerry would get everything out in the open, and the company would have to pull the stuff back before someone got hurt." Her eyes filled with fresh tears. "If I'd known what would happen, I never would've told."

Clay squeezed her hand. "It wasn't your fault."

Turning her head, she stared at the floor. A shamed flush stained her hollow cheeks. "I—I knew your daddy hadn't done nothing," she whispered. "But I was too scared to tell."

The realization that Hallie actually knew which of the men had killed her brother sent adrenaline coursing through Clay's veins. After years of speculation and research, the final revelation was within his grasp. He wanted to grab the woman's shoulders and shout the final question but couldn't risk spooking her into silence. Somehow he managed to maintain an even tone. "Who did it, Hallie...who pulled the trigger?"

Her head snapped up. She began to shake violently.

"Please. I have to know." Clay couldn't keep the desperation from his voice. He was so close. The final elusive answer was within grasp and he couldn't let go, not now. Because he'd seen the police chief aiming a gun at Lainey, Clay blurted, "It was Clark, wasn't it?"

Confusion clouded Hallie's eyes. She stammered, "N-no, he weren't even there. Reeves called him after—" She paused to lick her lips and take a deep breath. "The chief, he cleaned everything up and put the gun in your papa's truck."

Stunned, Clay sat back on his heels. He'd been certain that of the four men involved, only Aldrich Clark was depraved enough to have actually done the evil deed. If it hadn't been the corrupt police chief, that left the coldhearted bastard who'd been willing to risk God knew how many lives rather than loose a precious penny in profits. Thinking aloud, he muttered, "Then it must have been Reeves."

Tilting her head, Hallie regarded him quizzically. "You really don't know, do you?"

Before Clay could respond, a weak but deliciously familiar voice called his name. He was on his feet in a flash and beside the sofa before his next heartbeat. "I'm here, Lainey. I'm right here." The emptiness in her dark eyes nearly broke his heart. He spun and snagged the nearest medic. "Is she going to be okay?"

"She's fine," the man replied. "Bumped her head when she fainted, that's all." After a reassuring slap on Clay's shoulder, the paramedic hoisted a metal case and followed his colleagues out the front door.

Lainey struggled to sit up. "Clay... are you all right?"

"Shh, honey. I'm fine." He slid an arm around her shoulders, urging her to lie back down. "You should rest." When she insisted, he helped her into a sitting position and gingerly settled beside her, eyeing the purple bruise on her forehead.

Wincing, she squinted up and laid a gentle palm on his cheek. "The paramedics said you brought the police," she whispered. "You saved me."

He turned his head to press a sweet kiss on her palm. "I brought the police, but it was your aunt who saved you. If she hadn't called me, God knows what would have happened."

Her brow creased adorably. "Aunt Hallie called you?"

"Hmm." He rubbed his face kittenlike against her soft hand. "A few nights ago I wrote down my phone number and asked her to give it to you."

Lainey's troubled gaze scanned the busy room and settled on her aunt, who was now surrounded by uniformed officers. "I remember you saying that you'd left a message for me. I never got it."

"I thought she'd thrown it away. Fortunately, she hadn't." Clay gently turned her face and searched her dark eyes. "Hallie is all right, Lainey. She's safe and you're safe. Your uncle and the others have been arrested. They won't be able to hurt you or anyone else again."

Lainey's lip quivered. A silent tear slid down her cheek.

Concerned, Clay brushed a strand of dark hair from her face. "It's all right, honey. The men who murdered your father have been caught. It's over now. It's finally over."

"You don't understand." She closed her eyes, squeezing out a fresh flood of tears. "They... didn't kill my father."

He couldn't have been more shocked if she'd reared up and kicked him. "You're confused," he murmured. "It's that bump on the head—"

"No." She took a shuddering breath. "When I was in the basement, Reeves said something and all of a sudden I remembered everything that happened the night my father died." Her eyes were enormous, wet and pleading. "I saw it," she whispered. "I saw who shot my father."

Clay's throat was dry as cotton. He waited silently as she grappled with the memories.

Finally she spoke in a voice that was quiet but firm. "While I was in the bushes, my father was on the front lawn arguing with Lloyd Reeves. Uncle Russ was there, too. He grabbed my father's arm and told him not to be a fool. My father called him a bad name and tried to leave, but Russ wouldn't let go. This skinny little person stepped out of the shadows. I didn't know who he was then. Later I learned it was Sandborne Hunicutt who...who grabbed my father's other arm while Reeves was putting on a pair of leather gloves—" Her voice broke. She covered her eyes for a moment, then shook off the weakness and went on. "Hunicutt and Uncle Russ held my father while Reeves beat him. I heard my mother screaming and saw the hem of her nightgown when she ran out to the porch."

A icy chill swept Clay's spine.

Straining to maintain her composure, Lainey took several breaths before completing the story. "Mother was screaming at the men to let my father go. There was a gunshot. M-my father slumped. When Russ and Hunicutt let go of his arms, he crumpled and fell on the ground. Mother ran down the steps and rolled Daddy onto her lap. She was screaming and screaming and screaming. At first I thought she was upset because Daddy got blood on her pretty nightgown. Then I saw Lloyd Reeves take the gun out of her hand."

Clay closed his eyes, his fingers trembling as he pressed Lainey's cold face to his chest. His heart ached for her, for the child who'd witnessed the ultimate horror, and for the courageous woman she'd become—a woman with the strength to overcome indelible atrocity to survive.

As the final puzzle pieces fell into place, Clay was sickened by all the ruined lives, all the years of deception and deceit. Obviously Reeves had to cover up the incident to protect himself and his company. What better scapegoat than the town ruffian whose wife was having a love affair with the victim? Framing a man for murder wouldn't have been particularly daunting when one's brother-in-law was conducting the investigation. Besides, Ben Cooper had been universally despised by the townsfolk, who'd doubtless been so relieved to purge the town nemesis that few had bothered to question contradictory evidence and judicial bias.

In light of what Clay had just learned, he now surmised MaryBeth Sheridan's disappearance was part of the treacherous scheme. The grief-stricken woman, distraught over having been the unwitting implement of her husband's death, would have been a pliable pawn for her duplicitous cousin. Clay now had no doubt that MaryBeth had been coerced into leaving town, although he still didn't understand why she hadn't taken her child.

In the circle of his arms, Lainey stirred. She sat up, wiped her wet face and spoke without looking up. "It looks like Catherine's book finally has an ending."

Clay traced her trembling jaw with his fingertip. "There isn't going to be a book."

She faced him incredulously. "Why not? That's what you came here for."

"I came here for the truth."

"And you found it."

"Yes. But I found so much more." He tipped her chin up. "I found the woman I want to spend my life with. I love you, Lainey, more than I ever thought possible. It makes me crazy to think how close I came to losing you. You are everything to me. You are my life."

"Clay, please." Her anguished expression cut him to the bone. "Don't say anything more."

He felt like he'd swallowed a brick. "I'm sorry if I've spoken out of turn."

"It's not that." She gestured helplessly. "You . . . you just don't understand."

"I understand that I love you." His thudding heart sounded like a funeral dirge. "But if you don't feel the same, I'll try to understand that, too."

A fresh flood of tears spilled from beneath her lashes. "I do love you, Clay."

It took a moment before he could breathe. "Then marry me, Lainey. Let me be part of your life."

Her beautiful mouth tightened as though the futile gesture could hold back the torrent flowing freely down her cheeks. Clay was both stunned and baffled by her unexpected reaction. He knew people cried from happiness, but these weren't joyful tears. They were tears of anguish, of pure torment. And he didn't know why.

Before he could summon the words to ask, Lainey reached out and took his hand. Her shoulders quivered. She lifted her gaze and searched his eyes. "You are the man of my heart, Clayton Cooper. I think I have always loved you...but I can't agree to be your wife."

Completely bewildered, Clay could barely respond. "Why not?"

A sweep of dark lashes concealed her eyes. "There's someone you have to meet first."

The sterile hallway loomed like a gallows road as Lainey trembled so violently she feared her knees might buckle. Outside these polished corridors the sun was shining and songbirds chirped homage to the beautiful autumn morning. Inside, Lainey approached her mother's room with increasing trepidation and unbearable foreboding. There was no choice now. The era of lies and deceit had ended. It was time for truth. And for Lainey to live with the consequence.

She touched the knob, pausing to skim a glance at Clay's stoic face. He seemed pale. Frightened. She swallowed hard and led him inside. Without waiting to gauge his reaction, she squared her shoulders and went directly to the gaunt woman's bed.

"Hello, Mother. How are you feeling today?" Lainey used a tissue to wipe the saliva bubbling from the corner of her mother's slack mouth. "This is Mr. Cooper. You knew him when he was a little boy."

Blinking away the vacuous stare, MaryBeth turned her head and blankly gazed past Clay to focus on a bare wall. "Aren't those Christmas lights just the loveliest things?"

Cringing inwardly, Lainey bit her lower lip and began removing her mother's grooming items from the nightstand drawer. "How shall we fix your hair today?" The cheerful question was betrayed by an annoying quiver in her voice. She forcefully cleared her throat, carefully avoiding Clay's gaze. "I think a French braid would be nice."

"I love Christmas," MaryBeth murmured. "My husband always brings me the most beautiful presents."

A scraping sound caught Lainey's attention. She glanced up in time to see Clay pull up a chair and sit beside the bed. "I love Christmas, too," he said. "And you're right, the lights are beautiful."

Tilting her head, MaryBeth extended her hand and favored him with a gracious smile. "Thank you for asking, but my husband takes care of our insurance needs. You'll have to discuss such things with him."

"I…see." Startled, Clay took the woman's proffered hand and slid a bewildered glance at Lainey, who feigned interest in separating her mother's barrettes by size and color.

MaryBeth turned toward Lainey. "I declare, aren't you just the prettiest thing. Do I know you?"

Biting her lip, Lainey laid the barrettes on the nightstand. "My name is Lainey."

The woman's gaze slid over Lainey's shoulder to an empty corner of the room. "Isn't the Christmas tree lovely?"

Before Lainey could respond, her mother's lips slackened, her eyes dulled and she retreated back into the abyss of her own mind.

Clay gently laid the woman's hand on the bedclothes. "How long has she been like this?"

Acutely aware of the pity in his eyes, Lainey turned suddenly and walked into the hall. In a moment, Clay followed. Lainey folded her arms and spoke without looking at him. "I realize that Mother probably doesn't understand what's being said, but I hate having people talk about her as if she's not even in the room."

"I'm sorry."

Lainey rubbed her eyelids. She was so tense that her shoulders ached and her neck felt like an overwound spring. "It's just that even the doctors and nurses discuss her as if she were less important than a piece of furniture."

"That must hurt you."

Something in his voice gave her the courage to look up. In Clay's eyes Lainey saw sympathy and caring, but not a trace of the revulsion she'd expected. "Yes, yes, it does."

Clay jammed his hands into his pockets. "Has she been like this since your father died?"

"I think so." Lainey blew out a breath. "I was told that when the police arrived, she was humming and rocking my father with a blank look on her face. At first the doctors said it was shock. When she never got any better, they kept coming up with new theories. I don't believe they really know why Mother has withdrawn into her own world, or if she'll be able to come back."

"Do the doctors think recovery is possible?"

"Anything is possible." Lainey stiffened her spine. "I won't lie to you anymore, Clay. No one believes she'll ever get any better."

"Including you?"

"Including me." Feeling sick inside, Lainey gestured toward a small reading area off the main corridor. "There are reasons I'm not more optimistic, reasons that you're entitled to know before we discuss . . . the future."

Clay's expression wavered between grim and grave as they settled into the private niche where Lainey finally related the entire story.

Over the next hour she held nothing back, revealing that even before the breakdown her mother had been emotionally unstable. In a voice that was strangely calm, Lainey explained how MaryBeth had always recoiled at the most innocent touch and been unable to either accept or offer kisses, hugs and other physical expressions of affection. Finally, Lainey spoke of her own fears, reinforced by her aunt and uncle, that she herself might carry some parasitic chromosome that might someday consume her heart, destroying her own ability to love.

Clay listened carefully, questioned occasionally, and was completely supportive throughout the ordeal. At the end, Lainey was drained, terrified yet oddly liberated. The horrible secret had been exposed. No matter what happened now, the burden of that murky deception had been lifted from her shoulders. She felt free.

Yet she knew that now, as she sat facing the man she loved with knees touching and hands entwined, the next few minutes would determine the course of her life. Every nerve in her body was stiff with anticipation of what Clay would say, what he would do.

For what seemed an eternity, he gazed silently down at their knotted hands. When he finally spoke, his voice faded like a whisper in the wind. "So all these years, you've lived with the terror that you might end up like your mother."

The inside of her throat felt dry enough to crack. "It could happen."

"No." He shook his head so slowly that the movement was barely perceptible. "MaryBeth was broken by tragedy. You gain strength from it."

Taken aback by that observation, she stammered, "B-but I've always been ambivalent, allowing other people to take charge of my life because I had no ambition beyond mere survival."

"That's exactly my point. You've always been terrified by the prospect of becoming a clone of your mother and God knows, I can understand that." Clay's ironic tone was a reminder that he'd suffered similar qualms. "Your aunt and uncle controlled you by constantly reinforcing those fears. But you survived. If that doesn't qualify as exceptional emotional strength, I don't know what does."

The concept was mind-boggling. Never in her entire life had anyone so much as hinted that there might be a core of durability beneath her compliant veneer. In fact, she'd been told exactly the opposite, led to believe that her future was an obscure void, a devouring emptiness into which the final vestige of her life would eventually drain. Now Clay was telling her that wasn't true. Even more startling, he believed she had value.

Apparently taking her silence as protest, Clay captured her attention by squeezing her hands. She looked up and was instantly impaled by his intense gaze. "It wasn't that long ago that you told me I couldn't be judged by the sins of my father. If that's true, then you certainly can't be held accountable for your mother's weakness."

She searched his eyes and saw truth. "It really doesn't matter to you, does it?"

"If you're referring to your mother's condition, of course it matters . . . because it affects you. I can only imagine how hurt you must be, loving her so deeply and realizing she may never even remember that you're her daughter. It makes my heart ache, but it doesn't change the fact that I love you." His voice dropped to a pleading whisper. "Marry me, Lainey."

"My mother will always be part of my life."

"After we're married, she'll be part of my life, too."

"And Aunt Hallie needs me. Uncle Russ may be going—" she couldn't choke out the word *jail* "—away. I can't leave her alone."

"I wouldn't expect you to."

"She needs me."

"I need you, too, Lainey." Clay gripped her shoulders. "Don't you have enough love to go around? Isn't there room in your heart for your aunt and your mother *and* me?"

"Oh, yes." She focused through a mist of happy tears. "I'm just not sure there's enough room in the house."

"We'll make room. Just say yes."

"Yes," she whispered. "Yesyesyes."

Clay's frantic expression melted into one of relief as he embraced her fiercely. She wound her arms around his neck and buried her face in the taut curve of his shoulder. Lainey finally realized that they weren't doomed to repeat their parents' tragedy. She and Clay actually had a future; the joyful prospect of sharing a loving, happy life.

And this time, destiny would not be denied.

* * * * *

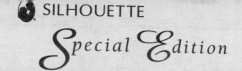

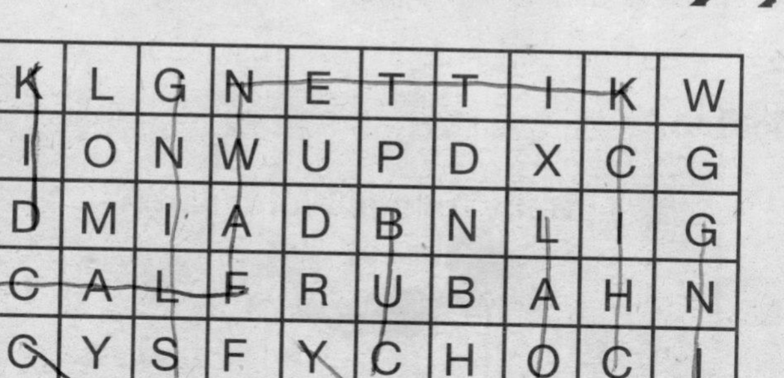

HOW TO ENTER

All the words listed overleaf, below the word puzzle, are hidden in the grid. You can find them by reading the letters forward, backwards, up or down, or diagonally. When you find a word, circle it or put a line through it.

When you have completed your wordsearch, don't forget to fill your name and address in the space provided and pop this page in an envelope and post it today.

Hurry – competition ends 31st August, 1995.

Post to:

Baby Animal Wordsearch
*Locked Bag 2,
Chatswood NSW 2067

Name ____
PLEASE PRINT

Address ____

______________________________ Postcode ____________________

CLOSING DATE – August 31st, 1995 BA495

COMPETITION OPEN TO RESIDENTS OF AUSTRALIA AND NEW ZEALAND ONLY. PLEASE TICK THE BOX IF YOU ARE A READER SERVICE SUBSCRIBER ☐

Harlequin Mills and Boon Reader Service is located at 3 Gibbes Street, Chatswood NSW Australia 2067. You may be sent promotional mailings as a result of this entry.

*New Zealand Address: Private Bag 92122, Auckland 1020

ONLY ONE ENTRY PER HOUSEHOLD PLEASE